Once Upon an...
Irish Summer

Once Upon an...
Irish Summer

Lisa T. Bergren

Once Upon a Irish Summer
© 2020 by Lisa T. Bergren

Published by BCG Press
7814 Potomac Drive
Colorado Springs, CO 80920

Printed in the United States of America

ISBN 978-0-9885476-6-7

Cover design by Timothy J. Bergren
Cover photography from iStockphoto

CHAPTER 1

Fiona pulled over to the side of the gravel road and shook her cell phone, as if that might shake the GPS pin loose. She knew it was silly, but couldn't help herself. Clearly Google hadn't mapped every part of the world. Looking at her screen, it appeared she was two miles from the nearest road, which was clearly not the case.

Part of her liked the fact that Google hadn't bothered to map this remote section of western Ireland; part of her was seriously irritated. She took a long, deep breath, trying to calm her nerves. *Focus on how beautiful it is, Fiona. You'll get there soon enough.* Descending from a craggy peak to her right was a long, sloping green hill, dotted with sheep just coming into their summer coats after spring shearing. To her left, the hill descended to a meandering, small river. Tidy farms were divided by hedges and rock walls, all seeming to run sheep. Fiona knew she could stop and ask for directions, but she preferred to find it on her own. If she was to meet her neighbors, she wanted it to be on her terms. Respect would not come easily in these parts, and if she was to do her research well, she needed their respect. *A lost American commands no respect,* she thought.

She still had hours of daylight left to find her rented cottage, and it had to be somewhere close. It had to be. She'd already taken three wrong turns trying to find Ballybrack Farm. Could the sign have fallen off the wall? In the pictures online, there'd clearly been a sign, as well as several images of a charming, white-washed, one-bedroom cottage "to let" for the summer. Fiona sighed and leaned her head on the steering wheel for a moment, gathering herself. This would have been far easier had she rented a place in one of the coastal towns. But given that it was high season, she couldn't afford it on a grad-student budget.

I can't wait to be out of debt. Working, she thought for the thousandth time in her life. Her parents couldn't either. To them, any degree after a bachelor's was folly. They would have preferred to see her follow in her older brother's footsteps and enter the work force a few years ago.

Fiona sat back and bumped the pad of her hand on the wheel. Her PhD would help her get a job. And to receive her PhD, she had to complete her dissertation this summer. And to get working on that project, she had to *get* to her cottage and get settled. Find some groceries. Put away her books and make sure she had a decent place to write. "Okay, then, Burke," she muttered. "One more try."

With a final glance at her phone, trying to judge the distance to the coast, then unfolding a paper map from the Galway car rental agency that only showed the major roads, she decided she still must be southeast of her destination. Finding a narrow turnout, she made a U-turn and moved down the road again, deciding to enjoy the drive rather than fret. Wouldn't she want to drive all these roads, in time? She was simply doing some exploration now rather than what she might do for pleasure later. How lost could she be?

A few miles later, she was rounding a broad, sweeping corner, grinning, when she glimpsed blue sky emerging between the gray, scuttled clouds rushing inland from the sea. Her eyes returned to the road.

The road.

She was on the wrong side. With a car coming at her.

There was no time to react. She slammed on the brakes and swept to the left, just as the other driver did the same.

Again, the wrong side.

With a sickening crunch, she jolted to a stop, her VW Up—barely bigger than a Smart Car—splashing a wave from the ditch to the hill. Her head hit something—the wheel? the window?—and she blinked several times, trying to clear her blurring vision. Trying to think. Had she just crashed? The very first rental car she'd ever been allowed to rent? Why had the airbag not popped out? *No, it was good it hadn't.* That might have sent some sort of automatic alert to the car rental agency. If you were only twenty-four and had never rented a car before and crashed it the very first day, did they take it away and never let you rent again? How was she supposed to get around all summer if they took it? What if—

"Miss! Miss!" said a man, rapping on her window with a knuckle. He opened her door when she belatedly turned her head in his direction. "Are ye all right?"

"What? Oh, yes. Fine, fine."

He squatted beside her, and Fiona briefly took in his broad shoulders, red beard, muddy jeans. His face was ashen, beads of sweat rolling down his forehead, despite the cool temperature. "Ye're bleedin', lass."

"Am I?" she lifted a shaking hand to her forehead, then noticed the red on her fingertips.

"*Look* at me," he said gently. "Keep yer chin in place and watch my finger."

She did as she was told and took his grunt as one of approval. Belatedly, she remembered she should be worried about him. The man she'd run off the road. "Are you all right?" She focused on his face. A kind, rather handsome face. Was it the blood on her forehead that had spooked him so? Or their crash?

"Ach, I'm well enough. Here," he said, handing her a handkerchief from his back pocket as the blood dripped down into her eye. "Sorry it's so dirty. It's all I have. Been out in the fields."

"That's all right," she said, ruefully meeting his gaze. He was only a few years older than she, but his eyes were startling. He was maybe, what? Twenty-eight? But his eyes... there was something in them that held experience, pain beyond his years. Or was he suffering now? Injured himself?

"I'm so sorry," she said. "I was a bit lost and I-I forgot. I was on the wrong side of the road. All the way from Shannon, I got it right. But when I got lost, I got distracted."

"Yes ya were," he said, giving her a look of consternation. "It's a miracle we didn't hit head-on. American, I take it?"

She hated hearing those words. *Way to blend in, Burke.* She nodded reluctantly. "Boston. But I'm here to let a cottage for the summer. Do some research. I was looking for Ballybrack Farm. Do you know where it is?"

He recoiled a little. "Ye're Fiona Burke?"

She narrowed her eyes. "Yes..." she said slowly.

"My grandda has been expecting ya. In fact, he sent me out to see if ya might be lost." Inhaling deeply through his nose he rose and looked about. For the first time, Fiona saw the hand-carved cane under his left hand, but no cast or brace on his leg. She knew he'd seen her take it in when she met his gaze again. He placed his right hand on the rim of her doorframe. "Think ye're up to helping me get my grandda's little wagon out of the ditch? It's a bit lighter than yer VW. Or should I fetch a neighbor?"

"No. No," she said, starting to rise and belatedly remembering her seatbelt. She colored, knowing he'd been watching.

"Hmmm," he said, his blue eyes taking in every bit of her action. Doubt drew the corners down. "Maybe ya need to be seen by a doctor."

"No," she repeated, now thoroughly irritated with herself. "I bumped my head. I was a bit dazed," she admitted, rising beside him. He was a big man, maybe eight or nine inches taller than she. "But it's not a concussion."

He studied her. "I thought ye were a doctor of history, not of medicine."

Startled, she glanced up again. "I don't have my doctorate yet, but I aim to have it come September." She paused. "You seem to know more about me than I do of you. I'm Fiona Burke," she said, reaching out a hand.

"O' course," he said, engulfing her hand in his. "I'm Rory O'Malley."

"O'-O'Malley?" she stammered. "But your grandfather's name is Caheny."

"That it is," he said, a half-grin on his lips. "He's my mother's father. But my father's kin are O'Malleys."

She shook her head. How had she not expected it? This part of County Mayo had to be full of Clan O'Malley. After all, at one time, the pirate queen, Grace O'Malley—the subject of Fiona's dissertation—had dominated much of it. And yet…

Rory let out a short, gruff laugh and folded his arms. "Ya look like ye've seen a ghost. But don't worry. I'm no Jack Sparrow, regardless of my peg leg," he said, lifting the cane and gesturing to it.

"Of course," she said, feeling the burn of a blush rising on her neck. She turned away from him and moved to the front of her VW to examine the damage, then to his grandfather's ancient, three-wheeled, tiny truck. The VW's bumper was smashed in on the left, splintered cracks over the whole thing. Her heart sank.

As much as her parents loved Ireland, they didn't understand her need to head off alone, even if it was a part of her education. They'd offered to come with her, to rent a summer cottage themselves, to keep her company. But Fiona had refused. She knew from the start that this would be the summer she proved herself to them. Show them that she was capable and smart and moreover, that all the money they'd sunk into her education—and the grad school loans she'd picked up herself—was not going to be wasted.

And what had she done now?

Wrecked her very first rental car.

By driving on the wrong side of the road.

—◊◊◊—

Rory hovered behind her, forcing himself to look at the vehicles rather than Fiona's fine, red hair, shimmering in the summer sun. She was a wee woman, but with pleasing curves, accentuated by the long-sleeved, scoop-necked, blue-black T-shirt tucked into her belted, figure-hugging khakis. Inwardly, he cursed his grandfather and his meddling, matchmaking ways. He'd not told Rory she was coming until that morning. And when he sent Rory out looking, he'd led him to believe it was some middle-aged, matronly scholar he might be looking for in a rental car, not a beautiful sprite who looked more Irish than half the girls in the village.

He tapped her hood, forcing his thoughts to her car. "Not as bad as it might've been."

She nodded, though she looked sick about it. "I got extra insurance, but it's the very first car I've ever rented." She put a hand on her head.

"Very first?" he repeated.

"I just turned twenty-four. They don't let you rent until then," she muttered, still staring woefully at the bumper. "And you know how these things go. They'll charge me a hundred-times what that bumper is worth to fix it."

"Who says they have to know?" He tapped his lips. "We've got all summer. This car is what? One or two years old? I bet we can find another bumper and replace it before ya have to return it. They'll be none the wiser."

Gratitude rounded her pretty blue eyes, laced with red-gold lashes. "Oh, you think?" she breathed, briefly reaching out as if to touch his arm, then catching herself. "That'd be amazing." She had a smattering of freckles across her nose, making her all the more adorable.

Rory turned away to his own vehicle, uncomfortable with how easily he was drawn to her. He'd avoided girls for years. *Ever since...* And wasn't he into brunettes anyway? He shook his head, rubbing his neck, again wanting to wring his grandfather's neck. Last summer, Patrick Caheny had found reasons to bring half the eligible young women from the village to come and call. Patiently, Rory had explained how each was not right for him, and that he was here to help out his grandfather and Great Uncle George for the summer, not find a wife and settle down.

When that had failed, Grandda had apparently decided upon a new tactic to entice a cute young scholar to come to Ballybrack Farm. For the entire summer. A woman he couldn't possibly avoid. *Canny old man...*

"Oh, good grief," she said, hunching down beside him.

"I'm sorry. I hadn't even looked at what I did to your…truck." He caught a bit of the fresh scent of her shampoo, slightly floral, and frowned, trying to concentrate on the injury to his grandda's lorry rather than her as he hurriedly rose.

"Is this an old Mazda?" she asked, rising with him. She ran her small hand across the rusty front hood and down the line of the old three-wheeler truck.

"It is," he said, following her along to the bed as she peered over the edge. "Running as fine as it did back in '57."

She cast him a wry grin. Her teeth were even and white. Her lips formed a sweet little bow—turning slightly up at the corners—until her smile faded and she resumed her careful examination. "This is amazing."

"There are several about the county. But Grandda prizes his own."

"As well he should. I'll pay to get it fixed. This is totally my fault."

Rory huffed a laugh and waved her away. "No need. We'll just pound it back out in the barn. It's not the first time this old thing has had to have a little work."

She put her hands on her hips. "You plan to fix it as well as find a new bumper for me? Are you a mechanic?"

"Spend any time on my grandda's farm, ye get some experience under a hood."

Again, those pretty eyes met his and he noticed dimples on her cheeks. "Well, if I *had* to get into an accident, you appear to be the right guy for me to run into."

CHAPTER 2

"Hop in," Rory said, gesturing to the tiny door on the passenger side. It felt a bit like a toy car as he clicked the door closed beside her. It hadn't weighed much when they'd pushed it free of the ditch—far lighter than her rental, which refused to be freed as easily.

Fiona paused. "Are you sure there's room? Maybe I need to sit in the back…" She eyed the tiny bed of the little Mazda truck, where she'd placed her most important duffel bag. Dung and straw clung to portions of the wooden floorboards. Clearly, this was a sheep-hauling vehicle. A primitive form of an ATV.

"Nah. It's filthy back there. It'll be tight but I think we can manage," he said, squeezing in. At most, there was room for one and a half of them, especially given his Viking-like personage, but she looked around for a nonexistent seatbelt while he settled in. He reminded her of Mr. Incredible with a beard, with his head hunched over so he could see through the windshield. "Not exactly American-sized," he said, eyeing her.

"Not exactly," she returned dryly. She looked back at her rental.

"It'll be okay. Trust me. I'll be back for it in two shakes of a lamb's tail, as my grandda likes to say."

"Two shakes, eh? Guess I can be that patient."

He turned the key in the ignition and the tinny engine

rumbled to life, sending a shudder through the whole vehicle. Rory reached to the gear shift between them. She tried to ease away, giving him some space, but there was precious little room. She gripped the door handle. She could feel his eyes cast over her—did he think her afraid?

Fiona wasn't. Perhaps she should be. Here she was, getting into a vehicle with a man practically twice her size, but she wasn't afraid. He'd known her name. He was her future landlord's grandson, sent to fetch her. And there was something about this land that made it feel like it might have been forty years prior, when times were more innocent and wariness was not a thing and neighborliness was. A woman picked up her mail and waved at Rory as they passed. A man, having sheltered his sheep across the road, lifted a hand—smoking pipe in it—in greeting, farther down.

A half-mile distant, they took a sharp right, weaving their way between two boulders that had clearly split eons ago, and up a long, winding hill road. "Welcome to Ballybrack Farm," Rory said loudly, over the whine of the ancient engine. He hooked a thumb over his shoulder. "That there was our fine front 'gates.'"

Rory shifted gears as they climbed up a steep hill, bouncing over some rocks.

The tiny truck had no shocks left, if it had ever had any at all. Fiona lifted a hand to the roof to keep from hitting her head on it and glanced back to see if her bag was still in the back. She half-expected it to have bounced out, but it was there, perched against the back gate. *Probably covered in sheep dung by now,* she lamented.

"Sorry," Rory said loudly, over the roar of the engine. "If I'd known I was truly fetching ya, rather than just leading ya in, I'd have brought my Jeep."

"That's all right!" she called, pressing a hand to the roof again when another bump almost gave her the concussion she missed in her accident. She dabbed Rory's handkerchief to her head and was relieved to see no fresh blood on it. Should she be worried? Her mother would be. She'd probably insist she go to a doctor, see about some stitches…

But around the next bend, her breath caught, and she forgot all about head wounds. The farm spread out on either side in sprawling, beautiful green hills dotted with sheep. A couple miles to the west, she could just make out the sparkling shimmer of the sea. A half-mile to the east, she could see a boy and his black-and-white speckled dog rounding up perhaps fifty sheep, moving them to a pen. Directly before them, in the heart of the farm, a middle-aged man hefted a bale of hay to his shoulder and carried it into a stone barn with a thatched roof.

"That's James," Rory said. "My grandfather's hired hand. Been with him since he was a boy. Up on the hill is his grandson, herding sheep."

"A thatched roof," she breathed, her eyes drawn again to the gray-stone barn. She glanced at Rory. "That's kind of rare around here, isn't it?"

"Yeah," he said, taking in her obvious appreciation. "It's a dying art. Grandda is one of the last to know it in these parts."

"It's so…romantic."

He waved at them. "It's fantastic if ya don't mind the snakes and spiders and rats."

She scowled at him. "Way to take everything wonderful out of it!"

He pursed his lips and dipped his head. "I love the old ways as much as the next, but I'm also a realist."

He pulled to a stop and an older, gray-haired man came out of the barn, his blue sweater telling her that he was helping haul hay. He brushed off his hands and came their direction. As he drew closer, Fiona guessed he was in his late seventies. Despite his age, he seemed strong, testimony to a lifetime of hard work. And while he wasn't nearly as tall as his grandson, he was still an inch or two taller than she.

"Ahh, brilliant. My wee grandson found ya!" he said, coming directly to Fiona and taking her hand in both of his. Deep wrinkles around his eyes told her that he smiled often. "Welcome to Ballybrack Farm. I'm Patrick Caheny."

"Thank you. I don't think I would've found it without Rory. But I'm afraid we've had a bit of an accident."

"Oh?" he said, lowering one of his giant, graying brows and lifting the other as he looked at his "wee" grandson, towering over him.

"This one tried to run me off the road," Rory said, giving Fiona a teasing wink. "We'll need the tractor to get her car out of the ditch."

"Ah, weel, it's not the first time that's happened about these parts. Are ya quite well, my dear?" His keen blue-gray eyes searched her and spotted the cut on her forehead.

"Oh, I'm fine," she said.

"Still. Best ya come and rest a bit before ya head out with Rory to fetch yer car. We'll put a kettle on and ye can put up your feet for a bit." He took her duffel from Rory and gestured to the tiny white-washed cottage on the far side of the clearing, one she recognized from the pictures. She followed his lead and fought the urge to look back at Rory, curious where he might be going now.

Patrick dug in his pocket and pulled out a key—probably fifty years old, judging from the size of it—and slid it into the lock. "It's a good thing ya reached out to me when ya did, Fiona. I've had several other inquiries about lettin' the place for the summer."

"I'm glad I got it," she said, entering before him, meaning it. Because the cottage was incredibly inviting. The main room was perhaps fifteen by ten feet and boasted an over-stuffed couch and wing-backed chair by a "wood-burner" stove. The furniture was old, but still in decent condition. In the far corner was a tiny kitchenette—a small fridge, a few cupboards, and two burners. On one was a Bialetti stove-top coffee maker, and in the corner was an electric kettle, which Patrick immediately plugged in and set to heating water for her tea.

"A cuppa will set ya back on ye're feet, once ye're ready," Patrick said.

"Can I look?" she said, gesturing toward the bedroom.

"Sure, sure," he said, waving at her. "Make yourself at home, lass. 'Tis yours for the summer."

Fiona moved into the bedroom, setting her duffel beside the double bed crowned with an antique, carved headboard. The bedding was a combination of neutrals—yellow sheets, cream down blanket, and an ivory hand-quilted spread, and it looked clean and cozy. She ran her hand across the old, rough, hand-plastered walls, thick with coats of paint. The antique desk by the window—the glass slightly wavy—looked out at the farm "courtyard" and the hill beyond it, reaching up to a rocky promontory that seemed to be col-lecting a ring of clouds.

She saw Rory moving toward the barn, twirling a ring of keys around his right hand, his left on the cane as he walked with the practiced gait of a man long-familiar with his infir-mity. He disappeared through the dark doorway of the barn and Fiona returned her attention to her exploration.

There was a dresser, but no closet. In the far corner she found the tiniest bathroom. A tight shower, a sink, a toilet. Hardly the "en suite" fixtures she'd hoped for, but serviceable for the summer. And in a cottage this old, she ought to be glad she wasn't facing a wash basin and an outhouse.

She heard the electric kettle boiling and returned to the main room to see Patrick settling tea bags in two cups. "Everything up to snuff?" he asked over his shoulder.

"It looks great. Do you let out the cottage every summer?"

"I do," he said, setting down her cup on a small table beside the wing-backed chair. "Do ye take sugar?"

"No, thank you." She took her seat, assuming that was where he meant her to perch.

"Ahh, don't know what ye're missin'," he said, dropping two heaping spoonfuls in his own cup. "My missus always said the sugar ya put int'a yer tea makes ya all the sweeter." He set to stirring it as he came to sit on the sofa.

Fiona refrained from asking if his "missus" was still about. The way he spoke, and the way the cottage felt, made her think Mrs. Caheny must've died some years before. The entire farm was tidy, but it was like it'd been a few years since it'd had a woman's touch. Patrick's own threadbare sweater, riddled with holes along the sleeves. The outdated linens on her bed. But it was just a guess, she reminded herself.

"Ya sure ye're not in need of a doctor?" Patrick asked, peering in concern at her forehead.

"I'm sure. You know how head wounds bleed—it looks worse than it is. And Rory checked my vision. He seemed confident I was all right." She took a sip of her tea. "Does he have medical experience?"

Patrick paused. "Of a manner. But I'll be lettin' my boy

tell ya about his background."

"Of course," she said, feeling chastened over her nosiness. But what was the big secret? *So maybe he's a medic...* "Thank you for letting me the cottage, Patrick. Are you wanting your rent money up front? I just need to get to town and an ATM to—"

"Ach, no," he said, waving her down. "There'll be time enough for that. Never had a renter yet who robbed me of what was due." He gave her a wink. "After all, I know where ya live."

"Yes, you do. Any rules I need to know about? Things about the septic? Electricity?"

"Ah, the usual. Nothing but paper down the toilet. Ya have enough hot water for about a five-minute shower, then it's over for a couple o' hours. No food waste down the kitchen sink. Throw scraps in a bowl before ya do dishes. Ye'll find a compost pile around the back of the cottage."

"Sounds good," she said, looking around. "So...what first made you decide to rent this place?"

"It was my missus's idea, about ten years back, to fix it up and offer it. The rent money covers our electricity bill for the whole farm all year, and I don't mind the extra company. Especially since my Orla died a few years back."

So, there it was. *A widower of only a few years.*

"It's good you have Rory this summer," she said.

The old man took a sip and gazed pensively out the window. "Aye. For now. There's no tellin' where that lad's heart will take him. But it helps that he has every summer off. Gives him ample time to return to me."

"He comes *every* summer? For the whole summer?"

Patrick met her gaze. "He didn't tell ya? He's a teacher. History." Was it her imagination, or did his eyes twinkle when he said that?

"H-history? No. He didn't say." *So he's a medic-mechanic-teacher...*

"Ach, well, ye'll likely have lots to discuss in the comin' months. Ye're here to research our own Grace O'Malley, aren't ya?"

"I am."

"Well then, ya have a livin' breathin' source right out yonder in our barn. Rory's been researching ol' Gracie since he was a lad, given that she's kin."

She considered him a moment. "Kin by what? Fifteen generations?"

"Give or take," he said with a nod, sipping more tea.

She narrowed her eyes. She was beginning to see what the old man might be up to. "Patrick, just so we're clear. I'm here to finish my dissertation. Not find a boyfriend."

His bushy eyebrows rose. "So ye're against having a boyfriend?"

"Well, not *against* it. I just don't need one right now. If you were thinking that Rory and I—"

"I had no further thought than this...Ye have a shared love of history. Who doesn't like a new friend who has a similar passion? And my grandson..." He set down his cup on the table, leaned forward and tapped his fingers together. "He's had a rough go of it for a time."

She didn't want to give the man false hope. Clearly he was matchmaking. But curiosity forced her to delve in a bit. "He's been injured..."

"Aye, in more than one way," he said, rising with his cup in hand to place it in the sink. "But again, that's my own Rory's story to tell, not mine."

She rose slowly, studying him. Trying to figure out if he

was baiting her curiosity or honestly respecting Rory's privacy. Something told her it wasn't respect that drove him. No, she'd had enough experience with older Irish to know that men like this relished a good tale. And yet they could be circumspect too. *No matter. I have the summer to find out Rory's story.*

Her focus had to remain on Grace's story first, though. *I have way too much to do to get wrapped up in some summer romance...*

The roar of a tractor engine brought her attention to the window.

"Ah, there's my boy," Patrick said. "He'll get ye back to yer car and put things to rights. He always does." There was a note of pride in his tone, the tiniest bit of boasting, salesmanship. As they walked outside and Patrick handed her the cottage key, Fiona figured she was likely one in a long line of potentials that he'd brought around for Rory to consider. *But by renting me the cottage, he's made sure I'll stick around,* she thought with an inward laugh. *Clever guy.*

Rory climbed off the bench of the old tractor and gave it a quick pat. "This old girl will get your car out of the ditch. She's got some years on her, but she's still strong."

"Ya remembered the hauling strap, laddie?" Patrick asked.

"I did." Rory gestured to the sturdy canvas strap and hinges that would likely connect the might of the tractor to someplace on her car so he could haul it out of the ditch. He turned to her. "Got your keys?"

"Right here," she said, patting her jeans pocket.

"Then up ya go." He offered his hand to help her up.

She took it and then reached for the iron wrung to the right of the seat, hoping she looked competent and not like some city-girl as she awkwardly climbed aboard. She moved to the other side of the seat and looked about, wondering where she was supposed to sit, if he was going to drive.

"Sorry," he said. "No passenger option, really. You'll need to hold on to me down the road."

"Oh. Right. O-okay," she said, her words emerging in quick, awkward succession, betraying exactly how she felt.

"Unless..." Doubt crept over his face. "Maybe my grand-da could give ya a lift? Meet me down there?"

She looked for Patrick, saw that he was already halfway to the barn, and said, "No, no. I'll be fine." She maneuvered behind Rory, figuring it'd be better to see what was coming and be able to brace herself when it did. The question was how. By holding on to his shoulders?

He leaned forward, started the engine again and the big tires began to turn. "Better hold on to me," he shouted over his shoulder at her. "Put a hand on either side," he said, tapping one.

"All right!" Tentatively, she laid a hand on either of his shoulders and loosened her knees, watching the road as intently as any skier anticipating moguls. Surprisingly, it was easier to negotiate the bumps while on her feet than it'd been in Patrick's tiny, old farm truck. Sure, she had to use his broad shoulders to steady herself a few times, but she'd managed to not dig her fingernails into him. And hopefully, her palms weren't sweating so much that he'd felt moisture seeping through to his skin. When they reached her car ten minutes later, she eagerly climbed down, not waiting for him to go first.

Rory didn't seem to notice. He was so nonchalant, it left her wondering how many times he'd done this—giving girls a ride on a tractor, hauling their cars out of the ditch and the like. Or maybe he'd never done it all. His face was hard to read.

He attached the strap to the back of the tractor, pulled it tight, then moved to her car.

"Oh!" she said, seeing the mud and water pooling beneath the vehicle. "I should do that!"

"Nah," he said. "Ye're still clean. I was replacing fencepost this morning, so I'm hardly in my Sunday best." He gestured downward, carefully set aside his cane, took to one knee—with a grimace of pain—and searched under her bumper. Finding what he sought, he hooked the other end of the strap beneath, pulled it taut, and rose.

He forgot his cane. He'd almost made it upright when he faltered, looked around in some fear, took a teetering step, slipped, and slid into the ditch.

—⁂—

"Rory!" Fiona cried, even as he slid into the water with a tremendous splash. Cold sludge seeped into his boots. Mud coated his jeans to his thighs.

"I'm all right!" he said, lifting a hand, taking a moment to gather himself. He'd been a fool. So eager to show her he had all this in hand that he'd forgotten to grab his cane before he rose. *You stupid, prideful, eegit!*

"Are you sure?" she asked.

He made himself look at her. She was halfway down the embankment, wringing her hands. Her cheeks were pink, her dainty eyebrows in an arc of concern. "I'm fine, fine," he said. "Just got a mite ahead of myself. Don't come closer. It's slick and ya might fall in too."

"Do you need…Should I get your cane?"

"Please," he said, swallowing down the bitter gall. He admitted it to himself then. It had felt so nice to have her hands on his shoulders, her relying on him to steady herself as they rode on the tractor. He'd wanted her to continue to look at him that way. A rock. A balance. Not some invalid given to slipping into the very ditch he was supposed to be helping her out of.

She handed him the tip of the cane, but as he looked about, he realized the embankment was too steep. He grimaced and then did what he had to. He turned on his belly, and using his elbows, forearms and his one good leg, army-crawled back to a place he could gain his feet again. Rory couldn't summon the courage to look at her as he finally stood up. He could feel the burn of a blush on his cheeks, and hoped his beard hid it. "Let's get yer car out of there," he said gruffly, passing by. "Make sure it's in neutral and then get well clear of it."

He threw his cane into the tractor cab with more force than was necessary, then made himself methodically climb the ladder. He turned the key and let the engine roar to life before he made sure she wasn't anywhere near her car. She stood on the opposite side of the road and well back, hugging herself. Had he alarmed her?

A wind was whipping up now, running across his wet pants and chilling him. His bad leg ached, seeming intent on mounting its own protest for his ill treatment. Falls always did that to him. It'd likely trouble him now for a few days, and he'd have to break out his brace.

What're ya doing, O'Malley? he wondered, as he gently pressed on the gas and began pulling her VW with the tractor. He'd wanted to impress her, he admitted to himself. Be the hero. *But your heroic days are over.*

He pressed on the gas a bit more and the strap seemed

to strain to its limit, making Rory briefly wonder if he ought not have looked for a newer one. Then the mud relinquished its prize and the little car popped out and up the bank. He continued to haul it forward until all four wheels were firmly on the road. He looked to Fiona. "Hop in and set the brake!"

She scurried over to the car and did as he had ordered. He put the tractor in park, clambered down and released the strap.

"Rory, thank you so much," she said, rising to stand between her car and the open door. "I'm really sorry you fell."

"No worries," he said, feeling his blush kick up a notch. "It's not the worst thing that's ever happened to me. Think ya can manage to find the farm now?"

He winced inwardly, even as she did so a little outwardly. He'd not meant to sound so harsh. He was mad at himself, not at her.

"Oh, sure. I got it now. Thanks again." She dropped into her seat and slammed the door. The engine started and she headed out, this time on the correct side of the road.

Rory watched her go until she rounded the bend, then he looked up to the sky, sighed, and closed his eyes. This was what happened when he got around women. He made a fool of himself. It just wasn't worth it.

He was here for the summer to do one thing—help his grandfather and Uncle George. Not find love. He didn't need that kind of risk. And no girl needed to risk her heart on him. He looked all right from the outside, he knew. But on the inside?

On the inside he seemed to keep limping along too.

CHAPTER 3

Unfortunately, Grandda was as determined to set the pretty little Miss Burke in his path as Rory was to avoid her. Three days later, he brought her around to "tour the barn," as Rory worked on replacing an old and rotting stable door on a stall. Molly and Murphy, the farm's border collies, followed along, as if they were tour guides too. Rory couldn't help but steal glances at her as they moved about the ancient structure, Patrick telling her one tale after another about his ancestors—fisher-folk for many generations "until they took to the land." Periodically, she'd pat Murphy's side or bend down to give Molly's face a good rub.

She looked adorable with her hair caught up in a high ponytail. She wore a creamy, thick fisherman's sweater above jeans that hugged her curves. Her feet were tucked into forest-green Wellies—a surprisingly sensible option for a girl who didn't want to worry where she stepped. He'd figured she was "city" enough that she'd wear shiny leather boots, rather than old, ratty rubber boots like the locals.

He was setting the door in place, measuring for the hinges, when she stole up beside him, hands tucked into the back pockets of her jeans. "Are you avoiding me, O'Malley?"

He turned away with the heavy door and leaned it against the far wall, glad for the excuse to not look her in the eye. "Me? No. Just busy as usual. There's always a thousand things to do around the farm, come summer."

"So I gather," she said, climbing up on the wooden pony wall and perching on the top, apparently ready to settle in and watch him work. "Mind if I ask you some questions while you're doing that?"

"Depends on which questions ya want to ask," he returned warily. He turned to an old, rusty toolbox and fished out a screwdriver.

"Your grandfather tells me you're something of a Grace O'Malley scholar yourself."

He let out a sound of derision. "Mostly folklore and hearsay. I doubt I know much more that ya can use in your dissertation than what ye've drummed up yourself."

"But that's exactly why I'm here," she said. "I've read every source I can find. Accessed rare documents in Oxford and Dublin. But being here in the county, I figured I could document some *oral* tradition about our pirate queen. It will help me flesh out my work."

"Hmmm," he said, thinking about old locals who'd told him more than a few tales about Grace O'Malley. He said as much to her.

Fiona's blue eyes sparkled with such interest he had to tear his own away. "That'd be awesome to interview them. Can you introduce me?"

"I can point ya in the right direction," he said, setting a hinge in place, marking where the screws were to go.

"Your grandfather...he led me to believe that older folks around here get a little suspicious with newcomers. That I'd get further if you were with me."

Of course he had, the meddlesome old fool. Rory used his efforts as an excuse to think it over. Once the screw was in, he looked at her. What would it hurt? To take her to the local pub, help grease the wheel?

"Those look like a local's boots," he hedged, still considering. "Not some Boston girl's."

"Give me some credit, O'Malley," she said. "I knew that if I came here, looking too much the '*sassenach*,' the locals would clam up tighter than a mussel waiting for the tide." She patted her thighs. "But let's start with you. What do you know about the pirate queen? Pretend I know nothing."

Remembering to reach for his cane, he rose and paused uncertainly. "Ya have to know everything I know already. Reading the books, your research. Your writing. Ya likely have it covered."

"Yes," she admitted. "You might be surprised at what I still have to learn. You know as well as I do that people talk. And they talk. For generations. It's been fifteen generations—give or take—since your ancestor Grace sailed these waters and lived on this land."

"Stories grow," he said. "Change. They're not really a reliable source."

"True," she said with a nod. "And yet somewhere in all those fish stories is a guppy that was the genesis. That's what one of my profs said once, anyway. I aim to record every fish story I can and if I can correlate a common guppy, it will help me flesh out my dissertation."

"And what is the bent of your topic?"

She looked pleased at his question. "I'm focusing on her life story, but mostly about how it was shaped by being a woman ahead of her own time. Historians believe she was abused by the men in her life and I'm certain she had to fight for everything she ever achieved—twice as hard as a man in that era."

He nodded. "There's a reason she was a legend."

"So..." She leaned slightly toward him and gave him a

small smile that sent a shiver of delight down his neck and back. How long had it been since a woman had looked at him like that? Really looked at him?

"...will you do it?" she was asking. "Rory?"

He started, focusing on her words again rather than his reverie. He paused, still considering. What was he getting into?

She frowned and pulled back a bit, clearly puzzled. "I'm not asking for a life-long commitment here," she said. "I'm just looking for a couple of introductions. For you to point me in the right direction."

"Hmmm," he said. "I'll think on it."

—⟋⟍—

Fiona watched the shadow descend on his face again. The shuttering of his eyes, as if he was closing her off. Why had she said that about commitment? He was just so intense...everything seemed to have far more weight than she would've ever intended.

"Miss Burke," Patrick called, from the open barn doorway.

"Yes, sir?"

"Care to join us for supper? I have a roast in the oven. Some potatoes. And some green beans to boot."

Her eyes shifted to Rory, who went about his work as if they'd never talked at all. "That'd be great, Patrick," she called. "Haven't had a chance to get back to the grocer's." And in her tiny half-fridge, she could only keep enough for a couple meals at a time.

"Good enough," he said, turning. "We'll eat in ten. See that ye wash up, Rory."

She smiled. "Yeah," she said lowly. "See that you wash up, Rory."

He grunted, working on the second screw. She left then. There'd be time enough to make eyes at Rory O'Malley, she figured, if she even wished to. The man was clearly complicated. One minute looking at her with an edge of wonder in those blue-gray eyes, the next acting as if she was nothing but a nuisance.

But as she set off for the main house—a two-story, tidy, white-washed-black-shuttered affair—he soon caught up. "Look," he said, tucking a greasy handkerchief in his back pocket. "It's not that I'm unwilling to squire ya about the county, making introductions. It's that I have responsibilities here. To my grandda and all."

"Of course," she said. "I'd never want to interfere in that."

"It's not that you're an interference," he said.

"No?"

"No," he said, his golden-red brows creating a ledge over his nose as they furrowed.

They walked on in silence a bit, and had just reached the stone steps leading to the front door when he took her elbow. "Fiona."

She took one step and turned to face him.

He dropped his big hand and shoved it in his jeans pocket. "I'm...I'm not..." He lifted his chin and a muscle in his cheek flexed. "Ya should know that I'm not looking for a summer...fling."

Fiona let out a laugh. "Uh...neither am I. Is that what you think I'm after?" She shook her head and climbed the next step, lifting up a hand. "Never mind. Maybe your grandpa can introduce me to some people." She faced him as she pulled open the ancient screen door, riddled with holes. "I don't want to be a bother."

She paused only long enough to see Rory scowl before

they entered the dark kitchen with its dropped low ceiling, inhaling deeply. "Patrick!" she said, spying him lifting a lid on a pot sitting on a decrepit circa-1970s stove. "That smells so good!"

"Good, good. Come in, lass. Make yerself at home. Do ya care for a cuppa? Or a pint?"

"Just a glass of water would be great," she said. "May I help?"

"No, sit, sit. I almost have it all ready. Well, Mrs. O'Sullivan almost has it ready." He gave her an exaggerated wink. "Orla saw to me hiring her when she was…Well, my beloved was a mite determined I wouldn't be blaming her death for my own decline. Mrs. O'Sullivan comes and cooks for us every other day, leaving us enough for leftovers on the next. She's especially happy to do so when Rory is about."

"I'll wash up and fetch Uncle George," Rory said as he passed through.

"George?" Fiona asked in confusion, for the first time noticing four places set at the old, stained table.

"Oh, yes," Patrick said, placing the lid back on the pot. "Ye haven't met my brother yet. He's a bit bats, you see. Got the Alzheimer's some years back and spends most of his time pacin' these halls and askin' me where he might find our mother." He gestured down the hallway, where Rory had ducked into what she assumed was a small washroom.

"That's hard," Fiona said. "I had a grandma with Alzheimer's too. It was tough, watching her go through it."

"'Tis a bitter way to end things," he said. "As a younger man, George was as sharp as a tack." He turned to drain a pot of cooked carrots, dumped them in a Baleek serving bowl and set it on the table. "Mrs. O'Sullivan makes me look like I can run a farm and host guests for dinner with ease." He snapped his fingers in dramatic fashion, flashing her a smile.

"Everyone should have a Mrs. O'Sullivan in their lives," Fiona said. "The world would be a happier place."

"Indeed," Patrick said.

Having seen Rory move on down the hall to fetch his great-uncle, she ducked into the wash room to clean her own hands. By the time she was done, Rory had returned. "Uncle George," he said gently, pulling the old man to a stop before her. "This is Fiona Burke."

"Fiona?" the man repeated dimly. His eyes searched hers, as if wondering if he should remember her.

"Fiona's let out the cottage for the summer," Patrick said, setting the cast iron pot on a trivet in the center of the table.

"The summer, ya say?"

"Yes."

Rory led him to a seat and pulled it out for him. Patrick winked at her and gestured to his right. "Miss Fiona," he said, touching her chair, already pulled out.

"Thank you," she said. Once seated, Rory sat down across from her, and Patrick took his own. The chairs and table were something out of a 1950s' sitcom—a metal and plastic combo that was once bright and clean. Now they bespoke years of use. Happy use, Fiona decided.

She was reaching for the carrots when she noticed all three men were waiting, hands clasped, heads partially bowed. *Oh, right. Grace,* she reminded herself. While she believed in—and thanked—the good Lord for her life on a weekly basis, she wasn't in the habit of table grace herself. But here in Ireland, she knew it was a thing. And judging by the framed, yellowed print of Pope John Paul, a newer one of Benedict, and a brand-new one of Francis, she knew that Patrick was a good Catholic and used to doing so. Was Rory too?

After grace, they passed the food between the four of them, and by the time she'd added potatoes, roast beef, carrots, beets, and some canned apples to her plate, it looked something like Thanksgiving to her. Each took a few bites in amiable—if awkward—silence, eager to dive into the food while it was hot. Fiona was hungry, she discovered with some surprise. The last days had been full, apparently making her crave a few more carbs than usual. Or was it being in this wild, wonderful country?

Patrick's knife and fork hovered over his plate. "So, tell me, lass. How did our Granuaile become the focus of your research?"

"Granuaile?" she said, knowing the Irish name for Grace, and savoring how his lovely accent rolled off the syllables as *Gran-you-ell.* "You mean other than the fact that she cut off her hair so she could sail with her father on the high seas?"

"Then was married off to the son of another powerful clan at sixteen?" Rory put in, pointing at her with his knife as he shoved a bite of beef in his mouth.

"Yes," Fiona smiled, welcoming this slight thaw between them. "Two kids later, she's widowed at thirty, but she's in her element." Fiona sliced into her own meat. "It wasn't every woman who could manage a fighting force of two to three hundred men."

"True." Rory gestured toward Patrick. "Grandda, do ya know she fished a future lover from the sea? The man was half-drowned. And then she bedded him."

"She also fought off enemies to save her infant son from Barbary pirates," Fiona quickly added, wanting to get past such talk. Would Patrick think it inappropriate?

"Don't forget she revenged her other sons too, in battle," Rory said. "It was due to her that they inherited anything at all."

"Not only that, but she survived imprisonment in Limerick jail and later Dublin Castle too."

Patrick laughed, looking between them like he was watching a tennis match. "You two pups aren't telling me anything I don't know. Next ye'll be eager to let me in on the big secret—that she met with Herself, as if all of Ireland doesn't know it already."

Herself. The queen of England, Fiona silently interpreted, smiling with them.

Rory laughed, the first time she'd heard him do so, and the sound of it was warm and deep. His grin transformed his face. He suddenly looked younger, even more handsome than before.

Rory glanced at his uncle, realized he was not yet eating, and turned to cut up his meat. "Go on, George," he whispered, touching the hand that held a fork as if the man had forgotten what he was doing at the table. "Eat up."

Fiona was moved by his tenderness and care toward the old, vacant-eyed man.

"Do ye intend to write about how Grace gave up the sea for love?" Patrick asked.

"But she didn't," Fiona returned in surprise. "Other than brief stints inland with Donal O'Flaherty, she continued to sail."

"That's not the way of it, according to some of the old folk," Patrick said. "Rory, lad, you really ought to introduce our pretty guest here to Laiose McCarthy. As well as Conor O'Rourke."

"Aye, I've thought of them, Grandda. But I—"

"Ya should also see her out to Clare Island," the old man interrupted. "There's likely a few folk out there who might remember the old tales."

Clare Island, Fiona thought excitedly. *Grace O'Malley's stronghold.* She swallowed a quick retort that she could find her own way to the ferry, remembering that she'd get farther, faster, with a local to introduce her.

Rory put a big bite of meat in his mouth and chewed. Both Patrick and she strived to ignore his scowl.

"Rory seems busy," Fiona began. "Perhaps you'd like to accompany me out to the island, Patrick?"

"Can't," he said shortly. "Molly's nearin' her time now."

"This will be Grandda's third litter of pups," Rory explained. "Ye've met Murphy and Molly."

"They're kind of hard to miss," she said with a grin. The border collies were clearly all about keeping everyone accounted for. Every time she drove into the farm, the handsome dogs circled her car and practically walked her to the cottage. "But Molly's expecting?"

"She's keepin' near the barn, more and more," Patrick said, "which tells me her time is approachin'." He turned to Rory. "Ya best see Miss Burke out to Clare soon. I make do around here all year, I can spare ya a few days this summer."

Rory huffed a laugh and shook his head slowly. He cast Fiona a sidelong glance, his meaty hands folded before him. "Ya can see what he's up to, throwing us together?"

"I see it," she returned, feeling a bit of a blush rise on her cheeks. "You're a bit shameless, aren't you, Patrick?"

"Well, lass, it remains to be seen," he said, cocking his head. "Whether 'twill be something I'm ashamed over, or something I can gloat about."

"Hmmm," Rory intoned, the sound of it like a rumble in his chest. He wiped his mouth with a napkin. "Back to yer subject matter," he said pointedly. "I've always found it fascinatin' that Grace was able to meet with Queen Elizabeth, and managed to then *leave* the castle, rather than get strung up in a cage like other pirates. Do ya think that plays toward your thesis of her being ahead of her time? Were they not both ahead of their time? Powerful women in a man's world?"

Fiona nodded. "Absolutely," she said, sitting back in her chair and considering him. "I delve into the fact that they were both women out of their time, leading in ways that women had not done so before. Perhaps it was their mutual admiration that granted Granuaile safe passage in and out of London."

"What about Grace's treasure?" George said, momentarily utterly coherent. The food seemed to have helped him.

All three of them turned to the man in astonishment.

"What did you say, Uncle George?" Rory asked, his long, golden-red eyelashes blinking slowly.

The old man slowly turned in his direction. "Say? I don't know, laddie. What did I say?"

"Something intriguing," Rory coaxed, patting his hand. "About Grace O'Malley's treasure. Do you remember somethin' of it? Where do you think it lies, Uncle?"

"Well," said the man, a bit of food clinging to the corner of his mouth. "If 'tisn't on Rockfleet Castle land, then it surely is in that hidden cove aside Howth Castle."

"Howth Castle?" Rory repeated, pronouncing it in the Irish way of dropping the "h."

"Howth Castle?" George said blankly, stabbing his last bite of carrot. "What's that ye say, laddie?"

Rory sat back and stared at him, then glanced at his grandfather, while Fiona waited expectantly.

"That's the most I've heard him say in months," Patrick said. "See there, lass? Ye're already good company for the men in this family."

Fiona shook her head. "Where is Howth Castle?"

"Over in County Dublin," Rory said. "Grace was said to have used a cove over there to moor her ship and sneak into Dublin undetected by the English. She came to call on Lord Howth one day but was refused at the gates. She was told the family was at dinner."

"Which she didn't take well," Patrick said. He rose and picked up Fiona's empty plate and carried it to the sink.

"No?" Fiona asked.

"No," Rory said, picking up his own plate and George's and walking to the sink, using his cane with one hand, balancing the plates in the other. "She retaliated by kidnapping Howth's heir. She only returned the child when Lord Howth promised to forever welcome any visitor to his dinner table, including her."

"To this day at Castle Howth, they always set an extra place at the table," Patrick said.

"Is it all true?"

"So goes the tale," Rory said with a shrug.

"That is fantastic. Exactly the sort of tales I seek."

"The woman cut a broad swath," Rory said with a partial smile, then seemed to catch himself—as if wary of this growing camaraderie between them.

"Indeed," Patrick said. "All the way to the Barbary Coast! But begin on Clare Island, lass. 'Tis a good place to start. She lived out there in that old tower for a good part of her life." He turned to Rory. "Go tomorrow. The sun should be shining, the seas calm."

"Why don't I stay?" Rory asked. "Keep an eye on Molly, as well as George? You could take Fiona out. Ye've always liked that ferry ride to Clare."

"Who is Molly?" George asked.

"Grandda's dog," Rory said, patting his great-uncle's shoulder.

Patrick frowned and brought a hand to his belly. "I tend to get a bit sick when I ride on boats these days." He lifted a brow of apology toward Fiona. "Perils of old age. No, I fear this trip is best left to ye young people."

When Rory again hesitated, Fiona shoved back a rising tide of embarrassment. The last thing she wanted him to think was that he had to take her anywhere. It hurt a bit, seeing him work so hard to try and get out of it.

She pasted on a smile as she rose. "No worries. You guys are so busy around here. I'll get myself out there and poke around, make some friends. I can be quite charming when I set my mind to it. Thank you so much for dinner, Patrick," she rushed on, interrupting both Patrick and Rory's retorts. "And please, I don't want to make a nuisance of myself at all this summer. I'm your tenant, nothing more. Honestly, I never expected anything more."

She turned to the lone man left at the table. "George, it was nice to meet you. Have a good night." He stared at her blankly—as if he'd never seen her before.

"Fiona," Rory began, moving toward her, leaning hard on his cane.

"No, really," she said brightly, feeling an odd tightening in her throat. Good grief, was she wanting to cry? "It's good. I'm good. It'll be fine. I'll see you when I get back. Good night!" With that, she fairly rushed out of the house, swallowing hard.

Why was she so hurt by his hesitation? Rory'd been clear about it—he wasn't here to find a summer romance. And he probably had to take such a hard line, given his grampa's overt matchmaking efforts. She couldn't really blame him.

But then, why did it feel like such an insult?

CHAPTER 4

"Well, I give ye the perfect opportunity to get to know that smart, pretty lass better, and ye throw it to sea!" grumbled Rory's grandfather. "Ye're too young, laddie, to be taking the path of old men!"

"Grandda, I don't need your help on this front. I'm…I'm just not ready for—"

"Bah!" said the man. "If ya wait for the perfect time to find love, go to university, or have children, you end up single, uneducated and childless." He punched him on the arm.

"Ow!" Rory complained in surprise, rubbing it and frowning at the smaller man.

"Perhaps I should punch ya across the jaw next time!" Patrick said, more agitated than Rory had seen him in years. "Knock some sense into ya."

"Grandda, ya don't know what I've seen. Afghanistan left me… What goes on in my head. It's…it's not the kind of thing…" He let out a sound of frustration. "Fiona isn't the kind of woman who wants a damaged man."

Patrick stilled. "Ye're not any more damaged than the next person, lad," he said, his tone gentling. "Sure, ye have some baggage, from yer time away. But everyone has baggage of some sort, if they've lived enough life. Why don't ya ask God what he thinks of Miss Fiona? The fact that ya both love Ireland and history? That ye're both here for the stretch of a summer?" He turned to fully face Rory, putting a hand on either of his much taller grandson's shoulders and shaking him a little. "Could this not be the good Lord's way of leading ya back to *life*, laddie?"

"Or could it just be my meddlesome grandda's way of trying to rope me into love?"

The older man continued to stare at him. George rose and shuffled over to them. Neither looked his way, but they could feel his concern.

"Would it be so very terrible?" Patrick asked softly. "To fall in love again?"

Again. Rory swallowed hard. Remembering Elizabeth. Returning from the Middle East, to find she'd taken up with his best friend. To remember her look of pity, as she took in his cane, his braced leg…a leg that never quite healed.

"Yes," he whispered. "It could be *very* terrible, Grandda."

"Or quite lovely," Patrick said, patting his shoulders, then his cheeks, forcing him to look him in the eye. "The question is, will ye take the chance at the lovely? Or keep yerself safe, avoiding the *potential* of the terrible forever?"

—⁓—

From the edge of his window, Rory watched Fiona drive out the next morning, obviously intent on catching the earliest ferry out of Roonagh Quay. He took in a deep breath and let it out slowly as she moved out of view with the familiar crack-and-pop sounds of gravel. Her little car disappeared around the bend in the road.

For the hundredth time, he considered Grandda's words. He resented the old man's interference. What right had he to wade into these waters? And yet he knew the man only had his best interests at heart. It had been five years since

Elizabeth had eviscerated him, since his best friend Max had betrayed him. It had hurt him more, in some ways, than his leg injury. Physically, a man had to take risks to live his life. Learn to walk again, press his limitations.

But he didn't have to do the same with his heart.

He'd built a life in Shannon since then. Made it through three years of teaching. Met a few friends down at the pub two or three times a week. But Rory admitted to himself that he kept them all at arm's length, really. It had worked, these last three years. It had kept his heart safe, allowed him to focus on improving physically. And yet now…

He faced the window and leaned forward until his forehead met the cold glass. It was a chilly morning but promised to turn into a brilliant early summer day. He hoped Fiona would take a seat inside the ferry on the way over to Clare, but he also hoped she'd venture outside on the way back to enjoy the view. The views from the boat were fantastic—Achill Island, the Nehin Mountain range, the rugged coastline and islands of Clew Bay, and the towering, conical Croagh Patrick. It had been years since he'd made the trip with his grandfather, but he remembered it well.

Why hadn't he simply agreed to escort her to the island? Who said that spending some time with Fiona had to lead to anything long-term? Why did he have to be such a navel-gazer? Had he not always found such men frustrating and weak?

He ran his fingers through his wavy hair. *Ya know exactly when ya became a navel-gazer, ya dolt. The day ya found Elizabeth in Max's arms.* He turned and sat down on the edge of his bed to put the brace on his leg, which he wore some days when it ached. It occurred to him then that he'd been bracing his heart for years. Caging it, all in an effort of protection. Even from friends.

Could his grandfather be right? Was it time to let down his guard, even a little? He opened the brace and re-strapped the Velcro, giving him a little more freedom. *That's what ya need, laddie,* he thought. *Just a wee bit more room in your Velcro.* It wasn't as if he was moving out without protection. Only loosening up the armor a tad.

He was older, now. Wiser than when he'd been with Elizabeth. He could protect his heart and yet live life a bit… broader now. Couldn't he?

This wasn't a life commitment. This was a trip to Clare Island. *Keep it in order, O'Malley, and you'll be fine.*

—⚊—

Fiona only lasted a couple of minutes on the sundeck of *The Pirate Queen*—the aptly named ferry to the island once ruled by Grace O'Malley. While it was a bright, clear morning, it was still damp and chilly, so she descended the steep steps down into the covered hold, where locals milled about, sipping coffee and catching up.

She went to a counter and paid for a cup of tea, then found a seat near a window, smiling as she listened to the people talking and laughing, noting their unique phrases. "How's the craic?" one asked a woman seated in the center section. It was the locals' way of asking how she was doing, or what was happening.

"Ah, ye know, the usual. Glad to be gettin' out to Clare on dis fine day."

A man moved into the bench seat behind her and was telling his friend to not "give out," which Fiona took to mean, in time, that he wasn't to complain about his wife, given that she put a fine meal on the table every night and had proven true over thirty years of marriage.

"Heya!" cried a man toward the back. "What's the story, O'Malley?"

Fiona didn't turn around. There had to be hundreds of O'Malley kin about these parts, especially en route to Clare.

But then she heard that laugh, a deep, warm sound, and the slap of hands as he apparently shook his friend's hand. She froze.

Rory was here. He had come after all. Why?

She resolved to pretend she hadn't noticed his arrival. No, after last night's rebuff, the dude could work a little if he wanted to get back into her good graces.

Moments later, Rory paused beside her red leather bench. "Mind if I take this seat?"

She glanced up at him and after a second's hesitation, slid closer to the window and gestured for him to take it, unsure of what to say.

He sat down, started to say something, then bit his lip. He leaned his cane between his legs, and put his big hands on the back of the seat in front of them.

"Second thoughts?" she said at last.

"Thoughts that I was a fool," he admitted. "The worst sort o' eegit. Forgive me?"

"Done," she said. "But really. I am a big girl, Rory, even if you have, what? Eight inches and fifty Euros on me?"

"Hey, now! Three stones, max," he said, patting his belly, and frowning as if she'd offended him. "Mrs. O'Sullivan's food isn't that good."

She smiled, relieved the tension had been broken. But he was a big man. Broad in shoulder, strong and lean, despite his injured leg. And he had to weigh fifty or sixty Euros more than she did. The guy truly resembled a Viking, with his rust-colored beard and bright, gray-blue eyes.

"Besides, I thought ya might take it into your head to borrow a car and drive the island," he said. "I couldna' lived with myself, if ye'd run another innocent off the road."

She gave him a sly, sideways glance. "I have it on good authority that you can walk most of the island in under an hour."

He frowned and leaned back, folding his arms. "On those wee legs of yours?" He pursed his lips doubtfully. "Maybe if'nya set off double-time."

"We'll see," she said, well aware he was teasing her.

"Now Clare is a lovely place. But the exhibit is nothing special. And Grace's old tower is in poor repair. What do ya hope to gain?"

"Well, there's something in seeing a place for yourself. Feeling, smelling, hearing what Grace might have once, too. And again, it's the people I'd love to talk to. Hear their stories. Gather the tales. So, yes, I'll stop by the exhibit, and I want to tour the tower. Capture a glimpse of what it must've been like for Grace to live there, back in the day. Feel it, you know?"

He nodded thoughtfully. "It's the best part of history, really. Imagining what it must've been like for people of the time. It's what I try to do with my students."

"What grade do you teach?"

"Fourth and fifth year. What you Americans call sophomore and junior."

"Did you choose that?"

"It's my preference," he said with a dip of his head. "They're not green to secondary school, and their heads are not yet at university. I find it's when they're most intent upon their learning. Perfect soil, as my grandda would say."

"Your grandda is something special."

"That he is."

Fiona paused, feeling the tension gathering between them again as both thought of how Patrick was clearly trying to play matchmaker. "How long have you been teaching?"

The ferry horn blasted then, warning of their imminent departure. People began to take their seats. A final few hurried over the narrow gangplank to board.

"Three years."

"Oh," she said. "I thought maybe you'd been at it longer."

"Are ya sayin' I'm old?"

"Well, not old, really. But what are you? Twenty-eight? Nine?"

"Twenty-nine, as of last month. Teaching is my second career."

Fiona considered that. "And your first was…"

"Mine sweeping," he said, blowing out his cheeks and rounding his eyes. "I worked for a non-profit that specialized in clearing roads and market paths for villagers in the Middle East, after soldiers departed. Got a little too close to one and blew apart this leg," he said, gesturing to his left, "and received a bit of a blow to my head as well. Proved to be a bit too much for my folks. They convinced me I'd done my bit for the world, and that I should return to university to pursue my other passion—history."

She paused, taking all that in. "Was it hard to convince you?"

"Not really. At that point, I needed to start over. In many ways."

Fiona figured he was now talking about some girl, but didn't want to pry. She'd had a significant relationship once herself—one that had left her feeling the need to "start over" too.

"I read once that the average adult has ten different jobs by the time they're forty," she said, "and twelve or more jobs in their lifetime. Do you think that's true?"

Rory considered that as the lines were cast off and the engine roared to life, slowly rotating them away from the pier and turning toward the open harbor. "The first ten I get, given all the jobs we have as kids and university students, then one or two after. But several more after that?" He paused, considering it. "Seems like a lot. All my life, I've watched my parents, my grandda do one. What about you?"

"Yeah, I come from a one-career parentage as well. My mom's a journalist—and still working part-time. My dad's a newly retired builder. Now he says his job is professional golfer."

Rory huffed a laugh. "That'd be the dream. Has he ventured on to any of our courses?"

Fiona thought about the crazy links course she'd seen beside the road on the way up the Wild Atlantic Way. There'd been massive hills and wild, untamed grasses lining them. "No. He's more of a perfected-greens guy, I think."

"Do ye golf yourself?"

"Not if I can help it. No patience. You?"

"Only when my mates drag me out. But few of them do anymore."

The engine picked up speed and great waves began to part before them as they cut through the icy-blue waters. But Fiona hadn't missed Rory's slightly dropped tone for that last bit. *Few of them do anymore.* Good grief, what had happened to this man? He didn't have friends anymore?

There was something inexplicably sad about him, just

under the surface. A grief that still haunted him. Was it his injury, or the events that led to it? Or something else?

"What about your parents?" she said. "What do they do?"

"My da's a retired maths teacher. My mum's a retired cook. They live in Shannon."

Fiona filed that away, surprised when her first thought was that his mother might be judgmental about her own meager cooking skills. *When exactly do you think you might be cooking for this man's mother, Fiona Burke?* Chances were she might meet them, if they came up sometime from Shannon. But Mrs. O'Sullivan clearly did all the cooking at the main house. And there wasn't a big chance she'd ever be entertaining in her cottage with the two burners. Not that she couldn't handle a dinner for two with Rory...

"Maths," she said awkwardly, interrupting her own troublesome thought pattern. "Back home in the U.S., we just call it math. Why the plural?"

"Well, there are multiple maths, yes?"

"I guess," she said, thinking it through. "But we use math as an all-encompassing term."

"What about siblings?" Rory asked, folding his arms.

"An older brother, Thomas, doing what my parents think I should've done."

"And that is..."

"Graduating with a 'practical' bachelor's degree, and getting to work."

"Ahh. I see."

"Now if I'd done what you did," she said, "gotten my teaching degree and gotten to work a couple years ago, that would've been okay. But taking on more debt? Aiming for a college professor job that is hard to come by? They think I'm foolish." She swallowed hard, a bit chagrined that she'd let all that spill out.

"Foolish? Nah. A gamble, yes."

She nodded. "It's true. It's a gamble. Lots of profs like to stay right where they are, enjoying their tenure. But I figure it's like any profession. If you know the right people and are in the right place at the right time, you get a job."

"True. So are ya hopin' that's back in Boston?"

"Ideally, yes." It was where she had the most contacts. As well as some ins with the faculty. "What about you? Brothers? Sisters?"

"A younger brother by five years," he said. "Who really has no interest but traveling the world at the moment. He's teaching English in China now."

"English?" she asked wryly. "Can it be called that with an Irish accent?"

He smiled good-naturedly at her teasing. "Aye. For the most part."

She turned to look outside, captivated by the skyline, lit by a sun gaining leverage in the sky. All around them were hundreds of small, shallow islands. Fiona knew Grace O'Malley had once used the biggest to hide and lay in wait to capture other ships—and the smaller, shallow islands to drive hapless ships fleeing her to ground. The much bigger, taller Clare Island stood out ahead, a silent, stubborn guardian to Clew Bay. It was easy to see why Grace had centered her operations there. With Clare at the mouth of the bay, and Rockfleet on land, she had clearly *owned* these waters.

In the distance there was a mountain range, one mount rising above the rest to command attention. "Is that…" she began, pointing.

"Croagh Patrick," he answered, "or in Irish, 'Curach Padraig.'"

"Which means?"

"'Saint Patrick's Stack.' Locals call it 'the Reek.'"

"Why?"

"It's based off an old word meaning 'rick' or 'stack.' Many climb it as a pilgrimage."

"A pilgrimage, huh?" she said, her eyes tracing the distant, high mountain. "Have you ever done so?"

"No. Always meant to. But then…"

She fell silent then, well aware that his hiking days might be behind him. *Way to go, girl. Open mouth. Insert foot.* But she dared to press. "Do you hike at all now?"

"Not like what I did, once. But this gains me a fair distance," he said, grabbing hold of the cane and batting it between his hands.

"Canes can be cool," she said, feeling both daring and honest.

"Think so?" he said, casting her a wry grin. Clearly, he could be charming if he set his mind to it. "Ya mean like in an aged professor sort of way?"

"Well, not in an aged professor way. But there is something distinguished, powerful in a cane."

"Even when the user is infirm?"

She paused and stared at him. "C'mon, O'Malley. Sure, you've obviously had an injury. But my gosh…" She shook her head slowly. "I'm not quite sure I've ever met a man as aware of his body—or his power—as you."

CHAPTER 5

She appeared to speak like she drove—without a lot of forethought. The last words seemed to fall from her lips, but then she caught herself. Pulled her chin slightly back. Looked to the sea. Then fished for her phone in her purse, settled it in her hand and scrolled, pretending that she'd not said anything notable at all.

But to Rory, her words echoed, and echoed again in his mind.

She thought him powerful. In spite of his injury.

His second thought shocked him, and sent a blush rushing up his neck he prayed she wouldn't notice.

Because his second thought was that he wanted to kiss her.

But it was gratitude that drove him. Not what any girl would want as primary impulse. She was pretty—God help him, she was pretty. But this? It was pure praise. Gratitude.

She thinks I'm powerful.

A woman thinks of me as a man. A whole man, despite my injury.

And in the midst of the thought, his own sense of strength seemed to transform, cascading back to before the explosion. When he played rugby and instilled fear in his opponents. Then fast-forwarding to the present. To the PTSD, that often threatened to send him into a panic attack, heart racing, sweat rolling down his face. To his brace. The ache in his leg. His constant reminder, his *handicap*.

And yet, for the first time, he let his mind rove over what he so rarely allowed himself to see in the mirror each day. His strong, hewn shoulders. Burly pecs. Chiseled belly.

He was strong. The injury, for as much as it had pulled him back...well, it had forced him to become stronger. In the arms and shoulders. In his balance. Even if it failed him at times, sending him down an embankment as he tried to hook a tractor to a VW. Or when a loud sound rattled him so badly it took minutes to recover.

But it turned out that women might be able to see his strength, in spite of it all.

Fiona had seen it.

He pulled out his own phone, pretending to scroll and tap, needing space, time to digest too. For so long he'd considered himself less-than. So far from anything resembling... powerful.

But this girl. This *woman*, thought him so.

They soon approached the cement quay and small harbor on Clare, with Grace's ancient castle keeping watch from the left. It was from there the pirate queen had reigned Clew Bay and beyond, keeping track of both the Irish who owed her homage and taxes and the interloping English on which she loved to prey.

As the ferry slowed, Fiona's eyes shifted from the tower house—a design favored by the chieftains of old—to the landscape sloping up the nearest peak, a roughly five-hundred-meter climb. He hoped she wouldn't wish to tackle that. If so, he'd wait for her down at O'Malley's tiny grocery and shop. Like so much else in this region, it was clearly run by kin—how exactly they were related, Rory wasn't certain.

Fiona flashed him a delighted smile and took the hand of the ferryman, offering help to passengers exiting the small gangway and down a few stairs. Seeing his cane, he lifted a brow and offered a hand to Rory too. But, after taking stock, Rory thought it a reasonable gamble. Stepping with his right leg first, he took the stairs, one at a time. After Fiona had so recently expressed her thoughts on his power, he wasn't eager for her to witness him fall on his face.

But she wasn't looking at him at all. She was already moving ahead, clearly eager to explore this place that had once been Grace O'Malley's domain.

—ɷ—

"Say, Fiona," Rory said behind her. "Do ya fancy a bike? The tower's right here, but it's a bit of a haul out to the abbey and the exhibit. And I, uh…well, I travel a mite faster on two wheels. If all goes well, we can go up to the lighthouse for lunch."

Fiona readily agreed. She didn't want the man to suffer, and she'd held her breath as he insisted on making his way off the ferry unassisted. Was that because she had been watching? Or just that he was stubborn? She'd looked to the tower and stepped ahead, pretending as if she did not fear for him at all. Now, as she followed him to the tiny bike shop— little more than a shack with walls thick with what had to be an annual white-wash—she wondered how she herself might handle such an injury. At twenty-four she felt like she could tackle anything. What would it be like to be a fairly young man, but know you could not?

As Rory negotiated a rate for the day and limped over to check out the vendor's inventory, she thought of his precious few words about his accident. She pictured a Middle-Eastern town. Dirt road. Mud or stucco houses. Rory sweeping the streets for land mines, until he came across one his monitor failed to warn him about. She was sorry he'd been injured. But she was glad he was—

"Fiona?" he asked, obviously for the second time. He waved at them. "Where are ya, lass? Back in the sixteenth century?"

"Oh! Sorry. Clearly," she said. She moved back toward the shop.

"Is this about the right size for ya?" the bike vendor asked, pointing to a small, yellow beach bike with fat tires.

"Looks like it," she said, straddling the seat and placing a foot on the pedal. It'd been years since she'd been on a bike. But didn't they say you never forgot?

Rory handed the man a credit card.

"Oh, I can cover mine," Fiona said.

"No worries. 'Tisn't much," he returned, waving on the man behind the counter to process it. After a few more instructions on when they were to be back, and a quick perusal of the map on the wall, they made their way outside and then to the tower house, just around the corner. Fiona's first twenty feet or so on the bike were a bit wobbly, but she soon settled in.

At the tower, they leaned their bikes against a neighboring rock face. "Oh," she said. "We didn't get any locks for them!"

"Ach, no worries," Rory said. He lifted his big hands. "We're on an island. Where would a bike thief escape to? Besides, I can keep watch while ya take a gander at Grace's castle."

She smiled and turned back to the tower house. She ran her hand along the ancient stones—thinking of Grace O'Malley's kin putting each into place—then out to the broad expanse of the sea. She glanced up to the roof, which had likely once been thatched or lead, and knew that from the top battlements, the pirate queen would have been able to see for miles and miles on a clear day.

Inside, there were remnants of a huge fireplace beside a great room where Grace would have once held court, as well as warded off the chill of an Irish winter. Fiona paused at each window, taking pictures of them, noting that from this level alone, Grace would have been able to see who was arriving and departing from the quay, who might be approaching from the farms above, and who was sailing upon the seas between here and Clew Bay. No wonder it had been her stronghold.

As she completed her walk around the perimeter, she belatedly noticed Rory was watching her as he leaned against the wall, arms crossed. He gave her a small smile as she approached.

"Did you just watch me do my whole survey?" she asked, a bit embarrassed.

"Is that what ya call it?" he asked wryly. "Ya had such a faraway look about ya. Imagining yerself in Grace's boots?"

"A bit," she allowed, slowly climbing over the boulders that surrounded the tower until she'd made it back to the road.

From there they set off for the abbey, just down the road. It really was a beautiful island, Fiona thought, with broad, deep-green hills sweeping down to the silver-blue sea, crashing with some gusto against the gray rocks below. The hills were dotted with white sheep, some of their wool clinging here and there to spurs in the barbed wire that separated their pasture from the road. They kept their bumpy quarters as neatly trimmed as a mower might.

"Why do they paint them?" she asked Rory. "The sheep?"

He looked to the three they passed, two with blue spray paint, one with blue and pink. "To know which are vaccinated and which are not. The woolies are kinda hard to tell apart."

She smiled at his use of "woolies," but wished they wouldn't paint them. It was not nearly as romantic to take pictures of spray-painted sheep as it would be of white ones.

After passing two walkers—they didn't call them "hikers" in Ireland—they saw no other people on the road. Around the bend, the white abbey came into view, and it was surrounded by tombstones, some of them tall, stone Celtic crosses.

Fiona sighed in pleasure. She'd read all about this place, of course, given that it'd been built by Grace's ancestors in 1224. But it was entirely different to be here. They left their bikes beside the entrance to the cemetery, approaching the abbey in an almost reverent way.

"This place has some of the finest medieval frescoes in Ireland," Rory said, stepping ahead of her and holding the top of the stone doorway as he bent beneath it to enter. Fiona followed without even tucking her head. They made their way down the dim hallways, into the nave, and then into the chancel, staring upward at painted figures of knights and stags and harpists.

"These once covered the entire ceiling," Rory said. "It must'a been quite the sight when the colors were fresh and bright."

There were still ancient pews and hymnals in the sanctuary. A candle flickered atop the altar in a soot-covered glass vestibule, with a picture of Mary and Jesus above.

"Do they still worship here?" Fiona asked quietly. To speak louder would seem intrusive.

"I'd wager so," he said, lifting a brow. "With a population of about a hundred and forty, Clare doesn'a have much need of another."

Fiona nodded, wondering over the idea of people worshipping in the same structure for hundreds of years. Back home, she worshipped at a local school, or once in a while, at a friend's home church. But even the oldest buildings in town were half as old as this place. *"If only these walls could speak, the stories they'd tell!"* That's what her grandfather was fond of saying.

They wandered toward an ornately carved tomb canopy over a nook in the north wall, which Fiona knew was widely held to be Grace O'Malley's final resting place. "Think she really is entombed here?" she whispered, bending to run her hand across the cool, limestone slab with a carved stallion, wreath, and helmet. She took in the wild boar at the center, and three bows, arrows affixed, pointing at the boar.

He shrugged. "It's as likely a place as any."

At the base was the carving of a galley with furled sails and five oars, as well as the name "O'Maille" and the family motto, "Terra Mariq Potens." *Powerful by land and sea.*

Fiona pictured the woman at sixty-seven, battle-worn, and finally at peace. Had they buried her with her sword in hand? For a long while she thought back on all she'd learned about Grace's final year.

"Is the exhibit attached to the abbey?" she asked, turning toward Rory. She thought she'd remembered that it was here, from her internet scavenging. With a start, she realized he'd gone to sit in a nearby pew, elbows on knees, head down. As if he were praying. Not watching her, as she half-expected him to be doing. *Silly girl,* she chided herself. *The man has more things on his mind than a redhead from the States.*

"Next door," he said, lifting his head, apparently unper-turbed at her gaffe. "I'll go and raise the priest. Fetch the key if necessary. It's early yet in the season, and as ya can see, we're the only visitors."

Which didn't bode well for a tourist-worthy exhibit, she thought. But she took a seat and waited as Rory disappeared down the hall into an attached building.

What had Rory been praying about? His life? His future? His past?

She frowned. *It's none of your business. Keep your mind on the goal, girl. Grace O'Malley. Not Rory O'Malley.*

He returned, following an aged priest. "Fiona, this is Father Michael. He's going to let us into the exhibit, even though it's closed for *renovation*." He gave the last word air quotes and a funny face from behind the priest.

"That is very kind of you, Father," she said, as the old, tiny man nodded at her and gave her a sad smile. "Thank you so much. Rory might've told you, I'm doing some research on Grace O'Malley," she went on as he turned to lead them to the exhibit hall. "Have you lived on Clare long?"

"If ya deem fifty years a long time," he said.

"That is a long time. As well as stopping to see your fine exhibit," she said, "I'm hoping to interview a few locals. Do you consider yourself up on all the Grace O'Malley lore?"

"Oh, aye," he said, rolling keys on an ancient ring until he found the right one, then sliding it into the lock. "I imag-ine if something's been told of old Grace, it's likely passed my ears. Let me go and fetch my tea and I'll return to regale ya properly. Do ya care for a cup?"

"Oh, no, thank you," she said.

"I would," Rory said. "I'll keep ya company while Fiona has a look about."

Fiona's neck tingled with anticipation as the priest flipped on fluorescent, humming lights, but her mood quickly plummeted. The exhibit was held all in one room, some of it as rudimentarily displayed as an elementary school teacher might, with curling cut-outs pinned to gray-cloth-covered bulletin boards. Here and there were some more sophisticated attempts. A circa-1980s computer, marked "out of order." A glass wall—that on one layer showed Grace O'Malley's domain in 1560—then with a slide to the right, the map of her "world" after she married Bourke in 1566. Then, with an additional slide, all that she considered "hers" when she died in 1603.

There was a small room with fading, framed pictures of the woman from over the centuries, probably culled from books and copied from museum archives. Fiona recognized most of them and used her phone camera to capture the few she'd never seen before.

She'd completed her perusal of the exhibit, chastising herself for her disappointment that she'd discovered nothing new, when Rory and the priest returned. The priest looked at her, gray brows rising in surprise. "Done already?"

"I am," she said, a bit sheepish. She suspected he might be quite proud of the place.

"Ach, well, 'tisn't much. All we could afford over the years, of course, but basic, as the kids say nowadays."

Fiona smiled. So the old man was in touch enough with his flock to know what the kids said. She liked that in a priest.

"That new section ought to be done in two or t'ree months. That'll give us a welcome boost. I only wish we'd gotten it done before the summer folk arrive." He waved at them. "Pity that ya cannot crack the whip with volunteers."

"Agreed," Rory said, with a comforting smile. He set his

mug of tea on an old table that had been set by the door—for someone to take ticket money? Or for study? "What if we sit here a spell? Fiona here would like to ask ya some questions. She's working on her doctorate in history, with a focus on our own Granuaile O'Malley."

"Oh, aye," said the man, falling into one of the two chairs with a grunt and grimace of pain. "Then perhaps ye can tell me a tale or two, lass."

"Probably nothing you haven't heard before," she said, as Rory brought over another chair from the corner, using it as his cane to stabilize himself. She resisted the urge to rise and help him, guessing he wouldn't appreciate it. "What I'm seeking is folklore, Father. They might seem like tall tales to you. But what I'm after is some new and fresh detail to add to my dissertation, not what the several historians who have published books about the pirate queen have covered. Have you read all those?"

"Oh, aye," he said, taking a sip of his tea. "All those folks have stopped by here too, o' course. Two sent a copy of their books to me after they were published, which I thought quite kind of them."

"It was," she said with a nod, making a mental note to send the man a copy of her dissertation when it was done.

The diminutive man continued to nod, his heavy-lidded eyes shifting back and forth as if searching the data-banks of his memory for a story that had not been told. "Ye must've 'eard that Gracie was the only pirate to have an audience with Queen Elizabeth and walk out free."

"Yes," she returned gently. "I researched quite a bit about that at Oxford."

"Oxford, eh?" he said, lifting one brow in appreciation. "And ye know that she saved her son from the Barbary pirates."

"I do," Fiona said, beginning to wonder if this was fruit-less. "Tell me more about what the locals have said over the years. What is the persistent rumor that gets folks talking, every time it comes up?"

"Well, that'd be her treasure," he said, without hesitation.

"I've chased a few trails on that front," Fiona said. "Seen all the episodes of 'The Pirate Queen's Treasure,' online." It was a low-budget affair, produced by the Irish, but had gained a cult-like following. After a scholar at Oxford had mentioned it to her, she'd tracked the show down online and watched with great interest. The host, Kiernan Kelly, was just a few years older than Rory. "Is Kelly still on the hunt for it?"

"Oh, aye," the priest said dismissively. "I wager he's dug more than a thousand pits about Rockfleet by now."

Fiona sat back in her chair. She'd have to interview that man too. She'd had no idea he was still actively searching.

The priest's eyes twinkled and he leaned forward a tad. "Mind ye, I doubt the queen would've ever hidden it at Rockfleet."

"No?" Fiona asked in surprise. Everything she'd ever read pointed in that direction.

"No," he said, shaking his head with some authority. "Think on it, lass. A woman didn't come to power and hold it for as long as she did without being quite canny."

"Go on," Fiona said quietly.

"No, I think if she did hold treasure…and that's a big if," he said, holding up a crooked finger in warning, "for com-manding the numbers of men she did, maintaining all her ships, took a fair amount of coin. But if she did hold treasure, she wouldn't have been fool enough to hide it near Rockfleet."

"Why not? That's where she spent most of her later years. It was where she always retreated to, most fiercely defended.

She died there."

"Have ya been there yet?"

"No, not yet."

He eyed Rory and took a sip of his tea. Rory stroked his beard, his gray-blue eyes dancing with some excitement. "It's true. It would've been a lousy place to hide treasure, given that it's not much more than a tower house surrounded by bog and hills, river and sea. It would've been better hidden here, on the island." He turned a questioning gaze to the priest.

"No, I doubt it's here either," said the priest, with a mischievous smile. He was reeling them in, building anticipation, and for a moment, Fiona wondered if he did the same with his congregants, when it came time for the message at mass.

"Do you think it's in the cove near Howth Castle?" she asked, remembering what George had said.

"Nah, not there."

"Then where?" Fiona said. "The woman traveled as far as the Barbary Coast!"

"Oh, 'tisn't that far," said Father Michael. "I think it's likely at *Caislean Achadh na nlur*. Or somewhere in between there and Rockfleet."

Fiona looked to Rory, who pursed his lips and lifted his ruddy brows. "Aughnanure," he said, translating the castle name for her.

Aughnanure, the tower house and castle grounds on the River Corrib, just off Lough Corrib, the massive inland lake north of Galway. "But that castle was built long after Grace was gone," Fiona said.

"Rebuilt," corrected the priest. "Long after the O'Flaherty's lost their land."

It started to click with Rory first. "Lost it to the invading

De Burgos," he said, leaning forward. "But the O'Flaherty's kept attacking them."

"The De Burgos," Fiona murmured, traction starting to take place in her mind. "The Anglo-Normans who built Galway?" She was a bit fuzzy on that part of history, given that it was well after Grace had died.

"That's the clan. And yet the O'Flahertys kept after them by land and sea," Rory said, his eyes shining.

"The question is why," Father Michael said, in his element now. "The O'Flahertys held land across the Connaught. They sailed many ships at the time, perhaps more, even after Grace died. The English were clearly going to rule the land. Why did they not simply abandon the land and take refuge on the sea?"

"Well, Grace was a tradeswoman," Rory said. "There was wealth in tallow and hides, wool too. But nothing near what the sea could provide."

Fiona's mind began to race. "Grace had a stronghold on Hen Island in Maum. I always wondered why—"

"Yes, lass, now you're thinkin'," interrupted the old man, setting down his mug and tapping his temple.

"You think it was to protect Aughnanure? Or a stepping stone toward recapturing the castle?"

"'Tis possible, right?"

Fiona sat back in her chair and folded her arms. "What made you start wondering about this?"

"When I came to Clare, I got to talkin' with the oldest man then living on the isle over a pint. He had been told of it in secret as a wee lad by his grandfather, and his grandfather in similar fashion. That there was some sort of clue to her treasure at Aughnanure as well as Rockfleet. He said it was tied to that plaque out by her tomb, the one with the bows and arrows pointing at the boar."

Fiona's pulse picked up. "Did Kiernan Kelly ever come to Clare, researching Grace too?"

"He did."

"Did you tell him of this?"

The priest pursed his lips a moment, as if trying to remember. "Ach, no. He came by, but the man was too big for his britches to ask me a thing. Claims he knows more about Granuaile than any scholar."

"I've heard him say that on his show," Fiona said.

"I've confessed to God more than once...It's given me a chuckle to think of the chancer digging in the muck of Rockfleet all these years. Grace's treasure might not be at Aughnanure, but I'd wager it's not at Rockfleet either. But based on that old man's story, there's somethin' in both that will point the way."

CHAPTER 6

Fiona's sea-blue eyes fairly sparkled with excitement, making Rory think about sailing the Atlantic on a brilliant summer day. They'd made the climb to the lighthouse and Fiona had tried to ask some questions about Grace of an ancient farmer beside the road. But the old man had been more interested in talking about the prospects of his "spuddies"—potatoes—than the island's most famous resident.

And as they coasted down the hill back toward town, he had to admit that he'd quite enjoyed playing escort to Fiona Burke. He liked her inquisitive mind, her gentle but forthright way with people, how she got lost in her own thoughts about life in a different age. Had he not frequently felt that way himself?

But he had never gotten so lost in it that the rest of the world seemed to fade away, as it seemed to do for her. Perhaps it was because he'd been to Clare's tower and the abbey before. But standing beside her at the ferry rail, looking out, he admitted it was more than that. Even when he'd stood in Saint Mark's basilica in Venice or in the Coliseum in Rome, he'd considered the history of the places at a distance. Was it because Fiona had a "character" for her story to hang her hat on, a pin from which her history could spool into a finite chasm she could enter?

"So," she said, nudging him playfully at the hip. "Tell me about your name. Rory. Were you named after the ancient king? Because the only other Rory I know is a female character on 'Gilmore Girls.'"

"Ya think my da would've given me a girl's name?" he nudged her back with his hip, immediately feeling the heat of a blush at his neck. He hadn't been so forward with a girl in...years.

She smiled, showing off her cute dimples and white teeth. Rory focused instead on the wake the big ferry was casting off beside them, a white, bubbly wash disrupting the silver sea. "Oh, okay. So then why did your 'da' name you Rory?"

"I was named after my great-uncle. He was two years younger than George. When they were but wee lads, he died."

"Oh," she said, all trace of humor fading from her face.

Rory chastised himself inwardly, hating that he'd brought an end to her high mood. Could he not have found a better way to say it? Or have deflected for another time?

"Did he look like you?" she asked.

"Yes, if ye're referring to the fact that I'm a ginger," he said. "Because that's all that my folks could really make out, when I was first born. That I had Rory's red hair. There's one in every generation, for us. How 'bout in yours?"

"More than one," she said, with a cock of her head. "But then, for a couple generations, gingers seemed to attract gingers, so the gene pool was against me."

"Against ya?" he repeated, about to tell her she was the prettiest girl he'd seen in years. But he caught himself. "I wouldna' describe it as such. Grandda says your hair is quite fetching in the sun."

"Does he now?" she said, casting him another teasing smile. "So you boys are sitting in your kitchen talking about my hair?"

Now he had to be blushing in earnest. It felt like he was

dead scarlet, with heat up to his hairline. "Well, I... It just-just was something he said one day."

She nodded and gave him one last, knowing glance before looking back out to sea, plainly holding her tongue—and blessedly, potential further torture.

He was sorely out of practice with women. At school, with most of his fellow teachers being female, he'd become rather adept at avoiding them all. He knew they gossiped. According to the school scuttlebutt, he was either gay, injured in a way that kept him from ever having an intimate relationship—which wasn't true, as far as he could tell—or too shy to approach a girl.

He'd allowed the rumors to stand without rebuttal, because together, the gossip formed an effective barrier wall. But that was in Shannon, away from here. It was different here on the coast, the place he called his heart's home. The place where he felt he most belonged.

And the very place Fiona Burke had wandered into.

—⟋⟍—

Fiona told Rory she was going to grab a Coke and pulled open the metal door that led to the indoor cabin of the ferry.

"Well now, how's she cuttin'?" said the young man behind the counter, giving her a wink and leaning both hands on the countertop.

Fiona smiled. "Not much. Just headin' back to the mainland," she said blandly, stating the obvious to try and cut him off from further flirtation. She'd had enough today to send her heart skittering. "May I have a Coke, please?"

"Ya may," he said, whistling a bit as he fetched a bottle from a glass refrigerator.

She handed him the exact change and with a brief smile of thanks, turned to the metal fixture on the wall to pry off the cap. Then she took a seat at a table, not ready to go back out and find her way in conversation with Rory again.

But then the giant man passed by the windows at the corner. She followed his progress as he made his way past a teen couple, then two old ladies, nodding sweetly to them, until he was visible through the windows at the bow. Carefully, he set his cane against a metal brace of the wall beside him and then lifted his face to the wind.

With his red curls dancing on either side of his neck, his broad shoulders and narrow waist, Fiona again thought of him as a throwback to his ancestor, a pirate queen, and her formidable husband. She imagined him in other clothes—a white, billowing shirt, long jacket and breeches tucked into polished boots. His hair a little longer, pulled into a leather band at the nape of his neck...

With a start, she caught herself and quickly looked to her bottle of Coke, took a sip, then pulled out her phone. She needed to get herself together. No more daydreaming about Rory, in any era. He was her friend. A fellow summer tenant. Nothing more.

Nothing more.

She saw that the ferry had its own WiFi and, spotting the password above the flirty counter boy, quickly logged in. Once her browser was open, she tried some keywords. *Grace O'Malley. Buried treasure. Treasure hunt.*

Six articles popped up on the first page, four of them about Kiernan Kelly. But she could feel the engines slowing. They were nearing the wharf. Quickly, she took screen shots of all six, saving them, knowing that the WiFi back at the farm rental was spotty at best. She'd already discovered she'd have to go to town if she really needed to do any Internet research.

Rory popped his head through the front entrance door and when he caught her eye, hooked a thumb over his shoulder, making sure she knew they were almost there. When he saw her raise her bottle, indicating she was just finishing up, he turned back to the deck, perhaps needing as much distance from her as she did from him.

But why did that thought make her feel a little sad?

She let out a low growl of frustration, drawing a concerned eye from an old lady to her right. But Fiona ignored her and stubbornly sat there, nursing her Coke until it was gone and the ferry came rumbling to a stop. Only then did she rise, throw her purse strap over her shoulder, and join Rory in the throng waiting to get off the ferry.

"So, I'd better take ya to Rockfleet when ya go," he said, when she came up beside him.

"'You'd better?'"

"With visions of Grace and treasure now in that pretty head of yours, you're likely to run another poor lad off the road. For the safety of my fellow countrymen..." He cocked a brow.

She smiled at his gentle teasing and folded her arms. "I assure you, I can find my way on my own and manage to not run another innocent off the road."

He cast her a playfully doubtful look.

"Or is it that you just can't resist the idea of getting in on the hunt for Grace's treasure?"

"I admit, the idea is pretty intriguing." He crossed his own arms. "Going to talk to that jackeen that's made such a to-do about it, and then moving on to get a mite closer to it ourselves?"

"Do you think he's still searching the fields near Rock-fleet?"

"I certainly hope so."

"You're as bad as Father Michael."

"Nah. *That* man's as fine as they come," he said.

———※———

A week later, Rory packed a lunch for them, ignoring his grandfather's sparkling eyes and barely concealed grin.

"It's good ye're looking after the lass," he said, crossing his arms. "It should prove a nice afternoon for ya both." He peered out the window and up into a cool, blue sky. It felt like one of the rare summer Irish days that the chill of morning would soon allow Rory to peel off his forest-green fisherman's sweater and just wear the T-shirt underneath.

Uncle George shuffled into the kitchen, still in his bathrobe and slippers, his hair disheveled. "Where are ya off to, lad?" he asked Rory.

"He's taking the lass to Rockfleet," Patrick said.

Rory shook his head. Nearly thirty, and to his grandfather and great-uncle, he'd forever be "the lad."

"The lass?" George asked, his eyes blinking in confusion. "Which lass?"

"Ya remember, George," Patrick coaxed, encouraging him to take a seat at their old kitchen table. "Pretty little Fiona Burke, who was here for dinner? The one lettin' the cottage?"

"Someone's lettin' the cottage, you say?"

Patrick sighed and poured a chipped mug full of hot water and set it before his brother, then plopped in a tea bag. "She is. Miss Fiona. She's on the trail of the pirate queen."

"There's a pirate about?" George said, looking agitated

and worried.

Rory shared a wry look with his grandfather. Some days George was more coherent than others. This was not that day.

Mrs. O'Sullivan arrived then, carrying two bags on either arm. Rory hurried over to take a couple of them, swallowing a groan. He needed to escape. *If Mrs. O'Sullivan learns—*

"Rory's off on a picnic with Fiona," Patrick volunteered. Rory stifled a groan.

"Is that so?" Mrs. O'Sullivan said, the corners of her gray eyes crinkling in delight. She was a lean, tough older woman, testimony of decades of hard work on her own farm and kitchens. And she loved both gossip and Rory. "Then ya best take these wit' ya," she said, reaching into a bag to fetch a plastic bag holding a dozen fresh ginger cookies. "Made them this morning." She leaned closer. "Ginger's good for your leg ache," she whispered conspiratorially. "And it settles the stomach."

"Thanks," he said, turning to stash them in the canvas bag that already held a couple cans of cider, a wedge of Kilree Gold goat cheese, and a wheel of Wicklow Baun, capable of going up against any French brie. Why did she assume he needed something to settle his stomach? How had she known?

"Take these too," she said, handing him a pear and apple after nosily peering into his bag.

"All right then," he said, turning to go. "That should be plenty. See ya later."

"Where are you off to?" George asked, confused again.

"George Caheny!" Mrs. O'Sullivan fussed. "Ye best get back to your room and put on some clothes. It's not civil to be loungin' about in nothing but your robe and slippers at this hour!"

Rory smiled and slipped out of the kitchen, half glad to escape the melee, half wishing to stay and watch it unfold. He went to the garage, lifted the dilapidated, creaking door, and took the keys for his Jeep from the wall. Fiona had offered to drive, but he couldn't quite imagine their outing being relaxing in that tiny metal box she called a car. Plus, he knew where to go. *And can keep us on the correct side of the road.*

The old Jeep roared to life. Rory wondered if there might be a small hole in the muffler. He'd have to see to it later. And he needed to check in on the status of Fiona's VW bumper. It was due to be delivered at the auto shop in Westport soon. But right then, all he could think about was Fiona, and the gift of spending another day with her. The days between their outing to Clare and now had dragged past, with him working about the farm and her holed up in her cottage writing.

He checked himself as he drove out of the narrow doorway, put it in park, set the brake, and went back to close the garage door. *Settle down now, lad,* he told himself. *This is a friendship, nothing more. The girl is here for the summer, not a lifetime.* Resolving to appreciate what it was, rather than fret about what it wasn't, he put the Jeep in gear and drove around the circle that passed the barn. He waved at the hired man, James, who was pounding a nail into a new fence crossbeam, and then Rory reached the tiny whitewashed cottage. Murphy barked at him and chased alongside. Molly was up in the field with the sheep.

Rory could see Fiona moving about inside the cottage through the four-paned front window. In a minute she came out, looking dead adorable in faded jeans, a long, cream-colored sweater that hung loose off her shoulders, exposing a cream-colored shirt beneath. He swallowed hard and leaned across the passenger seat to open the door for her. Getting out and opening it seemed more like something someone would do on a date. And this was not a date. This was nothing but two friends going to check out an ancient tower site. *Nothing but two friends*, he repeated to himself.

"Good morning," she said, climbing in and stowing her backpack on the floor in front of her. She perched a metal water bottle between her slim thighs and reached for her seatbelt.

"Good morning," he returned, wrenching his gaze away from her legs. "Sleep well?"

"Not so much," she said, as Rory set off down the winding drive. "I guess my head was too full of questions."

"Questions. Such as?"

"If Grace did indeed have treasure, where did it come from? Was it amassed over time? And some say she only went to Spain once, but I've found sources that record multiple voyages. Given that her father already had well-established trade routes, it's really not totally crazy to think it could have happened. There's another written record of her meeting with a Spanish sea captain. What I'm wondering about is what she was trading. Broadcloth? Clothes? Down in the Pale—that part of Ireland in the sixteenth century that was distinctly English." She paused to take a breath and check to see if he was still with her. He grinned over her enthusiasm, nodded in encouragement and she went on, "the English gentlemen wanted everything they were accustomed to having. Silks, spices, dates, dyes."

"As well as wine, coal, and iron, like any city of the time," he put in.

"Yes," she said, excitedly touching his arm as he shifted gears. "Of course you'd know this! So tell me, do you know what Grace might have been trading that was of great value?

Research tells me she did a fair trade in fish and tallow, but that couldn't have been enough to garner *treasure*, could it?"

"Well here in the West, the Connaught and the Connemara, look about for yourself," he said, as they exited the road and joined a two-lane highway. He gestured left and right to the green hills.

"Right, yes!" she said. "Wool, yarn, hides, along with the tallow. Of course."

"But fish was the primary source of income," he said. "This land was considered settled by 'the wild Irish.'" He hung a left and gestured outward as the curving coastline spread out before them. "Our bays and inlets were perfect for any fisherman with a taste for herring and cod. It was truly the best fishing grounds in Europe. Our rivers produced salmon and other fish too."

"And others came to trade for it?"

He nodded once. "It's said that six hundred sails came from Spain to fish every year in Irish waters, and the king was willing to pay a thousand Euros for the privilege. Now it was with Galway they traded for the most part, given her favorable harbor. They had no one to compete with them. Except for..." He lifted a brow, waiting.

"Grace," Fiona said, her pretty mouth rounded in a silent "o."

"Grace O'Malley ruled these waters off Mayo. If her fish trade went through Galway, you can bet they were paying for it. But I'd think a pirate would find other means to conduct the trade herself. And as you said, there are resources that point to the fact that she did establish trade with them."

"So she would've traded fish for spices or other items that would be of value."

"Or she simply took their gold and headed home," he said. Fiona fell silent, undoubtedly thinking of what Rory was—a chest full of Spanish doubloons. Or more…

In time they reached the inlet off of Clew Bay which led to Rockfleet, and Fiona impulsively gripped his elbow. "Is that it?"

"It is," he said, unable to hold back his own grin of anticipation. He hadn't been inside since he was young. An Internet search had told him that the castle had been closed a few years ago, due to safety concerns. He wished he could get her inside; she'd love to tour the interior. But they'd have to satisfy themselves with a walk around the outside, and then search for the infamous Kiernan Kelly.

Which wouldn't be all that difficult, it appeared. Because on the crest of a hill a bit north of the tower, several white tents, a large RV, and a small satellite dish were perched. In the field before them was a team of five men and women, running metal detectors over the ground in what looked like an organized sweep. He'd heard stories of Kelly covering every inch of the swamps and fields around Rockfleet and then going back a second time, he was so convinced the treasure was there; it appeared the rumors were true.

Fiona's attention was solely on the tower. She leaned forward in her seat, looking up as they neared, and when Rory pulled to a stop, she was out in a matter of seconds. He grinned and hopped out too, reaching in to grab his cane, then hurrying to catch up with her. She had crossed the fenced walk that led across the muck surrounding the castle to the tower doorway.

"I hate this," Fiona said, tapping the fence with distaste. "It doesn't belong here."

"Well, if ya were here without it, you'd need your Wellies on for this side. And you're lucky it's not high tide."

"True. But what about this?" she said, pointing with

distaste at a garish white sign that had been tacked directly on the ancient door. It read, "Carrickahowley Castle (or
Rockfleet Castle) – Caislean Carraig an Chabhlaigh – Notice – This site will be closed for the duration of works, for
reasons of health and safety." Then it went on with the Irish
translation.

An old, wooden, hand-written sign above it—half-miss-
ing—said something about "key available in garage window
to left," hearkening back to the days of his boyhood when
anyone could let themselves in. For a while after the old tower had been restored, tourists were allowed to enter between
certain hours. But later, when the old girl's masonry had apparently proved unsafe, she was locked up tight again.

Still, Rory couldn't resist trying the small cubbyhole with
the wooden door to the left.

"Anything?" Fiona asked, lifting the rusted, circular metal ring on the front door and letting it fall, cocking her ear as
if memorizing the sound of it.

"Not a thing," he said ruefully. "Anyone comin' to answer?"

"Sadly, no," she said.

He looked to the creek beside the tower, still running
high, given that it was early summer. He gestured to it. "Back
in the day, the water was higher, surrounding the castle. For
protection as well as to allow Grace to bring her ships right
up next to it during high tide. I don't know if she dredged it
or dammed it or what."

"Some say she slept with a rope tied from her ship up
into her bedroom," Fiona said, placing a small hand on the
gray-stone wall and looking upward. She began to make her
way around to the creek-side of the building. "Tied it to her
bedstead," she added over her shoulder.

He carefully followed her across the uneven ground. The

last thing he wanted to do was fall in front of her again. She stepped back from the wall, the better to see upward, trying to peer up to the arched window fifty feet above. "Is that it?" she asked, eyes wide. "Grace's bedroom?"

"That's what they say," Rory said. "Careful," he added, reaching out to steady her when she wavered on her rocky perch. But her attention was again solely on the tower.

"Do you think it's true? The rope bit?" she asked.

"Probably not. It's a bit gammy, don't you think?"

"Gammy?" she repeated, eyes narrowing.

"Yeah. Ya know, problematic. Why would she do it?"

"To be the first to know if someone was trying to make off with her ship?" she guessed.

"Or so she could take another rope and glide down across the ship rope, right down to the deck."

She grinned with him. "Like some sort of pirate ninja, eh?"

"She was a legend, after all." He followed her as she picked her way around the perimeter of the tower. "So not only is this place of scholarly interest, it's a bit of an ancestry touch-stone for you, isn't it?" He followed her several paces into the lush, roadside grasses where she turned and looked back at the tower from a distance.

"As a Burke? Or Bourke?" she said.

"Aye."

She smiled up at him. "I confess I was a bit peeved at Grace for divorcing my grandfather—fifteen-times removed. I wouldn't have minded being related to her."

"She did have that wee babe after divorcing him…it's still possible ya are."

"I suppose."

"What do you think made her marry him, then divorce him?" he asked, staring up at the twenty-meter high tower alongside her. He could feel the subtle warmth emanating from her body. Or was it his imagination?

"Their relationship was pretty convoluted. Yes, she divorced him, once she took Rockfleet and their year of 'trial marriage' was up. But they remained in cahoots for decades. She was pivotal in helping him secure the coveted MacWilliam seat."

"Because she thought so much of him or because it would benefit Herself?"

"Perhaps both."

"Why didn't she do the same to Donal O'Flaherty then?"

"Well, she was just a kid when they married. And they had several children together. Even though it was an arranged marriage, and Donal was difficult, I think Grace loved him," Fiona said definitively.

"Difficult in what way?"

"Biographers say he was even more aggressive than she, constantly seeking battle. They called him 'the Cock,' as in a rooster, always picking fights, defending his territory—either real or imagined. I've come to decide their marriage wasn't easy, and they probably argued a lot, but I like to think it was passionate. Like Italians, you know?"

Rory smiled, watching as she paced a bit, warming to her subject. He liked watching her think—and how passionate she was about Granuaile. *I could watch this lass wax on for a good week and not grow tired of it.*

"Fourteen years into their marriage, Donal was hunting along Lough Corrib—oh, I can't *wait* to go there!" she said, suddenly gripping his arm, as if visualizing the vast inland lake from pictures in her mind. Her eyes, with that faraway look, suddenly snapped tight on him. She shook her head a little. "Wait. Am I boring you? You know all this, right?"

"Not all of it," he said with a grin. "Besides, it's fun to watch ya warm to your subject." He waved his hand. "Go on."

"Donal was ambushed by a band of Joyces. They were in constant dispute over Hen's Castle. You know that, right? Is that taught to every child in school? Do *you* teach this stuff to the kids?"

He paused, considering his words. "Ireland's history is rather vast. I fear Grace O'Malley is only mentioned a bit in lectures about the warring clans and in our unit on seafaring trade."

"Travesty!" she said, pretending to be shocked.

He held out his hands, silently laughing. "But she has a full spread in our textbook!"

She folded her arms in mock indignation and Rory wondered if he could ever think a girl was more adorable. "Maybe after this summer with me, I'll convince you to create a whole unit on her."

"It could be," he allowed. They began walking up the road, toward where Kiernan Kelly's crew was at work. "I didn't remember the Joyces killed Donal. And I knew Hen's Castle was named after Grace, but I never knew quite how."

"Yes!" she said, flashing him a grin and walking backward for a few paces. "I need to go there too."

"There's not much left of it…" he warned.

"I know," she said forlornly. "I've seen pictures." The castle had long ago been ransacked for building blocks for other nearby structures.

"So it was called Hen's Castle, given that Donal O'Flaherty was the rooster, and Grace his wife?"

"Exactly. But I bet she didn't take too kindly to that moniker." She snapped off a green head of waist-high wheat waving beside the road and began mindlessly dissecting it as she went on. Rory found himself staring at her small, dexterous fingers, and reminded himself to concentrate on the path ahead.

"After Donal died in 1560 she avenged his death and assumed leadership of the clan on behalf of her young sons. But I think she was uneasy inland. She longed for the sea. On the water, she *knew* how to lead men. By '64 she was back in Umall and settling on Clare Island, and she set to maintaining both the O'Malley and O'Flaherty clans' vast holdings."

"'Maintenance by land and sea,'" Rory put in, quoting the famous O'Malley motto. "With her three hundred men at arms. Brilliant. So how'd she get tied to old Bourke?" he asked, hooking a thumb over his shoulder toward Rockfleet's tower.

"The English were moving in on Mayo. Grace was probably feeling a bit exposed, out on Clare. And here was Richard-in-Iron Bourke," she said, gesturing back to the tower herself, "who owned the big ironworks, a man who supposedly wore a chainmail vest every day."

Rory let out a low whistle at the thought. "If she felt adrift, she'd found her literal anchor."

"In name and land only. As soon as she had moved into his castle, her ships at anchor, she divorced him."

Rory sucked in his breath. "Tough break for the man who was 'Iron Man' before Tony Stark was even thinking about a fancy suit…"

She smiled and then moved down the path. They'd reached the huge, white RV—so big, Rory wondered how the crew had managed to get it down the Connemara's winding, narrow roads—and they could see the logo on the side. "Kiernan Kelly—In Search of the Pirate Queen's Treasure."

He glanced down and around the neighboring hills. From here the tower seemed small in the distance. But he let out a low whistle when he took in the vast number of holes dug across one farm and then the next.

Fiona knocked on the trailer door.

After a moment, it opened. Rory was behind it, so he couldn't see who answered.

"Hi, I'm Fiona Burke. I'm a grad student, working on my dissertation on Grace O'Malley. I was wondering if I might speak to Mr. Kelly for a minute."

But then the door was opening wider and Kiernan himself was walking down the three metal stairs, pushing back his wavy dark hair from his brow with a practiced move. Rory stiffened involuntarily. He loathed this sort of man.

Kiernan flashed the dyed-white smile Rory had seen a few times on TV and reached out a hand to shake Fiona's. But he didn't drop it right away. He covered it with his other for a moment, clearly checking her out before turning to Rory and giving him a cursory greeting and handshake, his eyes a bit dismissive when he discovered the cane.

What a jackeen, Rory thought.

"What can I do for you, Fiona?" He leaned an arm against the RV and perched a booted foot on the step. Again, it was like he was setting himself up for a shot. Rory swallowed hard and looked away, not wanting to ruin anything for Fiona.

She gave Kiernan a soft smile that made Rory a bit sick. Was she falling for his act? "Mr. Kelly—"

"Kiernan, please."

"Kiernan, you probably overheard me. I'm Fiona Burke, and I'm working on my dissertation. I hear you're a noted O'Malley scholar."

"Some say that I am," he said, with false modesty.

"I was wondering if I might ask you some questions. Could I come by and interview you sometime?"

"Well, out here," he said, crossing his arms, "I'm rather busy."

Busy making your crew do all the work while ya lounge about inside your RV doing your hair, Rory thought darkly.

"Oh, absolutely," Fiona said. "I get that."

"But I could meet up some evening. I always like to talk about Grace O'Malley with others who share my passion." His eyes flicked to Rory, as if wondering what their relationship was, exactly. "We could meet for a pint in Westport. Both of you if…" his words trailed off.

"Oh," Fiona said, following his glance to Rory and back to him. "Rory doesn't want to tag along on all my research. He has his own things to do this summer."

Rory found his mouth dry. *Tag along. Own things.* Her whole tone said *We're just friends. Never mind him.*

Kiernan seemed to brighten a smidge. "You're here for the summer?"

"All summer. Nothing to do but research Grace and finish my dissertation before I head home."

"Brilliant. Where are you staying?"

"I'm staying about twenty minutes south and inland from here," she said.

Not we. But "I," Rory noted. But wasn't that okay? Why should she reference him in this discussion?

"There's a pub in Newport that's class. That's about halfway. What about Tuesday? At the Axe & Oak?"

Rory stepped closer again. What was he doing? Trying to get himself invited into their meeting? She was doing research. Not trying to date the man. And even if she wanted to, what business was it of his? She was absolutely right to use those words, that tone.

They *were* just friends. Right?

CHAPTER 7

Fiona watched Rory's stiff movements as he shuffled down the path at a quicker pace before her. He seemed agitated. Or miffed?

"Just the man I thought he'd be," Rory said under his breath as they left the path and returned to the road that rolled down to the tower and his Jeep.

"Meaning?" she asked, confused.

He glanced at her. "So full of himself."

She raised a brow as they kept walking, catching the cadence of Rory's uneven gait. "Did you expect something different?"

"I...I guess not."

Her expectation of the obvious seemed to diffuse whatever was bugging him. She'd seen Kiernan's casual glance to his cane, the subtle dismissal in his dark eyes. Undoubtedly, Rory had noticed it too. How many times had he seen that in another? Felt less-than, just because of his injury and the cane?

Or was he feeling an eensy bit jealous that she was meeting up with Kiernan later?

They walked in silence down the road, each lost in their own thoughts. Why did the thought of him being a bit jealous please her? She had no business diving into such a thing. There was a time in her life that a summer romance would have been welcome. A distracting, engaging fling. Someone to share fun memories with. But with this being her twenty-fourth summer, Fiona figured she was old enough to know better.

No, this summer she'd keep things strictly in the Friend Zone.

But then Rory's hand brushed past hers and it sent a weird bolt of electricity up her arm. How long had it been since she'd walked hand in hand with a man? Three years, she calculated. The summer she and Mark had broken up, deciding they were right for each other, just not right enough for marriage. The summer she decided she might not ever be right enough for anyone and threw herself into her grad studies. She swiftly shoved her own hands into her jacket pockets.

"Cold?" he asked.

"A little," she hedged. Not much was missed by those keen, gray-blue eyes.

"Should warm up soon." He peered up toward the sun and then to the horizon as if he could sense it. There was a big part of Rory that was inherently *settled*.

It was smaller things in his life that threw him off.

Like Kiernan asking her to meet up at the pub.

"Fiona?" he asked, and she realized she'd been staring at the tower again, lost in her thoughts. He gestured toward one of the Kelly crew in a gray sweatshirt, coming to the bottom of the hill, making a methodical sweep with a metal detector.

"Oh!" She moved toward the young man and waved, realizing what Rory had. This was a good chance to get inside Kiernan's tent, so to speak.

"Hi!" she said, when the sandy-haired man neared.

He pulled off his headset, paused to look over his shoulder, then edged up to the barbed wire fence and shook her hand.

"I'm Fiona Burke. I'm researching Grace O'Malley for my college dissertation."

"Savage," he returned with a nod, then reached over to shake Rory's hand too. "I'm Dylan. Just on Mr. Kelly's summer crew. So I've read a few books on the queen."

"Awesome. Have you worked for him other summers?" she asked, glancing past him to see the others drawing nearer.

"This is my second."

"Ever find anything interesting?"

"In regard to the queen?" he asked, glancing over his own shoulder as if now worried the others would overhear. "Nah. Most of the stuff we find predates or postdates her. Others have, though. But you've probably seen most of that on the show."

"I have." Pottery shards, coins, an axe head that all were sixteenth century. They'd even found remnants of a sixteenth century ship in the mud beside Rockfleet, but not enough to exhume and preserve.

"Mr. Kelly's on the trail of something big, though. That's why we're back here, covering old territory with these bad boys." He lifted up his detector. "The old ones could only detect about a-third of a meter. These go three-quarters."

Twelve inches for the old, Fiona silently figured. *Now thirty.*

"That's good for land like this," Rory said. "Prone to flooding and all."

"That's what Mr. Kelly says. So here we are."

A pretty blonde approached him, clothed in the same gray Kelly crew sweatshirt. "Hi," she said casually to Fiona and Rory, before eyeing Dylan meaningfully. Clearly, she didn't like that he was talking to them. "Ready to head back up the hill?"

"Sure, sure." He gave them a look of apology and turned to go.

"Thanks for your time," Rory said.

"No worries!" He slipped his headset back on and resumed his work, the blonde five paces behind and just to his right.

They watched as the three others turned, lifting hands in silent greeting. In this pattern, the five would not miss an inch of soil.

Rory let out a low whistle and looked about. "That's a lot of ground to cover that way."

"Meticulous," Fiona agreed.

"And tedious. Did it seem like the lad wanted to chat, but the lass shut him up?"

"It did," Fiona said, turning toward the Jeep. "But if you're working for a treasure hunter, you've probably signed some agreement to keep your mouth shut. Kiernan doesn't want anything out there that he hasn't carefully curated himself. There's probably more money in his production and syndication of his show than he'll ever find in treasure."

Rory opened the car door for her. "Especially if he keeps searching here, and the treasure is elsewhere," he whispered, giving her a conspiratorial grin before slamming the door.

He went around, climbed in, and set his cane on the floor behind her seat. "Is that what ya were doin' with Kelly, then? Up there at the trailer? Playin' him along?"

She pondered his wording. There it'd been again, that note of irritation. But she decided to let it slide. "If I'm to get any information out of Kiernan—especially if he's issued a gag order on his crew—I'm going to have to handle him rather shrewdly. Right?"

Rory glanced at her, wrist resting on the steering wheel,

and a slow smile of appreciation spread across his face. Because he'd found a new reason to admire her? Or because she'd essentially given him a reason to excuse her amiable exchange with Kelly up by the RV?

He turned the key in the ignition and the Jeep roared to life. "So where to, now? Westport House? Or Lough Corrib?"

"It's a beautiful day," she said. "Let's go on to the lough for initial reconnaissance."

"Lovely," he returned, as he popped the Jeep into neutral and set the brake. "I know the perfect way to start."

He reached for his cell phone, searched his contacts, and pressed a button. A minute later, his face broke out in that wide grin Fiona was quickly coming to love. It made his eyes crinkle at the corners and betrayed a hint of a dimple in his cheek. He had a manly profile—high, rounded cheek bones, a strong, straight nose.

"And ye? How's the craic?" he said, talking into his cell. He listened for a while. "Good, good." Then, "Brother, I'm on my way to the lough with my friend, Fiona. I was wonderin' if ya could set us up with an outboard. Do ya have any today to let?"

Again, he listened. "I know. It's dead lovely out. I knew they'd be in short supply."

More listening. "Brilliant. I'll take it. We'll be there as soon as we can." He hung up, set the Jeep into gear and headed down the road, a faintly smug smile on his face.

"I take it we're going for a boat ride?"

"Indeed," he said, lifting a brow, but not sharing any further information. Clearly, he had some fun secret up his sleeve. She'd let him keep it for a while, given that she'd gathered the vitals—they were going out on the water. Water Grace O'Malley had once sailed. Lough Corrib was the largest lake in Ireland, covering over a hundred square miles.

"Did you know that in the twelfth century, they cut Ireland's first canal on Lough Corrib?"

"I do. 'The Friar's Cut,'" he said, turning onto the highway.

"Well done, Teach," she said. "A gold shiny history star for you." She looked over at him. "I bet your students love you."

"Why do ya say that?"

"I don't know," she said, suddenly regretting her words. Would he misinterpret them? No, it was right to praise your friends, wasn't it? "There's a steadiness about you. An assuredness. A certain command. I bet it calms your students. Gives them the right zone in which to learn."

He flashed her a doleful look. "Ya clearly haven't met some of my students."

"Well, sure," she said. "There's always gotta be a certain number of attention-deficient kids. Or your standard troublemakers. You knew that going in. But tell me the truth. How many history teachers are there at your school?"

"Three."

"And of those three, whose classes are the most well-behaved?"

He paused, clearly uncomfortable with her press. "Mine," he admitted at last. But there was a softening about his eyes, recognition that she had seen something in him that was true, without ever having stepped into his classroom. He glanced her way, gave her a small, closed-lip smile, and they drove on a while in silence.

Around them the countryside opened up for a while into land reminiscent of the Scottish highlands—sweeping hills, rocky promontories, rushing brooks. When they drove into a dense forest, lush with life, Fiona cracked her window so she could smell it. The earthy, loamy odor reminded her of the summer trip to Ireland she took with her parents when she was a kid.

"Smells good, eh?" Rory asked.

"You can smell the green," she returned, staring outward at a hundred different shades of the color. Pistachio, avocado, moss, sage, fern, and shamrock were a few that came to mind. "There's good reason to call it 'the Emerald Isle.'"

"Hmmm," he agreed with a nod. She liked the sound of it when he "hmmm'd." It was a deep, rumbly utterance from his chest, the very sound of deep contemplation, she thought.

"Have ya been to this part of the Isle before?" he asked.

"I think so, but I'm not sure. I was just a kid when we visited as a family."

It had been her parents who instilled a love of all-things-Irish in Fiona and her brother. Over a summer vacation, they had spent a month traveling all over the island. The road grew curvy, and she saw they were edging the beginning of the lake. She remembered they'd spent time along fresh water as well as the sea, but she'd only been twelve or thirteen that trip, and now couldn't remember which lake it would have been. But then they passed a sign to Ashford Castle—a place Fiona remembered visiting and eating in the castle's "dungeon"—but she didn't ask Rory to stop. Ashford was beautiful and a fun kid-memory, but not really Fiona's sort of thing now. She preferred the old, abandoned ruins she could have to herself over castles turned into five-star hotels.

But as the forest gave way to beach and the wide, blue expanse of Lough Corrib, Fiona gasped. "Oh my goodness," she said. "I have been here before! And I'd forgotten how pretty it is!"

"Just wait," Rory said, downshifting as he slowed, then turned down a narrow drive with a faded, peeling sign that read, "Corrib Boat Lets." The road was so narrow, with rock walls on either side, that Fiona found herself praying no one was coming the other way. She supposed if they did, Rory would just pull to a stop and one of them would volunteer to reverse until they found a pull-out. But wide-open, at-least-two-lane American roads were still too recently experienced for Fiona to be fully ready for this...

At one point, she sucked in her breath.

"Whatcha doin', lass?" Rory asked. She noticed his brogue got stronger when he was either amused or angry.

"If I hold in my breath," she said thinly, still not exhaling, "I make the car skinnier."

"Is that so?" he said, eyebrows forming an arch.

She exhaled at last with a grin. "You didn't know this?"

He smiled with her as the road opened up into a parking lot near the water. Before them was a long dock, with several canoes, two rowboats with outboard motors, and a restored, wooden Chris-Craft boat at the end. She'd heard him inquire about the outboard rowboats on the phone and get shot down. Getting out on the water in a canoe would be lovely, but her stomach was already rumbling. How long would Rory want to paddle?

"Umm, maybe we could go find a pub and grab a bite to eat before we do this?" she asked, as she got out of the Jeep and faced him across the top. "I might have more muscle power with some fish 'n' chips in me."

"No muscle power needed," he said, reaching into the back seat and pulling out a plastic bag. "I brought our lunch. And we're taking the wooden boat at the end."

"The Chris-Craft?" she said incredulously, as amazed

that the man had thought to pack a picnic as she was that they were going to be able to take that beautiful beast out on the water. Going to school in Boston, she'd seen a few restored models, and one in a museum. But to ride in the rumbly, long gem would be an experience of its own.

"I knew you'd like it," he said as she came beside him.

"Want me to carry that?" she asked, lifting her hand for the bag.

"I have it," he said, a little proudly. Or was he just wanting to keep her from peeking in to see what he'd brought? What would a man like Rory pack? PB&J? A dried sausage and a loaf of bread? A full-on charcuterie platter? *No, not in that kind of bag...*

A brunette spotted them and turned to greet them, glancing at her clipboard.

"Hi, I'm Rory O'Malley. I gave Aidan a ring on the way and he said you'd save the Chris-Craft for us?"

The young woman smiled and shook his hand and then Fiona's. "Lucky ye are. Been out on the lake before?"

"More than a few times. Aidan has shown me the shallows," he said, as if anticipating her questions.

Fiona left them to complete their prep-talk, moving toward the old, beautiful boat. The leather had been restored and the wood refinished, perhaps many times. Even now it was drying out and flaking in places. But the vast majority of it gleamed, a shiny, rich-hued wood with polished silver accents. Fiona climbed down and into it from the pier, plopping down into the captain's seat, placing her hands on the wide wheel.

The crinkle of the plastic bag landing in the seat beside her brought her head up. Rory tossed in his cane, sat down on the pier and carefully clambered aboard, always with a handhold to steady him, she noted.

"So how does an American classic end up on an Irish lake?" she asked, rising from the seat that would need to be his.

"Aidan's father is a boat-builder himself. He's collected probably twenty or more different boats over the years from around the world, and a few grace his operations like this one around Lough Corrib." He reached for the picnic bag, moved it to the seat behind him so it was out of her way, and then sat down to review the laminated card the dock girl had given him.

"How many docks does he run?"

"Six. My mate runs the one down in Oughterard, but he's responsible for this one too."

Fiona did a long survey of the lake, from left to right, where it disappeared around a bend. But she knew it went on from there.

Rory flipped a few switches, waited a minute for the bilge pump to empty and something else to happen, then turned the key. The motor was so loud, coughing and sputtering, Fiona blinked in surprise. She'd remembered the rumbling. She'd forgotten how *loud* that rumbling was.

He laughed when he saw her face. "No worries! I have a plan!" he fairly shouted over the engine. "Ready!" he called, looking to the pier. Fiona looked up and saw he wasn't speaking to her, but rather the dock girl waiting to toss in two orange life jackets. She'd unwound their ropes from the cleats and tossed them in. After giving them a smart salute and a smile as they drifted away, carried by the current, she turned to greet her next boat renters. Fiona looked back at Rory. *I really hope he knows what he's doing.*

But as he put the boat into gear, and then shifted, looking left and right, then dead ahead, Fiona at last got to see him as she had imagined him on the ferry and elsewhere. As a ship's captain, utterly in charge.

He glanced at her, surprised to find her staring at him. "What?"

"Nothing!" she shouted over the rumble of the engine. "You just look 'right' here."

"So ye're saying I look wrong elsewhere?" he shouted back.

"No!" She shook her head. "You know what I mean. It's like you're where you belong!"

He smiled. "Ya look happy yourself!" he called, as she sat on top of the back of the passenger chair, letting the wind blow in her face. Rory opened up the motor and sped along the center of the lake.

And she was happy in that moment. Happier than she'd been in a long time. Being here, in this amazing place, with this very nice man, in this fabulous boat, on the trail of the Pirate Queen. *Bliss*, she thought, closing her eyes and feeling the cool air off the water flow past her face. *This is what bliss is like.*

CHAPTER 8

She caught him staring at her this time. He couldn't help himself. In that moment, with her beautiful red hair dancing behind her in the wind, her eyes closed, a slight smile on her full lips, she looked so happy. What he saw mirrored what he felt inside. So in spite of the beauty all around him, he couldn't seem to look at anything but this beauty beside him.

When her deep blue eyes popped open and immediately went to him, he jerked his face away and then kept sweeping the horizon, as if he'd been scanning left and right the whole time. But he was certain he was turning scarlet; he could feel the heat of it on his neck. She said nothing, God bless her, but she'd seen him staring. He knew she had.

Thankfully he had a way to distract her, ahead. Potentially a historical site that even wee Dr.-Burke-to-be did not know about. When he turned the boat in an arc toward the big island, lush with trees, she threw him a questioning glance.

"Inchagoill Island!" he called over the rumble of the motor. "I have a picnic spot in mind!"

"If there's food involved, I'm game!" she returned.

He smiled, and that utter sense of wellbeing returned to him. Being here on the lake on such a fantastic day, with such a pretty girl, driving this boat, well, it was about as perfect as it could be. Just as they approached the docks, an Ashford Castle ferry left the dock with a load of tourists.

If he'd timed it right, there wouldn't be anyone else but day-trippers for a couple hours.

"Throw out the fenders, mate," he called to her as he slowed, nodding at the plastic bumpers that would keep the wooden boat from scraping against the dock. He knew Aidan would kill him if he brought his dad's boat back in anything less than pristine condition.

She hurried to do as he asked, and he slowly motored near, quickly reversed when they came alongside, and brought it to a stop. Fiona gave him a surprised look. "Where'd you become so adept with driving a boat?"

Holding on to the boat's window, then the edges, Rory moved to the ropes to wrap them around the dock cleats, pretending her praise didn't affect him as it did. "Growing up with Aidan, I had little choice. If we weren't on this lough come summer, we were on another. Any time my grandda could spare me, I was on the water."

"How'd you become friends with him?"

"He's a classmate from Shannon. We were wee lads together, up through secondary, when his da moved up here. But we've seen each other every summer, hanging out on these waters. Except…"

Dark memories sagged about him, like a cold, wet towel. "Except?"

"Except for the years I was in the Middle East," he finished hurriedly. He straddled the boat edge and offered her his hand to help her out. She took it and hopped out.

"Have ya heard of Inchagoill before?" He grabbed his cane and the picnic bag and carefully got himself to the dock too.

"No," she said. "But it's beautiful."

He hid his grin. It was hard not to constantly feel schooled by this wee sprite who held so much Irish history in her pretty head. If he hadn't admired her so much, it would have taken his ego out for a beating. But instead, he'd enjoyed sharing the tidbits he knew that could round out her comprehensive knowledge. And it delighted him to help her find new aspects she could chase for her dissertation, be it this lead on Granuaile's treasure or something else.

"I take it I *should* know of it," she said, falling into step beside him down the long dock. "Given that it's a ferry stop and all."

He gestured over to the bigger, taller stone pier that the ferries used for dockings. "It's called 'Island of the Stranger,' or 'Island of the Foreigner,' because local legend says that none other than St. Patrick himself settled here. He and his nephew arrived in Cong to spread the new religion in the fifth century, but the local chieftains and Druids wouldn't have it. So they banished him for a time. Here," he said, waving about.

They entered the forest on a well maintained path, climbing a hill toward the ruins. "Patrick and his nephew Lugnad were building a small church, but then his nephew died. Patrick buried him here."

"How awful," Fiona murmured as they reached the old graveyard and the ruins of a small, roofless sanctuary with a narrow door. "Can you imagine? To be on a mission from God, only to be banished here—lovely as it is—and then your only companion dies?"

"It must have been a dark night for the saint indeed," Rory agreed. Memories of Rory's own friend dying in his arms flashed through his mind, and he tried to shove them away. Bryan had been a bloody mess, with shrapnel lodged in his chest, head, and shoulder. Barely moving. Rory had dragged himself over to him, not yet aware that his leg was mangled, and that he couldn't rise. He'd held him as the man choked on blood—

"Rory?"

His attention jerked back to her, to the present. "Sorry." He hurried over to a standing stone, a pillar that reached his waist and was covered in crosses. "They call this the Stone of Lugnad," he said, gesturing down at it. "Maybe his burial stone. It's been here for about 1600 years. And look here, he said, bringing her around to the other side. This inscription reads, 'Lie Luguadedon Macc Menueh.'"

"Which means?" She squatted down in order to see it better, then reached for her phone and took a slow video of it.

"'The stone of Luguaedon, son of Menueh.' Menueh was Patrick's sister. It's the oldest inscription of its kind in Ireland. The second oldest in all of Europe."

"Where's the oldest?"

"Rome, in the catacombs."

"Cool," she said, staring at it in awe. "Think Patrick carved it himself?"

"I dunno. Could be. But it's fantastic, isn't it?"

"It is," she said, rising.

As he followed her into the tiny light-stoned church, he thought about holding her in his arms. Thought about pulling her to him, in this quiet place, and gently kissing her. She'd fit so nicely against him. He could imagine tipping up her chin...

Rory swallowed hard. His earlier thoughts of keeping this to a friendship were obviously quickly fading. He had to get ahold of himself. He was just shaken by his memories of that Afghan street, the bomb. Searching for distraction. And Fiona didn't deserve to be treated as a mere distraction.

Fiona turned in a slow circle. "Saint Patrick was *here*,

working on these very stones himself."

"Well, that's the story anyway. Some say that it could be dated to the sixth or seventh century instead."

"There's always gotta be the doubters," she said, resting her hand on a moss-covered wall of stones all cut in various sizes, but meticulously placed. "But doesn't the fact that it remained unfinished seem to mirror the story that his nephew died? Grief might have knocked him to his knees for a while."

"Hmmm," Rory said. "It has that capacity." He ran his hand along the stones, heading back to the narrow doorway and out. She followed him. Together, they turned for one last look before heading over to the other structure.

"Here," she said, coming close to him and lifting her phone. Let's grab a selfie together."

Rory tried to smile, but he was probably late. He'd been too surprised at the sudden, warm nearness of her small body, the graze of her back against his chest as she pressed closer for the picture.

She slid her phone into the back pocket of her jeans as if she hadn't noticed any awkwardness from him, thank God. "It could have been grief that stopped Patrick," she said, looking back to the sanctuary. "Or maybe the chieftains lifted their banishment and let him off the island?"

"Could be," he said, kicking his toe in the gravel at his feet, trying not to look at her. He pointed ahead. "This other structure is the Church of the Saints. It was built around 1180 by Augustinian monks from the abbey in Cong. Whatever success Patrick had—or didn't have—in this region, his legacy stirred up a fervent faith for quite a few behind him."

"Indeed," she said, pulling out her phone again to take close-up shots of the eroded heads that decorated the archway of the Romanesque church. She handed him her phone. "Will you take a pic of me here? I want to post it on Instagram. It's how my folks and friends are following along with me this summer."

"What? Oh, sure," he said, framing her in the arch and taking the picture. His mouth was dry. She looked radiant, with her red hair glowing in the summer sun that streamed through the trees, her body framed in the arch.

"Who were these guys?" she asked, looking up at the carved faces again.

"The ten saints of Lough Corrib, they say."

"And who were they?" she asked, wandering inside.

"I have no idea," he admitted. "Not sure anyone does."

Halfway down there was a preserved archway, perhaps a support for the long roof at one time. And at the far end, an alcove—probably used for the Elements of the Sacrament—and what appeared to be a stone altar.

"Do you think it once had a thatched roof?"

"It's a good guess. The monks used this island as a retreat. They had wooden huts between the two churches for centuries. Now the only action the island sees is visitors like us."

"No one lives here?"

"Not for a long while. Once a year, they hold a mass here for fishermen and all who travel on the lake. I hear that gets quite a turn out."

Rory paused at the doorway, wondering if it was wise, to take her to the viewpoint. Would it be better just to picnic on the boat? Aidan would not appreciate any spills...and it truly was one of the prettiest places he'd ever been to. He was itching to share it with her.

He shoved a hand into his jeans pocket. "We could picnic at a spot I know, just up the hill, or back in the boat. Your call."

"Ooo, let's picnic on the island. Lead on!"

She flashed him an open, trusting smile, and as he turned, Rory felt a pang of regret. Even if he wanted to pursue something with her, this woman didn't deserve a man with baggage. No woman deserved that. It was better to pour his energies into his students, then go to the pub for a pint and a bite, then head home alone. He remembered her pegging how he ran his classroom and how the kids responded. That was where he belonged. That was where he could live his life best and serve God with what he had left.

But as she followed behind him, her boots crunching through the leaves, it felt right to have her with him.

Just a friend, he began to chant in his head. *Like a sister.* He started to think of other women he'd set firmly in that category, and managed to enjoy ongoing friendships. Given that three-quarters of the staff at the secondary school were female, it was pretty hard to avoid them. But he'd done it. Marjorie. June. Sheila and Sorcha. Emma. He'd managed it with all of them, had he not?

He tried to picture being on this outing with any of them. How he'd treat them. But none of them made him want to pick them up and threaten to throw them in the water from the dock, like some primary school lad desperate to see the girl he liked respond to him. These feelings... well, these hadn't been percolating inside his head and heart since...Elizabeth. When he started dating her eight years ago.

And he remembered too well how it felt to have his heart torn in two when Liz chose Max over him while he was in Afghanistan.

No, Rory would just have to visualize one of his friends

when speaking to Fiona. In a few days, it would start to feel normal.

It had to.

—⁓—

Rory seemed to grow distant, even as she trailed right behind him. Was it something she'd said? Or did the big man simply need some quiet time? The morning had been rather action-packed. Maybe he wasn't used to so much…activity. But he'd seemed to be totally having a blast out on the water.

They emerged from the forest, onto a rocky outcrop that gave them a sweeping view of the lake. "My gosh," she said, putting a hand to her heart and staring across the water and then turning in a slow circle. She hadn't realized they'd gained this much elevation on the gently sloping path. And from here, she could see at least twenty other smaller islands, as well as towering mountains in the far distance. She pointed. "Are those…"

"The bens of the Connemara," he said with a nod.

Bens, she inwardly translated. *Peaks*.

Directly below were partitioned segments of land, walled in crumbling stone, which spoke of old farming operations. Some fields were a bright emerald, others a golden mossy green. Flowering bushes surrounded their lookout. The lake glittered below them, as if in silent invitation to return. "You're right, Rory. It's a perfect place for a picnic." She sat down on the rock and clapped her hands. "Now show me what you brought me to eat before I pull out my phone to Google edible flowers in Ireland."

"All right, all right," he said with a laugh, seeming to soften a bit. He handed her the bag and she opened it with all the delight she felt on Christmas morning. There were two beautiful wedges of cheese, a loaf of bread, fruit, a couple cans of cider, and… "Cookies?" she said in wonder, immediately opening the zippered baggie. She took a bite of the soft ginger confection and closed her eyes in pleasure. "Mmm, did you make these?"

He let out a huff of a laugh as he sat down beside her. "That would be Mrs. O'Sullivan. She baked them this morning and insisted I bring them. I'm sure Grandda was a bit miffed when I accepted."

"Well, I'll try and save him a few. Maybe. These things are delicious."

"Do ya always eat dessert first?"

"On occasion. When the dessert is worthy." She enjoyed the look of surprise on his face. "What sweets are your favorites?"

"Ah, Mrs. O knows I'm partial to her ginger cookies. But I like a good Carrageen moss pudding with raspberry sauce myself."

She blinked in surprise. "That sounds…disgusting."

He looked at her skeptically. "Truly?"

"What is it?"

He held out his hands and scowled as if he were certain she must've had it before. "Well, it's made with a red seaweed that's cleaned and dried and then boiled with milk. When it's heated, it creates its own gelling agent."

She shook her head. "And that is…good?"

"O' course it is! Well, once they add in sugar and egg and vanilla. I wager we'll have it in heaven!" he said, sounding dismayed that she had no idea what he was talking about. He unwrapped the goat cheese and pulled a knife from his back pocket. He cut a slice for her and handed it to her on the back of the knife, then another for himself, as she tore a chunk of the white soda bread to eat with it. "What about you? What's your favorite dessert?"

"Pretty much any homemade baked good, fresh out of the oven. Ooo, and a good gelato. Preferably both, together."

He smiled and handed her a can of cider. "Sorry it's not cold."

"That's all right," she said, cracking it open and taking a sip.

"What's your favorite gelato flavor?"

"Oh, in Rome, they have so many! Have you been?"

When he nodded yes, she said, "There's the most amazing gelateria off of Piazza Navona. Did you go to that one? They have flavors like lavender and thyme, candied ginger," she added, lifting the remains of her cookie, "even truffle mushroom!"

"Well that sounds revolting."

"It wasn't, oddly. But as much as I had fun trying them all, my go-to is stracciatella, the vanilla streaked with chocolate syrup. There's just something so satisfying about it. The creaminess of the vanilla, the chocolate. What about you? Favorite ice cream or gelato flavor?"

"Hmmm." He thought on it for a minute. "Pistachio or coconut, for gelato. Or rum raisin."

"Strange. I'd pegged you as an Oreo man."

He gave her a wry look. "Guess ya have more to learn about me, eh?"

"I guess so."

They chatted on, eating the delicious brie-like cheese with slices of apple and the goat cheese on slices of pear.

—⁓—

Fiona took out her phone and took a panoramic shot of

their view, then a quick pic of him. "Oh, quit scowling," she said, lifting the phone to show him. "You look good. One more shot of us," she commanded, switching the camera to face them. Again, she leaned close, so close that Rory could smell the light, clean scent of her shampoo. He was just taking in the fact that her body was touching his from shoulder to waist, when she moved away. "What's your number?" she asked. "I'll send these to you."

He related the number, thinking he'd appreciate the pictures to remember this day. Why was it that he never took any pictures himself? He really hadn't since...

Since Afghanistan. Back then, he'd take pictures for the charity operation he worked for, as well as to send home to Mum and Da. Maybe it was time he started to document this chapter of his life. To remember this pretty girl, this fantastic day, the feel of driving the beautiful, restored boat, the taste of this picnic...

He perused his last bite before placing it in his mouth. "Good on Mrs. O's part," he said, lifting the slice of crisp apple laden with creamy cheese. "She's the one that added the fruit at the—"

A gunshot rang out, very close. Rory and Fiona froze.

And then there were more.

CHAPTER 9

The shots were so close that Fiona was just forming the thought that maybe—possibly—someone was shooting at them, when Rory growled, "Get down!"

He grabbed her by the waist and rolled off the rock to the grasses below. They rotated once more until they landed, hard. He was partially above her, and stayed there, as if intent on shielding her.

"Stay down!" he whispered, peering around. His face was red, his eyes wide and manic. His fear set her own heart to pounding.

More guns sounded off, several at a time, and Fiona flinched.

"Are ya hurt, lass?" he asked, taking an assessing look down the length of her body and back to her face. He touched her cheek. "Were ya hit?" he asked urgently.

"What? No. I'm okay! Just…scared. Who is it? Why are they shooting?"

His head lifted. He listened intently. For what? Danger? The shooters, coming near? His eyes shifted rapidly back and forth.

But then they heard more shots. They were distant. Perhaps on the other side of the island. She studied him, waiting for him to understand it too. But he remained where he was, on high alert, sweat running down his face.

"Rory," she said carefully, "I don't think they're shooting

at us. I know it sounded close but—"

He held up a warning finger to his lips.

What was this? What was happening to him? It was as if he really expected people to be coming after them, any minute.

But the only sound she heard was the wind through the long swaying grasses about the rock, and in the distance, a lonely ferry horn.

The color had drained from his face, leaving him ashen. His eyes remained wild and distant.

"Rory," she said softly, but he did not answer, just lifted his head and continued to scan from left to right, as if a sentinel on duty. His breath came in short pants. It was as if he wasn't fully present with her. As if he was reliving something horrible.

His accident, she thought. *The bomb in the Middle East.*

"Rory," she repeated, laying a hand on his chest with all five fingers splayed, desperate for him to focus on her. She could feel his heart still pounding as madly as hers had been a few seconds ago. "Could it have been... Could it have been hunters?"

"It's the wrong time of year for that."

They listened for a while longer, and in time, his breathing gradually slowed, and the taut lines in his face eased. Did he think his attackers were moving away?

"Maybe skeet shooters?" she tried.

He looked into her eyes then, as if fully recognizing at that moment what he had done. His rash grab-and-roll tactic would probably leave her back bruised in a few places, but landing here, with him, she knew his whole goal had been to save her from whatever terror he'd imagined. The crease in his brow grew deeper as regret and embarrassment began to dawn on him.

PTSD? she wondered.

It has to be. And gunshots are one of his triggers.

"Ach. Fiona, I… Of all the thick moves…" He pushed away from her, and as he did so, she noted the pang of loss that rang through her. It had felt good to be beside him. Practically in his arms. Cared for. Protected. And he was leaving her side for all the wrong reasons. Embarrassment. Frustration. Fear.

He stumbled away from her now, reaching for the cane, high on the rock, finding himself six inches short.

"Here, let me get it." She scrambled onto the rock and across it to the cane. She could feel the awkward tension between them as she handed it to him. Still, he took it and stood up straight for the first time, then ran a trembling hand through his hair.

More shots rang out in the distance, and he flinched. "Ye're dead right," he said, sounding utterly disgusted with himself. "It's probably skeet shooters. I don't know…I should've thought of that at once. They like to set up on isles like this and shoot over the water. Since we're between ferry drops they probably thought they were alone." He met her eyes briefly, even as a deep blush rose like a crimson tide on his cheeks above his beard. "Can you give me a minute? I need to…I need to take a walk."

"Of course," she said softly. She watched him limp off down the path a ways and pause in the shade of an old, gnarled tree with small leaves. He set down his cane, reached up to take hold of a branch and then bowed his head, rubbing the bridge of his nose. He pulled off his sweater, as if unbearably hot, and she could see his broad back expand and relax with each, long, deep breath he took. A panic-diffusing tactic?

She'd gotten to know a couple of returning students during her years at Boston College, army vets back on scholarship. Over time, they'd shared their struggles with PTSD, which so many of them had. And she'd learned it was a long road back. Not an impossible road. But a long trek of dedicated therapy for sure. Was Rory even doing any therapy for his?

She busied herself with gathering up the remains of their picnic and then pulled her legs up to her chest, resting her chin on them. The lake sparkled. Boats made their way down the invisible boundary line at the center that marked the border between County Galway and Mayo. Men and women were fishing. A child rode on an inner tube behind a motor boat. All was moving on on this bright, beautiful day, oblivious to the trauma that Fiona had just witnessed.

Was this why the man was still single? Had women fled from him once they saw this side of him? Or did he work at keeping women far away, so that he'd never be this emotionally exposed? Had he only let her in a little because of their shared passion for history and the fact that she was living on his grandfather's property?

Dear God, she prayed, *show me how to handle this situation. Show me how to ease this tension. Diffuse it. And please, please comfort Rory. 'Cause I have no idea how to.*

After about fifteen minutes, he limped back to the rock and stood before it, rubbing the back of his neck.

"Do you want to talk about it?" she asked carefully.

"Not really," he said, avoiding her gaze.

"Fair enough. Back to the boat, then?"

He didn't answer, just set off, aiming for the trail.

She grabbed the bag and followed behind him, wondering if she should say anything more. Force him to talk about it. Maybe he needed to?

But she wasn't the right person for it, was she? She was not his girlfriend, nor was she a therapist, and their friendship was too new and fragile to wager on such a bet.

—⟪⟫—

Rory had never been so eager to hear the roar of the Chris-Craft's motor. It would soon fill the uncomfortable silence between them, cover his pulsing blood, thundering in his ears. What had he done? Had he scared the poor lass half to death? Ruined their entire day? They still had hours left with the boat, but truthfully, all Rory wanted was to retreat to the farm.

Still, once they were back in the Chris-Craft, he forced himself to pause and say, "What would ya like to do now? Head south past Hen's Island? See the river mouth that leads to Aughnanere?" He hoped he had done so with enough invitation that she would ask him to do it if she wanted to. He'd rather not disappoint her. Not any more than he already had.

Her eyes searched his when he dared to meet them. "No," she said. "All this fresh air has wiped me out. We've seen Rockfleet, a place I've fantasized about seeing for years, and now Inchagoill, a place I'd never heard of before. And I've been on another waterway that Grace herself sailed. I'd call that a successful day. So…head back?"

He could hear it in her voice. She half-wanted to stay and make more of this bright afternoon. But she sounded shaken too. He'd scared her. *Eegit. Losin' your ever-lovin' mind like that! And in front of her!*

He put the boat in gear and they trolled away from the island for a bit before he gradually sped up. The roar of the motor and the wind soothed him, settling his speeding heart-beat the farther they got from Inchagoill. He dared not look Fiona's way. He couldn't bear it if he saw pity in her eyes.

Again, he concentrated on the wind off the water, the deep, loamy smell of rotting soil on the edge of the lake, and a hint of fish. Anything to get his mind off of how he'd fairly tackled her and rolled off the rock.

"Did I hurt ya?" he called, thinking of it for the first time. Forcing himself to ask.

"What?" she asked, pushing aside wind-swept hair from her eyes.

"Did I hurt ya, when I took ya down to the grass?"

"No! No." A hint of a smile tilted the corners of her lips. "I thought it was kind of cool!"

"What?" he asked in irritation.

"I've never had a man try and save me before! It was all kind of…bad ass! Like we were in a movie or something!"

Rory huffed a laugh and rolled his eyes. He was well aware she was trying to make him feel better about it all, and for a moment there, he had. But then he wondered: *If someone really had been shooting at us, what would I have done next?*

Would he have been frozen in the moment, lost to his past terrors? Or could he have managed to move, to actually get Fiona to safety? Defend her?

It was like he'd disappeared in the moment. Entered a fugue, some said it was like. A swirling tornado of memory. Because the first shot had put him on alert, but the next group of shots that followed had sent him cascading back to that dusty Afghan street where one bright morning he and Bryan had gone to pick up some fresh fruit and banter with the locals. It was something they'd done many times before, but that day, they were surrounded and fired upon. Aid workers, with big red crosses on their backs, fired upon.

It had been the American Marines who had saved them. Told them they were lucky they'd chosen to shelter in a "friendly's" small one-room home, rather than with a different family who might have turned on them.

He'd never forget their faces—a young father, mother, and two tiny children, huddled in the opposite corner of the house from him and Bryan, the open door between them.

Sunlight and shots streaming inward, the bullets sending little dust-clouds into the air as they tore apart the far, earthen wall.

It had taken days for his ears to stop ringing and his mind to stop swirling from the chaos. He had been so sure, so very certain he was about to die. He'd curled up in that corner beside Bryan, hands against his ears, wondering if it'd hurt when the killing bullet pierced his skin. He wished he could write one more letter to his parents, his grandda, his brother. Send an email, or even a text. To tell them he loved them.

He should've gone home then, he supposed. But he'd stayed. They were doing good work, saving countless innocents from blown-off limbs or losing their lives. There were plenty of children and women and old people hobbling about on makeshift crutches as it was. So he and Bryan had made a pact to stay one more year. "To save another hundred," they'd said.

And on month seven of that year, Bryan lost his life and Rory got an emergency trip to a German hospital, then eventually made it home.

But he returned forever changed.

—⁊⁊⁊—

They'd made small talk all the way home in the Jeep, but by the time they reached Ballybrack Farm, Fiona knew that they both found it a relief to part company. Rory's questions and comments had seemed perfunctory, forced, and in response, she sounded much the same. Before long, she'd asked him to turn on his favorite local radio station. "I want to get my Irish on," she coaxed with a smile.

But his own had been tight-lipped.

At least the music had filled the silence, much like the roar of the boat had. When he dropped her off in front of the cottage, she saw Patrick walk to the front door of the barn and lift his hand in greeting.

Murphy raced across the yard to greet her, tail wagging. "Hi, Murph, hello," she said, petting his neck and then patting his side as he leaned against her legs. "Where's Molly?"

She leaned through the Jeep's window. "Think Molly is having her pups?"

"I don't know. Maybe. It's odd she's not out with Murphy. At least to see who's arrived."

"That's what I was thinking. You'll let me know when it happens?"

He hesitated. "Yes."

She could have let him go then, but couldn't resist another try to reach him. "Rory, in my book, this day will go down as one of my favorites, no matter how it ended. Try and stop beating yourself up about it, okay?"

He stared back at her in surprise. "Okay," he said slowly.

"I'm going to head up to Westport tomorrow. I have an interview set up with Abigail Callaway. She's in from Dublin."

He obviously recognized her name. She was Grace O'Malley's principal biographer. "Good on ya." He paused, looked at the steering wheel, and back to her. "And Fiona…

I… Well, thanks. It was a mostly brilliant day for me too."

They shared a rueful smile and then Fiona turned and went to her cottage.

Once inside, she let the deep shadows and quiet cool settle around her as she slumped to sit on the squeaky bed for a moment. There was so much about Rory O'Malley that was straightforward. And yet clearly there was a great deal that remained beneath the surface, just out of reach.

She flopped to her back and laid the back of her wrist on her forehead, feeling oddly feverish. She was probably a bit sunburned and windburned. Neither of them had thought of putting on sunscreen or wearing a hat. It had simply felt too good.

Fiona reached for her phone and scrolled through the pictures, stopping on the one she had secretly taken of Rory, in profile at the helm of the Chris-Craft. She'd wanted to remember him in that moment, when he seemed so at ease and yet so in command at the same time. Impulsively, she hit the button to message it to him. "It was a good day," she typed beneath the photo.

And then, determining that whatever mental-emotional work Rory had to do needed to be done by him—not her— she sent it off.

—⁓—

Rory, wrapped in a towel after his shower, padded into his upstairs room and sat down on the bed. A light was flashing on his phone, telling him he had a message. Wearily, he picked it up and saw that it was from Fiona. He quickly opened it.

"It was a good day," she'd written, and attached a picture of him that he hadn't noticed her taking. He tapped on it, made it bigger, and really studied it. In that moment, he looked like he longed to be all the time…Relaxed. Happy. Soaking in the sun, the wind, and yes, even the woman by his side.

He tossed the phone to the center of his bed, rose and then stared in the mirror after combing his hair and beard. He heard the slam of the front screen door as Grandda left. He'd mentioned he thought Molly might be beginning to whelp; he was probably heading to the barn to check on her. But Rory's attention remained on his reflection.

He saw the dark shadows beneath his eyes, evidence of the nightmares he frequently experienced. The weary lines around his mouth, denoting the toll his injury and recovery and daily pain had taken. Then he went back to the bed, grabbed his phone, and opened Fiona's picture again, staring at it.

Rory closed his eyes and rubbed the center of his forehead, hoping to ease the tight tension. "Lord," he prayed softly. "I want to be this man, *this* man that Fiona captured today. Not the sad bloke I see in the mirror tonight. Help me to deal with my memories and heal. Help me to live now, in the present, instead of circling back and back to that day in the desert." He heaved a heavy sigh. Then, "Thanks that this was a mostly good day. And be with Molly as she brings her puppies into the world. Amen."

There was no bolt of lightning, no holy presence that Rory felt in the room. But he did feel his burden ease a bit. It was something to even put some of his feelings into words. A start, he decided, pulling on a sweater and jeans, then his Wellies, in order to go join Grandda out in the barn. He couldn't stay in his room. He needed distraction from his swirling thoughts.

He headed down the stairs, peeked in on George, asleep in his customary chair, the TV blaring, and then made his way to the barn. He walked across the yard, hands in his pockets, sneaking glances at Fiona's cottage from the corner of his eye. Was she hard at work, writing? Taking notes? Reading those articles she'd screen-shot on the ferry? The sun and the wind threatened to send him to bed early. Maybe she was even in her pajamas already.

He imagined her in pajamas for a moment. Not the silky kind, but what he expected she'd wear. Something cotton and comfortable and yet still utterly adorable on the lass, making them no less sexy than the satin. Rory could see her, cross-legged on her bed, papers strewn about her in a half-circle, tackling twelve different things at once. Then he shoved the images from his mind. "Ya have no business thinkin' of her that way, O'Malley," he grumbled to himself.

Murphy was sitting by the barn door, as if keeping watch. Rory slid the door along its rusty bar, then waited for Murph to come in after. But the dog seemed reticent. "All right then," he said, "have it your way." He closed the door behind him to preserve the heat. Grandda had set up a whelping pen in the center stall of five, using the heat from the horses, goats and two ailing sheep in the others to generate some extra warmth for the old girl. She'd had two litters over the last eight years. This would be her last. Grandda figured it took too much out of a dog to have more than three. He'd choose the best female of this litter to carry along the dog's prize-winning bloodline.

Rory saw the gold extension cord leading into the pen, and the stall door was open. Inside, his grandfather had a heat lamp set up, as well as an extra light. He'd helped usher in enough pups over the decades that he felt comfortable serving as midwife, but Rory knew his vet was on speed-dial if necessary. He set his hand on the corner post and watched the old man stroking the panting dog, speaking low and sure to her.

"How close do ya think she is?" Rory asked softly.

"Oh, I think we'll see her first pup in the next half-hour or so. She's already had two contractions. And the rest will come fast. If not, I'll need to bring in Doc Ames." He eyed his grandson. "If ya don't see hide nor hair o' the second pup within the first hour of number one, there might be trouble. Two hours? Ya call the vet. If there's trouble, ya could lose the rest of the litter."

"Got it," he said. Rory didn't intend to raise sheepdogs himself. He only wanted to understand the process. Know this part of his grandfather's history and life. *For what?* he chided himself. *To pass along to children? Children you'll likely never have?*

"Ya were dead quiet over supper tonight," Grandda said. "I expected ye'd be all news after yer day with the pretty miss."

"Hmmm," Rory said, not sure what to say next.

Patrick let a moment go by before pressing. "Was it a good day?"

"Mostly," he said. "We went out to Rockfleet. Met that man from TV, Kiernan Kelly."

"Oh?" said the old man, lifting a grizzled brow. "What'd ya think?"

"That he's just the person I expected, after watching his show."

"That good, eh?" Patrick said with a knowing smile.

"That good."

"Is that what brought ya home in a low mood?" He returned his attention to the dog, softening the question by not looking directly at his grandson. *Handling me*, Rory thought, *as adeptly as he does Murphy or Molly.*

Rory moved into the pen and leaned against the side wall, setting his cane in the corner, crossing his arms. "The man was a jackeen, and irritated me, yes. But 'twasn't that."

His grandfather remained silent, waiting.

"I took her out on Lough Corrib, over to Inchagoill Island. It was a fantastic day, o' course. Aidan even let out his da's Chris-Craft to me."

Grandda lifted an appreciative brow.

"We toured around the ruins, then went to the top for our picnic. It was perfect, really. One of the best days I've ever had."

"But?"

Rory swallowed, looked down and toed aside a pile of hay with his boot. "Then there were gunshots. A lot of gunshots." He ran his hand through his hair, feeling perspiration gathering on his lip, even remembering it. "Skeet shooters, most likely," he added with a mirthless laugh.

"And?"

"And like an eegit, I tackled the lass. Took her down to the ground, fearin' that we were under attack or somethin.'"

Grandda took that in, stilling his hand on Molly's head for a moment and bowing his own. He heaved a sigh and looked up at Rory then. "All these years later, it still troubles ya so?"

Rory nodded. "Well and for certain it's a classic case of PTSD. The doctors told me so. I just thought 'twould be better by now."

"Ya endured a great deal, Rory. Think ya need to talk to someone?"

"I did. For a good year, I did. It only helped so much." He shoved off the wall, grabbed his cane and paced out into the center of the barn and back. "But that was *then*. I want what God has for me *now*, Grandda. To have days like I had today with Fiona, without those memories castin' a dark shadow over all of it." He resumed his pacing. Murphy barked to be let in, and Rory went to pull aside the door. "Set to take on the role of the nervous father, are ya now?" Murphy was not the sire of Molly's pups. But the two were tight companions.

When he returned to the stall, Patrick said, "In my experience, the only way to wrestle shadows back into their rightful place is to drive 'em back with light."

"Brilliant. And how, exactly is that done?" he asked, rubbing the back of his neck, which was as tight as his forehead.

"Well, now. That's a good question." Patrick considered the dog in front of him. "Do ya remember old Dexter? That dog I had when ye were but a pup yerself?"

Rory nodded.

"That old dog was a gem. Won me more than a few blue ribbons over time. But one summer, that dog came up against a ram with a big set of horns who'd decided he'd had about enough of good ol' Dex. Unfortunately, the ram had 'im cornered and before Dex knew what was what, he got rammed good. He was fairly crushed against those stones."

Grandda looked up to the corner lantern and rubbed his mouth, as if remembering that awful day. He shook his head. "When I found the poor pup, he was still there, in the corner of that pasture, with the ram up on the crest of the hill, proud as a peacock. He'd fair crushed Dexter's kidney; I was sure we would lose him. Only Doc Ames's quick action saved him."

"So did he ever run sheep after that surgery?" Rory said,

figuring where this was going.

"Not for a while. A good, long while."

"How'd ya get him out there again?"

Grandda gave him a gentle smile. "One ram at a time, my boy."

He leaned down and laid his head on Molly's belly. She was panting now, and rose to pace back and forth. Patrick gave her a good rub, bowing his face to hers. "That's okay, lassie, that's okay. Soon it will be time."

Molly stilled, sat down and stiffened.

"There you go, sweet girl, there you go," Patrick coaxed. "That was another contraction," he whispered to Rory, checking his watch and noting the time.

"She can hear ya, ya know," Rory said with a smile.

"I know it, I know it."

After a moment, it seemed to pass and the dog resumed her panting. Murphy resumed his pacing, whining, as if well aware of what was transpiring. He'd likely been present for her last two litters too.

"So with old Dex, when he was fully healed and back up on his feet again, I knew he'd become shy with the sheep because of that mean old ram. So at first I let him hang with the female sheep only. Then after a while, a good long while, I introduced a beta ram. Once he'd found his way with that one, I let in a slightly more stubborn beta ram. And so on. You follow me?"

"I do. But I don't know if it truly applies to me..."

"Sure it does, lad," Grandda said. "Sure it does. Think on it some."

"Hmmm." Rory rested his chin on his hands, watching as Molly endured a second, and a third contraction. An hour later she'd had ten, and now they were coming more quickly.

She kept checking her hind end and Grandda drew closer, rubbing her head, scratching her ears and neck, speaking soothing words all the while. And then the first pup arrived.

Grandda reached for a clean rag in a pile beside him and quickly rubbed away the amniotic sack, clearing the pup's nose and mouth. "Awww, there ya are, lassie," he cooed, when Molly pressed in, licking her puppy. He grabbed hold of a clamping tool and attached it to the umbilical cord, then snipped it.

Rory laughed as with a grin, Grandda lifted the black and white puppy up to show him, her tiny pink paws splayed. He took the cloth and rubbed the sweet little bundle some more. "A good, tough scrub is good for their lungs," he said, as the tiny puppy began to mewl and cry. "There ya go, lass, that's what we want to hear."

He lowered the puppy down by Molly's head so she could lick her again. "If they don't start crying right away, ye can take them like this," he said, showing Rory how to secure her head and neck, "and then swing them like this." With that, he used a broad, swinging arm to use gravity to help do the work, but Rory laughed in amazement.

"Grandda! Aren't ya hurting her?"

"Nah," he said, bringing the adorable mewling pup to rest beneath his chin. "If ya have them securely in your hands, it can only help, especially if they might be aspiratin'."

"I see," Rory said wryly. He loved seeing his grandfather in his element. It reminded him of being a lad and following him every step of the way, every day. Literally placing his smaller boots inside the bigger boot prints of his grandfather's on a muddy path. How he'd have to stretch to match his stride…

And now Rory was a good foot taller and twice his size.

Grandda would have to stretch to match his boot prints, these days. And yet he felt like half the man. His grandfather had weathered his own storms over the years. A bout with cancer. A sheep virus that almost forced him to sell the farm. Losing Grandma, three years ago. That had been the hardest. But still here he was, moving on with his life. Seeing new puppies into the world. Welcoming him, George, and James and Mrs. O, all as family, in a way. And now Fiona too.

"When I grow up, Grandda," he quipped. "I want to be just like ya."

His grandfather looked up at him in surprise. "Ya already are, laddie, in here," he said, thumping his chest with a fist. "Ya just have to remember it in here," he said, pointing to his head.

CHAPTER 10

Fiona was up with the sun, stretching on the old, squeaky bed. It frequently awakened her at night, what with its sprung coils in a few places, and others that complained when she turned over. At first, she wondered why Mrs. Caheny hadn't replaced it, when she'd shown such meticulous care in choosing the bedding and refurbishing the charming cottage. But after a few nights, and learning to sleep on the diagonal, she'd made peace with the old thing. A bit of living history, this old mattress had obviously welcomed more than its fair share of sleeping bodies over the years.

She ran her hand across the covers. Had Rory and his brother slept on it, during summers they spent with their grandparents? Had there been cousins? Aunts and uncles? Some people might get creeped out by such thoughts. Her mother definitely would. But to Fiona, it simply felt like she was the latest member of the family to be welcomed in at Ballybrack Farm. As if the mattress was saying, *I was good enough for them. I'm probably good enough for you.*

It made her feel like she belonged with them. And more and more, she thought, rubbing her bare arms against the morning chill, she found herself drawn to them. And Rory. Definitely Rory.

She ran a brush through her hair and pulled on a thick sweater and jeans. Then she pulled her hair into a ponytail and slid on her fuzzy slippers. Moving to her tiny kitchenette, she poured water into the European pot's bottom, added grounds to the center and screwed it together. She set it on the burner to heat, and rummaged in the half-fridge to see if she had any eggs. She didn't. And all she really wanted was another slice of that salty goat cheese Rory had brought yesterday. On a crisp piece of toast.

She padded over to the window, wondering if the men in the main house were awake yet. Pondered going over, asking the neighbors if she could borrow a slice of cheese. Would that break the ice? But as she stared at the front door, through a misting rain, she saw Rory emerge, pulling up his hood as he stepped out on to the tiny stoop. He made his way down the steps and across the yard.

She slipped to the side of the window, at first assuming he was heading her way and not wanting him to think that she'd sat there all morning, waiting for him like some creeper. But that made no sense; it was too early. So she peeked and sure enough, he was striding across the yard toward the barn, clearly not intending to stop at her cottage. She opened the door. "Good morning!"

He paused and turned toward her. "Ye're up early," he said, stepping toward her, his rubber boots mushing aside the wet soil. But he stopped five paces away, as if he dared not get closer. "It's not even six."

"I passed out last night after our big day. Why are you up so early? Chores?"

"Nah. Well, yes, I'm to feed a few sheep." He gave her a conspiratorial smile. "But Molly had her puppies last night!"

"She did? Why didn't you come get me?"

"By the time it was done, it was late. And your window was dark. I figured ya were dead to the world. Sounds like I was right."

"True. Well, let me just finish my coffee, then may I come see?"

"O' course. Grandda is out there already. Practically had to drag him out of the barn for a few hours last night. Bring your jacket and your Wellies," he said, peering upward. "It's soft out."

"I'll be there in a sec," she said, taking in his term for misting. Soft. She'd have to begin a list of colloquialisms to keep them all straight. But her mind was more on the okay-ness between them this morning, after the awkwardness of yesterday afternoon. "Thank you, Lord," she whispered, walking back to the two-burner stove. Turned out puppies might be a way better ice breaker than cheese.

She couldn't wait to see those tiny, wriggling bodies. It made her miss her own golden retriever, at home with Mom and Dad.

Thoughts of them made her do the math, wondering if she could call them. The six-hour time difference always seemed like a hurdle. It was either too late or too early when she was ready to sit down and give them the scoop about how things were going. She knew they followed her on Instagram, so they knew she was alive, but they'd appreciate a text, at least.

Hi, Mom and Dad.

Doing well here in Ireland. Settling in on that adorable farm I showed you, exploring, and today will go and interview Abigail Callaway, the O'Malley biographer. But first...puppies! A litter was born last night. Off to the barn to see them. Let me know how YOU are.

Love you!

She pressed "send" just as the coffee finished percolating. She poured it into an insulated mug, screwed on the lid, pulled on her hooded jacket, switched her slippers for boots, and moved into the "soft" morning. It was an apt term, she decided, as she made her way to the barn. The mist made everything more mellow. The clouds, the sunlight...even the rusted metal roof on the shed seemed a bit less sharp in this weather. Maybe she could wrap such words into the text of her dissertation, lending further authenticity to her work. If so, she really would need to begin cataloguing them all.

Fiona had only been out to the old barn with Patrick, on her initial tour, but not again in the ten days she'd been here. She liked old barns, and always wished she'd had cause to visit one in her younger years. Pitch hay. Feed chickens. Set hay into troughs. The closest she'd come was taking horseback riding lessons at the city stables.

She slid aside the door and entered the barn, pausing to shake off the drops clinging to her jacket and to push back her hood. Patrick looked her way and then Rory rose, two little, mewling pups in his giant hands.

"Oh my goodness," Fiona cried, striding toward them. "Have you ever seen anything so adorable?"

"A few times, yes," Patrick said benignly.

"Well, of course, you've seen it before," she said, chiding him slightly, "but isn't it new all over again when you see a fresh batch?"

"Aye, ye have it right, lass," he said. He looked weary, as if he'd only gotten the few hours of sleep Rory had mentioned. He seemed more stooped this morning, a bit more... fragile.

"May I hold one?"

"Sure and for certain," he said, gesturing down to the pile

of towels that Molly had made into a nest.

"Molly won't be bothered that I'm taking one?" she whispered to Rory.

"She's too tired to care much," he said. "Tomorrow might be a different story. Wait for me or Grandda if ya want to hold one in the coming days. New mums can get a bit nippy."

"Fair enough," she said. She started toward the pile of seven puppies, but then pulled back nervously. "Why don't I just hold one of yours?"

He smiled, laughing at her, but she didn't care. Her eyes were solely on the pup he handed her, a beautiful female with black ears and cheeks and eyes, but a brilliant white that began in a stripe down her forehead, spread out across her mouth and dominated her chest. "Aren't you just the prettiest?" she cooed, holding the puppy under her chin as the tiny dog grunted like a pig and squirmed against the warmth of her skin. "Do you smell that?" she asked Rory, widening her eyes.

"What?"

"Puppy breath! I haven't smelled that in years! But isn't it the sweetest? It's one of those smells you could identify anywhere." She lifted the little bundle up in two hands to see her better. "When do their eyes open?"

"In a few weeks," Patrick said.

"Have you named them yet?"

"Do ye always have so many questions?" the old man asked.

She laughed under her breath. "You have no idea. Especially when I'm excited."

"Hmmm," Rory agreed.

Fiona smiled and cradled the puppy to her chest.

"I've never been one with a gift for names," Patrick said.

"My Orla was always the one to do it. Now…" He lifted his gaze to Rory, then Fiona. "You two can see to it."

Rory paused.

Hoping to ease the odd tension she felt rising, Fiona said, "Don't the people who buy the puppies like to name their puppy themselves?"

"They do. But we always send them home with papers, certifying the dog's breeding. And in those papers, the pup is named. It often gets changed, of course. But that's how we do it anyway."

"I see. Well, this will be fun. I can do it, Rory, if you're not into it."

"Go on with ya," he said, with a shrug.

She swallowed her disappointment, thinking that it might be a further means of breaking the ice between them. But she was being silly. It was just naming dogs. Temporary names, not names their owners and families would probably use in the future. "I-I'll have to think on it for a bit. Get to know them a little."

"Hmmm," Rory said. He turned to his grandfather. "Why don't ya go in and rest for a bit? I'll keep watch on the pups for a while. James will soon be here too."

"A good suggestion, that," Patrick said, putting a hand to his lower back. "I'm not as young as I used to be. Will ya be about today too, Fiona?"

"This morning, I am. Then I'm off to Westport."

"Ah, yes. Rory tells me you're to meet the great Abigail Callaway. She's somethin' of a legend, around County Mayo. Thanks to her, our 'Queen of Connaught' got a bit of what she was due."

"Agreed. I'm looking forward to it. Rest well. And congrats on all these beautiful puppies!"

He lifted a hand as he walked to the door and slid it aside. He was just closing it when his head jerked up and around. "Fire!" he cried. "*Fire!* Call the fire department, Rory!"

Then he disappeared from the doorway.

Startled, Fiona and Rory set the pups back by their mother in the whelping pen and ran after him.

Fiona's mind raced. Was it the cottage? Had she forgotten to turn off the burner, in her hurry to get to the barn?

It wasn't her cottage—it was the main house. Smoke was seeping from the frame of the corner kitchen window, flames visible inside. Patrick was just reaching the front steps when they left the barn.

"Grandda, wait!" Rory hollered, hobbling madly across the yard, moving faster than she'd ever seen him move. "Grandda, don't go in! Yell at George to come out!"

But with one last, grim look at him, Patrick was already opening the door, crying his brother's name.

Rory thrust his cell phone into Fiona's hands at the front stoop, then plunged inside the smoky house. Dimly, she realized that someone had answered her call. Someone was asking what her emergency was.

"F-Fire! We have a fire here!"

"Address, miss?"

"Ballybrack Farm! County Mayo, on Road 303! Please send help!"

Her heart in her throat, she waited for the men to emerge. *George. Patrick. Rory.*

The operator assured her that help was on the way. But what did that mean here in Ireland? In the States, help usually arrived in town within what? Ten minutes? An hour? She'd never called an emergency line before.

She had to see what was going on. Tucking her mouth

into the neckline of her sweater, she took a deep breath and plunged inside the house. Rory was in the back, yelling at his grandfather, in the kitchen. "Where's the extinguisher, Grandda?"

"It's there! In the back closet!" he cried, beating at the flames that were now engulfing the wall and cabinet above the stove with a towel, but clearly losing the battle. "On the side!"

Fiona spied George, standing in the corner, eyes wide and dazed. He was still in his open bathrobe, his boxers and white undershirt exposed, his hands outstretched. His hands…

Quickly, she went to him and took his elbow, her eyes burning in the smoke. "C'mon, George. Come with me. You're hurt." She led him to the laundry room on the other side of the entry and to a utility sink, gazing in horror at his brown, charred palms. Had he tried to put out the fire on the stove with his bare hands? Hurriedly, she turned on the water, but just as she was about to pull his palms under, she thought she remembered something about the treatment of burns this bad was different. That you weren't supposed to pour water or press ice on them. The skin was too delicate.

George was ashen and wavering. Probably going into shock, she assessed, hearing the sound of a fire extinguisher spewing liquid in the kitchen. She glanced over her shoulder and watched as Rory sprayed left and right, putting out the flames licking up the cabinet and ceiling, then lower. He was getting it under control.

George, on the other hand, was looking like he might faint at any moment. "Here, George, come outside with me," she said, leading him to the front door and out to a tattered, splintering bench seat. She helped him sit, then lie down, then went to fetch a blanket and pillow for him. She gently took his hands and laid them atop the pillow, somewhat elevated. His eyes were wild and vacant. His lips moved as if he was trying to say something, but failing.

Fiona ran a hand over his head. "You're hurt, George. Maybe in shock. Help is on the way. Stay right where you are."

Thankfully, she thought she heard the tinny sound of a siren in the distance. Help was arriving, she hoped.

Rory found them, then, his clothing covered in extinguisher foam. "Is he all right?" he asked, his forehead wrinkling in concern as he moved toward them.

"His hands are horribly burned," she said, wringing her own. "And I think he's going into shock. Are *you* all right?" she asked, taking Rory's hand. Wondering if this excitement elicited any of the trauma response she'd witnessed on the island.

"Me? I'm fine, fine," he said, pulling away.

She saw the beads of sweat at his temples, the gray tone of his skin, but if he didn't want to acknowledge it, she wouldn't either.

CHAPTER 11

After the ambulance set off with George for the hospital in Galway, and the fire department declared the house fire totally extinguished, Fiona followed Rory back into the kitchen, with Patrick coming right behind her. They took in the foam on the floor, the blistered walls, charred cabinets, and gaping hole in the counter. "If you hadn't found that extinguisher," she said, looking about, "you might have lost the whole house."

"Thank God we didn't," Patrick agreed. "Have I ever told ya about the time my mum set the house afire with an iron, laddie?"

"Ye've told me," Rory said. "Grandda, we might o' lost you and George as well. What were ye thinkin', goin' after him? Did ye not hear me call ye to wait?"

Fiona wished she could hide, well aware this was swiftly entering a very personal conversation. Should she try and slip out the door?

"What would ya have had me do, lad? Leave my very own brother to die? Ya saw him! And look! We got it out!"

"Why'd ya not grab him and go? Why stop and fight it?"

Patrick frowned. It was a logical question. "I didn't think. I just acted," he said with a shrug. "I'm glad ye both were wit' me." He rubbed his eyes—still bloodshot—and looked around the kitchen, appearing a bit shocked himself.

Rory heaved a sigh and put a hand on his shoulder.

"Grandda, ye're not as young as ya once were. When I'm not here—even with James and Mrs. O—I think ya have too much to manage. Between the farm and George, it's enough to keep a man half your age busy. Maybe it's time to consider finding a home for George. Someplace where he—"

"No," Patrick said, slicing his hand in the air to stop him. "This is George's home. This is where he belongs. Here. With me. Until he breathes his last. If I go first, then I suppose it will be up to yer mum and da to decide. But as long as I'm livin', George *stays*."

Fiona had never seen the older man so angry and serious. "I-uh, I'm gonna just head out. Obviously you guys have things to discuss."

"There's nothin' to discuss," Patrick growled, looking at Rory, not her. "I've decided. Now if ye'll excuse me," he said to her, his tone gentling a tad. "I must go check on the pups. Doc Ames is due any minute."

With that, he turned on his heel and strode out of the burned out remains of the kitchen, letting the front door slam behind him.

She turned partway to face Rory, and seeing his weary, drawn face, set a hand on his folded arm. "I'm sorry. These kinds of things are tough with families. My gramma had Alzheimer's when I was in high school. Knowing what to do, what was best, was hard to figure out."

He lifted his own bloodshot eyes to meet hers. "What'd your family do? Keep her with them?"

"No," she said. "She went into a memory care place."

Rory looked out the soot-coated window. "My mum and da—they can't take care of George. They're just retired, their home is tiny, and they just want to travel now. If Grandda dies, we'd have to put George in a home."

Fiona nodded. "What's the plan with this place? Will your mom and dad take on the farm at some point? Maybe move here?"

He shook his head, and she could see how miserable he was. "They might for a while. But it's not really their thing. If I don't take it over within a few years, then we'd probably sell."

Fiona took this in, feeling the echoing ache in every word. "And I take it teaching is more lucrative than farming?"

He gave her a wry smile. "Hard to figure, but yes. Grandda barely scrapes out a living here. He invests every dime back into the property and livestock. And now he has this…" he said, gesturing toward the blackened kitchen.

"Did he have insurance?"

"With a five thousand Euro deductible," he said. He shook his head. "I shouldn't burden you so…I'd better phone my folks. I need to figure out what I should tell them."

Fiona considered him. "Start with the fact that everyone is okay, then tell them about the fire and George going to the hospital in Galway. And maybe…that you think your grampa and George need…"

"Someone with them all the time," he finished wearily.

He looked so overwhelmed by this that she reached out and took his hand. "Hey. It'll be okay. These kinds of transitions come for every family. And you're right. If Patrick won't send George to a safe place, you need to find a way to make this home safer for the both of them." She squeezed his hand and then dropped it. "Right?"

—⁓—

Rory's pulse had picked up when she took his hand. Had she felt it?

"Right," he said. She made sense to him, calming him when Grandda had done little but agitate him, *the stubborn, old eegit.*

"Now why don't we get going on some repairs?"

He blinked at her. "We?"

"Absolutely," she said, breaking away and turning to peruse the damaged kitchen. "I haven't spent a thousand hours of my life watching HGTV for nothing." She rolled up the sleeves of her sweater.

He huffed a laugh. "That so?"

"Totally. Do you suppose we can tear out some of this?" she said, touching the charred corner of a cabinet. "Get it cleared out and then go to town to price out cabinets, counters, a new stove, flooring? This place looks like something out of the '50s. Maybe it's time for a good refurbishing? I bet you could make a dent in it for the five thousand Euros you'd just have to pay the insurance company, if you do the work yourselves. I could help. Are the walls okay?"

He blinked again, a bit dizzy. The wee sprite was ready to wade in with a sledge hammer and help him manage this mess? "I...I think we need to wait for the insurance company to come this afternoon and take some pictures. Give us an estimate on what they'll cover, that kind of thing. And the county inspector's goin' to come 'round, make sure the structure is sound, and all."

"But that wouldn't keep us from *planning* the new kitchen, right? Somebody needs to go check on George in Galway. The EMTs said they might even release him later today. Your grampa will likely want to stay here with Molly, given Doc Ames has yet to come, and he's expecting those visitors to survey the damage. What if we say hello to George, find out what time he'll be released, then check out what they have at the Home Depot—"

"Home Depot?" he asked in confusion.

"Lowe's?" she tried.

He shook his head.

"Well, whatever big home store you have."

"*Home store*," he repeated flatly.

"You don't have home stores? Like big, big hardware stores, but with appliances and gardening supplies, flooring, cabinetry?"

"Maybe in Dublin. Not much like that in Galway."

"No?" She stared at him in surprise and then lifted her eyebrows and tapped her lips, thinking. "So much for the one-stop shop. This is going to take a bit more time...but Mrs. O'Sullivan is going to need something to work on, and when she's not here, you boys are going to need something to cook on. At least a microwave and burner."

"Maybe a burner's not such a good idea," Rory said. "If George isn't supervised twenty-four-seven. And your kitchen isn't really big enough for all of us."

She snapped her fingers, her eyes growing round. "I've got it. Until we figure out supervision for George, you could use a barbeque."

"Like they have in Texas?" He couldn't resist the urge to tease her. Seeing her light up and her mind whirling five-hundred-kilometers an hour lifted his spirits. Half his contemporaries in Shannon had a barbeque, but not many folk in this part of the country did.

She laughed, and her grin did his heart good. "Like they have in every state in America. I know quite a few people who barbeque in their backyards all winter long."

"Backyards?"

"Gardens," she supplied.

"You Yanks are a strange bunch," he teased.

"*We* are? You should try being an American girl smack-dab in the central coast of Ireland…"

He smiled. "I'm glad ya are. It's good to have ya here." As soon as the words were out, he wished he could reel them back in. His heart shrank. Had that been too forward? A friend could say that, right? "I needed a sounding board," he pushed on. "And diversion."

"It's been a big couple of days," she said.

Her tender response encouraged him to venture forward. "I tell ya what. You help me pull this kitchen back into workable order, and I'll take ya to what we called the 'pirate cave' as kids, sometime soon."

"Ooo. You do know the way to this girl's heart." She paused awkwardly with the last word, perhaps saying a bit too much herself? A tinge of a blush rose on her cheeks before she moved a few steps away from him, staring up at the remains of the cabinets. "Maybe this is a blessing in disguise. Look up there, Rory, past the drop ceiling."

He edged closer to her and saw what she did. A beautiful tin ceiling, five feet above.

"If your grandfather approves, we could tear this whole drop ceiling down. Paint that pretty ceiling above." She rubbed her hands together. "Ooo! Want to take measurements? Then we could at least start on getting some prices while we're in town."

"I can do that," he said.

"Great. I'll just be outside. I need to make a few calls while I have a signal. I was supposed to meet with Abigail, but she'll understand why I should delay."

"Are ya sure?" Rory asked. "I could head to Galway on my own."

"No, that's all right," she said, shaking her head. "My head's here with you and Patrick. And in Galway, with George. Grace O'Malley...and Abigail, just need to wait."

She left then, and Rory smiled, touched that she'd made them her priority. And she'd be a help with George, when they picked him up. Her sunny, attentive personality seemed to be a boon everywhere.

He rummaged through a few drawers, but seeing no measuring tape, thought he'd check on Grandda—make sure they were getting on all right—and tell him their plans. He couldn't forever remain the golden grandson, never willing to tackle hard subjects. And somebody had to do it this summer before he left. He'd worried about them last year. Now this proved his concerns were warranted.

He went outside and gently closed the door, not wanting to interrupt Fiona's phone conversation. But as he passed by her, he wished he'd let it slam. Because she wasn't talking to Abigail yet; she was talking to Kiernan Kelly about their meeting at the pub tomorrow night.

Rory didn't know why it bothered him so much. It was logical that she speak to everyone who was an "expert" on Grace O'Malley in Ireland—be they self-proclaimed or truly so. She needed to flesh out her dissertation. *And the sooner she gets it done*, he thought, *the more time she'll have on her hands.* Time to hang out with him, watching the puppies, touring around?

Or if she got enough, would she simply head home early? The thought actually caused him to misstep, and he narrowly caught himself. *No*, he told himself, *she wouldn't.* She'd already let the cottage for the whole summer. And didn't she need time to study, to prepare to defend her thesis, once it was done?

He slid open the door and saw that his grandfather was shoveling pitchforks of hay into an ailing cow's trough. "Doc Ames going to tend to her too?" he asked.

"Hope so," Patrick said.

"Do ya have a measuring tape out here?"

"Sure. Over on the ledge by the door," he said, gesturing to Rory's right.

Spying it, he grabbed it and tossed it back and forth between his hands. "I thought we'd go to Galway and check in on George. Find out when they're going to release him. Then Fiona has it in her head to price out cabinetry and the like for a refurbishment of your kitchen."

Patrick smiled knowingly. "I see. The lass doesn't let the grass grow beneath her feet, does she?"

"Seems it."

"What do ya think it will cost me?"

"Well, you said you had a five thousand Euro deductible, right?"

"Aye."

"We're hoping to do it for less than that. Do ye have that on hand?"

"I will," he said, nodding at the pups. As champion border collies raised by Patrick Caheny, they were quite valuable. But Rory knew his grandfather likely had already spent that money ten different ways in his head.

"Listen, Grandda. I'm sorry I pressed ya on George. It's just that—"

"I know, I know," he said, holding up his hand. "Ya mean well. But I know what I want to do for m' brother. And while I have breath in my lungs, I aim to do it."

Rory figured he'd leave it there, for now. Talk to his folks and see what they thought. "Fiona thinks we ought to find something for us to cook on, in the meantime. We were thinkin' a new microwave, and she has it in her head we need a barbeque. Things George can't set on fire."

"A barbeque, eh? When we have a perfectly good pub in town?"

"Maybe she'll show us some American cooking."

"Maybe. Make your best call, lad. Need some money?" He made as if to search his pockets.

"No, Grandda. I'll catch up with ya when ya settle with the insurance company and sell your pups. You'll be calling them today too? Arrange for an inspection?"

"Yes, yes," Patrick said, rubbing the back of his neck.

Rory hesitated. "Should I stay? If it's too much—"

"Nah. Go on wit' ya and yer handy excuse to have the lass by yer side." He poked his pitchfork playfully, but then lowered it. "But ya won't forget our George…"

"I won't forget, Grandda. We'll go there first."

"Thank you, laddie."

Rory left then, thinking of the tender bond between the older men. He wanted to find a way to honor his grandfather's wishes. To keep George at home with him, but without leaving Patrick knackered out. *Or without a home.*

CHAPTER 12

"Ye were talkin' to Kelly, huh?" Rory asked her, as they climbed into the Jeep.

"And Abigail Callaway," she said, ignoring the barb in his tone, if she noticed it at all.

"Was she miffed, with ya not comin' today as planned?"

"At first," she said. "But once I explained, she was quite understanding. I'll meet up with her at Westport when she returns next week."

"That's good." They drove down the winding road to the highway, where he saw that James was turning in. He pulled over and ran down his window. "Can't keep away, even on your week off?"

"Heard that ya tried to burn down the house around ya in my absence." He lifted his chin. "Your grandda need some help today?"

"He wouldna' say no."

"Right then. I'll be about." His eyes moved over to Fiona and he gave Rory a knowing wink.

Rory rolled up his window and ignored him. "So how many kitchens have ya remodeled in your twenty-four years?"

"Oh, I haven't ever remodeled a kitchen."

He glanced at her in surprise.

"What? How hard can it be? I've seen a ton of demo and renos done in record time."

"Hmmm," Rory said. "Have ya done any DIY projects?"

"No, but I can find reference on YouTube like a boss," she said. "If you can find it on YouTube, you can figure out anything."

"I see. Well, I can probably cover the cabinetry and countertops, the ceiling, plumbing a new sink if we need it, but I'll have to hire an electrician. I'm guessing with the house being as old as it is, we may as well make sure those are up to code. And at that point, I take my hall pass as a history teacher and let the journeyman do his work."

"Or journeywoman."

"Sure, sure," he said, accepting the correction. "We'll have to be spare with the budget. Grandda doesna' have much. He can go as high as five thousand Euro, but he'd rather not."

"Got it. Well, maybe we can take the doors off the cabinets around that central burned section, and paint them. Then we could add new ones where it burned around the stove somehow. We'll have to check out the options to make sure it looks right. Or go super-low budget on the cabinets if you want to replace them all. Obviously, you need room in the budget for a new stove, wallboard and paint. Oh and a barbeque!" She slipped off her boots and put her sock-covered feet up on the dash. "Do you mind?"

"Not at all." He sneaked another glimpse of her small feet and the colorful wool socks he'd had no idea were beneath her Wellies. They were cute. Girly. Nothing like his plain blues. And he liked that she was becoming so comfortable with him that she could do such a thing.

"I'm amazed at how your neighbors rolled in with the firemen," she said. "It seemed like Patrick had just cried, 'Fire!' and they were rolling in like they'd heard him."

"Well, ya know farmers. They always have their nose to the wind, checking for weather. And smoke."

"It all was just so…assumed," she said.

"Assumed?" he repeated, not following her.

"Back home in the States, I think we've lost something of what your grandfather and George have. It's almost an assumption that people will look after each other here. Not just to respond to a fire. Like James, coming in on a day off. Just because he cares."

"They wouldn't do that in the States?"

"Oh, I'm sure some would. I just think the likelihood is greater here."

"Hmmm."

They drove along in silence for a while, each lost to their own thoughts. Rory wondered if she'd ever move from America. Choose to live someplace else. *Like, Ireland, you eegit? She's an Irish scholar. Not a wanna-be immigrant.*

—∿—

Fiona thought of their conversation half the way to Galway. She knew it was likely different here in the country than it was in the big city. But by and large, the Irish were plainly more kind than Americans were. Especially these days. Back home, more and more people seemed to become further entrenched in their own political, religious, and philosophical camps, never venturing to reach across the divide on the socials, let alone in real life.

She pulled out her phone and searched for Ed Sheeran's "Galway Girl," and pressed play. "Are you a fan?"

"Sure," he said with a tiny shrug. "It's hard not to like the guy, even though he's English. But if you're wantin' music with an Irish flair, I should take you by a few pubs on certain nights."

"A pirate cave? And now pub singing? It sounds like you're trying to distract me from my task of writing, Mr. O'Malley."

"Just trying to do my best to be a friend to a lonely Bourke descendant."

She took that in, that casual *friend* reference. Was he trying to make it clear to her, his intentions, despite the invitations? She sighed, inwardly. It was okay with her. It really was. If he needed to draw the line, she wouldn't try to cross it.

At least, she didn't think she would.

Because more and more, Rory drew her.

She knew she really should have bowed out, worked on her dissertation today, or seen through her meeting with Abigail Callaway. What did going to a hospital to pick up George, or to hardware stores and wherever else they needed to go to price out kitchen replacements, have to do with her goals for the summer?

Her professors wanted her to "fill in some of the cracks" in her dissertation. She wasn't entirely certain what that meant. She only knew that one of her profs had spent the summer in Rome, sitting at a café staring at the Pantheon as she wrote about it. Another had spent the summer in a 9th arrondissement apartment in Paris, as he finished his dissertation on Napoleon. She had figured if she came, what she needed would simply arise on the map before her. But she admitted to herself that this was a detour. Procrastinating by volunteering to join Rory in Galway, help him with George and the kitchen. Be a friend to him, as well as her landlord.

At least Rory's an O'Malley, she decided. *I can chalk it up to spending time with one of Grace's descendants.*

As if reading her mind, he said, "So, you're meeting up with Kelly tomorrow night?"

"I am. At the Axe & Oak."

"Just watch yourself with that one. He has a reputation of getting a bit forward with girls."

She considered him. Again, there was a tinge of jealousy to his tone, but right after his friend-zone comment, she had no idea what to make of it. Maybe he was just warning her. Like her brother Thomas might. "Don't worry. I'll keep him in his place. Or shoot his face full of pepper spray."

He cast her a small smile, as if wondering if she really carried a canister. *Let him wonder,* she decided.

Rory pulled up in front of the contemporary hospital in Galway and they hopped out. She noticed he was quiet. Perhaps anxious about the state in which he'd find his great-uncle?

They checked in at the front desk, then elected to climb the stairs to the second floor rather than wait for the elevator. Down the hall they found George in his room, sitting in his hospital gown, hat and coat, his hands bandaged up.

"There ye are, my boy! They say I can go home." His smile faded as he looked to Fiona. He blinked several times. "And who are *you*?"

"I'm Fiona Burke," she said with a smile. She knew from experience that it was easier to just go with the flow with people suffering from dementia, rather than trying to remind them. Because the memory simply was not there. "I'm renting the cottage at Ballybrack. So you'll be seeing me quite a bit this summer."

"Are ye feeling better, Uncle George?" Rory asked.

"Right as rain, my boy. Right as rain." He paused and squinted. "Tell me again who ye are? Are ye Alex?"

"No, that's my da. I'm his son, Rory. Listen, I see ya have your coat on and everything, but we brought ya some clothes." He glanced at Fiona. "And I need to make sure the doctor is really ready to send ya home." He threw a questioning glance at Fiona.

"I'll go and ask," she mouthed, hooking her thumb toward the door. She went to the nurses' station and said, "Excuse me, can you tell me if George Caheny has been cleared to leave?"

The nearest nurse pulled out his chart and took a look. "Yes, I just need to discuss his treatment plan with the nearest kin. Is that you?"

"His great-nephew, Rory, is in with him now."

"Right then," said the nurse. "I'll join them shortly."

Fiona went back to the doorway and Rory came around the privacy curtain. "Is he really cleared to go?" he whispered.

"Yep. Nurse will be here in a minute to go over his treatment at home."

"Sorry about the shopping expedition," he said, smiling ruefully at her. "I thought it'd take until tonight to get him out."

"No worries," she said. "George is our priority. The barbeque and cabinets can come later."

She took a seat and watched the nurses, aides, doctors, and patients move down the busy hall while Rory finished helping George get in his clothes. She suspected that with his hands bandaged so, it was going to take some doing.

Her cell rang and she fished it out from her purse. "This is Fiona."

"Hi, Fiona," said a deep voice. "This is Kiernan Kelly."

She closed her eyes and stifled an inner groan. Rory was right. The way he even said his name seemed to assume she would faint dead away at the moment she heard him utter a word. "Kiernan, hi."

"I had another thought about tomorrow. An O'Malley scholar should really see Bunowen Castle."

"The old O'Flaherty castle?" she said, trying to remember what she could about it. "I thought it was on private land."

"It is. But I have a friend in Ballyconneely who is friends with the owners. I've secured permission for us to tour the property tomorrow afternoon. Want me to pick you up at four?"

She frowned, swallowing her irritation that he just assumed she was available, hours before they were scheduled to meet. But to see the castle where Grace had lived for sixteen years, born her children... "I'd love that," she returned honestly. "But there's no reason for you to come all the way out to pick me up. I'll meet you there at four. I appreciate it, Kiernan."

"Of course," he said. Was there hesitation in his voice? Surprise? Maybe women rarely turned him down. "Right, then. I'll see you at Bunowen, tomorrow at four." He hung up without a further word. Was that an Irish thing or an irritated-man thing?

Rory and George emerged from the hospital room, this time with George fully clothed and his presumably smoke-drenched outfit in a bag. Rory and Fiona walked out with George between them. This time, they elected to take the elevator down.

"So, that's it?" Fiona asked George—really Rory—as they waited. "They're not worried about your breathing or anything?"

"His chest x-ray was clear," Rory said. "And he's always struggled a bit with emphysema, so that's a relief. That's why they wanted to keep him overnight."

"Spent some time in the mines, ya know," George put in, touching the front brim of his hat.

"I didn't know that," she returned.

"He was an engineer," Rory supplied. "For over forty years, he was often down below."

The elevator dinged and they made their way out through the foyer and to the car. Fiona tried to encourage him to sit in the front seat.

"No, no, my dear. Ladies should sit in front," he insisted.

"Really, George. Fiona doesn't mind," Rory said, clearly wanting to keep an eye on his beloved uncle.

"Fiona? Who is Fiona?" he said, growing irritated.

"This is Fiona, beside you. She's renting the cottage for the summer."

George turned to her and his eyes lit up. "My goodness! What a bonny lass! Ya shall be a fine addition to Ballybrack Farm. We're all just men there, you know. Please, take this seat," he said, gesturing toward the front seat again as if it were a gold carriage instead of the Jeep.

Rory shrugged, giving up.

"Thank you, George," she said, slipping into the Jeep, just hoping her action would settle him.

George didn't want the seat behind Fiona for some reason, and came around with Rory to the other side and got in the seat behind him. Fiona tried not to look, but she couldn't resist stealing a quick glimpse. Rory was extraordinarily patient with his uncle. For a moment, she daydreamed about watching him in his class at school, interacting with the kids. She bet they loved the gentle giant.

Rory sat down in the driver's seat and they were off. "Hopefully we can beat the traffic," he said, glancing at his watch.

"That'd be great," she said. She looked forward to the drive home, through some of the most beautiful landscape the Connemara had to offer, with steeply climbing mountains, small lakes and swaying grasses. She'd loved the trip down already and wondered if she could get Rory to stop in a few places so she could take some photos. She needed to post on the socials to reassure her parents that all was going well, as well as share this beautiful country with anyone else who was interested.

Rory had just pulled onto the highway when George said, "Aren't ye going to introduce me to yer girlfriend, Alex?"

"I'm Rory, Uncle George," he said, a tinge of red at his neck. "And this is Fiona. Remember? She's not my girlfriend. She's renting the cottage this summer."

"*Not* yer girlfriend!" the old man said, sounding bewildered. "Why not? She's quite bonny."

Rory laughed under his breath and winked at her. "That she is, Uncle George."

"And lass, do ye not think Alex is quite handsome?"

Fiona smiled and swallowed, trying to just go with it, not make a big deal of it. "He is. Sometimes he reminds me of a Viking."

"A Viking!" George said. "Well there were a few of those in these parts in the early days. Alex likely has some of their blood in him."

"Do you, Alex?" Fiona said, warming to the game.

"I assume so. My father says that that's the family lore, anyway. And some cousin did a deep dive into the family genealogy and claimed it was true."

"Have you ever done one of those tester kits? See what your DNA tells you?" she asked.

"Nah," he said, shaking his head as if that was a silly idea.

"I know who I am, already. I may have Scandinavian blood, but Ireland fills my soul. Irish is who I am. That's good enough for me."

Fiona leaned her head back against the rest and watched as the city and suburban sprawl gradually gave way to periodic farms, more houses, then eventually wide open land. *Ireland fills my soul*, he'd said. She was beginning to understand that. Though she'd visited before, and been researching an ancient Irishwoman for years now, there was something different about being here now.

She'd heard someone say that Ireland called the Irish home as clearly as Jerusalem called to the Jews. Is that what she was sensing now? That deep, primal pull toward home? Something that seeped from her roots, her very DNA that had granted her blue eyes and red hair? What would it be to claim as Rory just had, "Irish is who I am," with pride and conviction and complete *connection* to this land?

"Say! Is this your young wife, Rory?" George asked, as if just waking from a nap and discovering her in the car with them for the first time.

"No, George, this is Fiona. She's renting our cottage this summer."

"Well, I'll only say this once, lad. Ye ought to marry such a pretty girl. Or another might snatch her away," he said, pausing to try and snap, then discovering his bandages, giving up. "Right from under yer nose."

Rory nodded, a bemused expression on his face. "Fiona and I are just getting to know each other, so it's a little early for marriage proposals. But I'll think on it."

"Good, lad. Good. But not too long?"

"Not too long," he said.

"Right, then. Good lad."

Fiona turned to the window so that George didn't see her grin. Rory was probably wanting to put duct tape over the old man's mouth. But as she stared out to the green hills, she daydreamed about what it would be like to marry a man like Rory. To live with him, beyond the summer. Where would they live? In Shannon, in an apartment? A little row house? Or could he find a teaching position here? She, in Galway?

She shook her head as if to clear it. She wasn't staying in Ireland after August. She'd return to Boston to present and defend her dissertation, then be on the job hunt for a university position. It was tight at Boston College—she doubted she could land a spot there. But maybe she could teach at the local community college for a while and keep up her relationships with key faculty, so when a position opened up...

But then her mind went back to Rory. He'd agreed she was pretty. Even if it was to appease his uncle, hadn't he said it with some serious agreement? She thought again of how he claimed his heritage. Of how he knew who he was, where he belonged. And how that was so, so dang attractive.

CHAPTER 13

Rory threw the bale of hay off the back of the truck down to the floor of the barn with more force than he'd meant to. The twine broke—and that always made it harder to move it. His grandfather looked up at him, lifting a brow. "Want to tell me what's got yer trousers in a wad today? Something's been eating at ya."

"I'm fine," Rory said, tossing another bale, this time more carefully. He grabbed his cane, moved a foot, and then set upon the next stack.

"As fine as a faerie in a hawthorn on land short of peat," Patrick muttered.

Rory smiled in spite of himself. He liked that old saying of his grandfather's, denoting agitation or fear. For centuries, the Irish equated the flowering trees as a likely home for faeries, and superstitiously avoided cutting them down. There were tales of those who tried—and ended up with broken axes and saw blades. Whole highways had been diverted to avoid an ancient hawthorn.

He didn't respond, but he admitted to himself that he was missing Fiona today. She hadn't sought him out or called out to him as he'd passed by her cottage this morning nor again this afternoon. And now he'd just seen her drive out, heading to meet up with Kelly at the pub, he assumed. But it was a bit early. He checked his watch. He'd thought she'd said it was an evening thing at the Axe & Oak. Here now it was only

3:30. He hoped she'd just elected to run an errand or stop somewhere else en route to her date.

No. It wasn't a date. It was merely a get-together for her to gather as much information from the jackeen as she could. And he wanted that for her. Kelly likely had some good stories to tell, stories that might help her flesh out what she already knew of Grace. It was just that Rory had seen enough of the tabloids to know there were plenty of rumors to spin tales about Kelly himself. No, the tabloids weren't really a reputable source. But given the sheer number of them he'd seen through the years, there had to be some kernel of truth. It didn't help that Uncle George subscribed to the daily. It was the only thing he'd read any more.

"Hey!" his grandfather yelled, as yet another bale burst at his feet.

"Sorry!" Rory said. Ruefully, he realized he hadn't really been paying enough attention. He might have sent that last bale directly into the old man's chest.

"Laddie," Patrick said. He rested his arms on the truck bed's edge and looked up at him. "Take a seat." He gestured to the bale of hay at the corner.

Rory heaved a sigh, took up his cane and did as he was told. He might outweigh the man by a hundred Euros, but when a grandfather took that tone, a grandson knew there was naught to do but comply. He eased down to the prickly perch and closed his eyes for a moment, taking a deep breath as the pain in his leg reached a crescendo and then gradually eased.

"Is it yer leg, then, that's botherin' ya?"

"My leg is but a part of it."

Patrick considered him a moment. "Are ya not gettin' on with Miss Fiona, then? Is that it?"

"I'm gettin' along with Miss Fiona *too* well, Grandda."

He dared to meet the old man's gaze then. But instead of the sorrowful, empathetic look he expected, Patrick looked as if he practically wanted to bust out into a jig. "No, Grandda. This is not good news. I—"

"Not good news?" He patted the flatbed boards with both hands, face full of glee. "'Tisn't good news! 'Tis grand news! Ye've finally set yer cap for a girl, and she couldna' be a finer choice, lad."

"She could be a finer choice," he said, irritated. "She could live in Ireland, not America."

"*Pffft*," his grandfather said, waving away his complaint. "In this day and age, ya can surely find a way."

"I don't know," he said, shaking his head and leaning down to rest his elbows on his knees. "She's headin' home, come September. She'll need to present and defend her dissertation. And that's where she'll have the most connections to find a teaching position at university. Her life is there. And my life is here."

"You listen to me," Patrick said, all trace of mirth gone from his face. He raised a finger—long crooked from arthritis—to shake at Rory. "Two things can keep a couple who are well suited from each other. If it is the wrong time—one person or the other isn't ready for a committed relationship. Or neither are," he said, lifting his hands. "But the other reason? Place? *Psssht*," he said, throwing aside a dismissive hand. "That's an adequate reason for when a man and woman were separated by a six-week voyage, not a six-hour plane ride."

He studied Rory. "Are ya falling in love with the lass? Is that why ye're in such a dark mood today, because she's off without ya?"

Rory stared at him. Love?

"Rory, man," Patrick said, his tone dead-serious now,

but gentle. "Do ya think ya could love the lass?"

"I, uhh…" Did he? Was this what he'd been wrestling with all day?

He leaned down and ran his fingers through his hair, pressing into his scalp, feeling the tension there. "Grandda, we just met. It's not even been two weeks."

"Bah. Ye're nearly thirty, lad. A man knows who he's looking for by yer age. Search yerself. Are ye in love with her?"

Rory considered it, his eyes shifting madly left and right. Love? Could it be possible? Even if it was, it was fruitless. "Even if I was, Grandda, she wouldna' have me."

His grandfather let out another sound of contempt. "A fine, strapping man like you? Why not?"

Rory took hold of his cane. "Because of this," he said, lifting it slightly. "And how the same injury hurt me here and here," he said, grazing his temple first, and then resting his hand on his chest.

Patrick considered him a moment. "Any woman worth her salt will see that ye're worth far more than the average man, despite your infirmities." He took a long, deep breath.

Rory shook his head, remembering anew how he'd been so spooked by the gunshots on the island and taken her to ground. Even the thought of it made his face burn. "It's not the leg, Grandda. I think Fiona can handle that fine. It's my head. My heart. I'm just not sure how I go about fixin' that."

"Remember that ram story I told ye? And how I brought Dexter back by having him face a bigger and bigger ram over time? That's what ya have to find a way to do, my boy. To dig in, dig deep. Root out the thing that's inside ya, like ya might the rot in a spud. And bit by bit, conquer it."

Rory knew what he was suggesting. He'd done some counseling, when he first got back from the Middle East. But not for a long while. And such work was hard. Almost physical, it took so much out of a man.

"Mrs. O'Sullivan's niece is a counselor," Patrick said. "She specializes in PTSD. Mrs. O says she's been trained in a new treatment process. Soldiers in the States have had good success with it, she says. They even use it for people who've suffered other traumas, she says."

"I dunno," Rory said, shaking his head. "It's—"

"Ya don't know? Don't know?" he frowned. It was his turn to shake his head and fold his arms. "Ya can't blame place—or distance—as the reason not to pursue Fiona, lad. Not if the truth o' the matter is that ye are not in a good place." His tone softened. "Ye're a Caheny. An O'Malley too. No matter what ye've suffered, ye have the strength in here," he said, tapping his head, "as well as here," he added, touching his chest, "but most of all there," he said, pointing to the sky, "to heal whatever ails ye."

His grandfather took a step away. "Regardless of what comes of this with Fiona, ye must tackle it, and tackle it soon. For your sake, first. But then for how it might benefit the both of ya, in time."

Patrick strode out of the barn then, presumably breaking for tea. But Rory sat there for a long while, thinking about his grandfather's words and staring up at the dusty rafters of the barn, where pigeons nested, fluttered about, and cooed.

"Is it possible, Lord?" he whispered, looking to the afternoon sun, piercing between the planks of the side walls, casting streams of light across the barn's interior. Could the good Lord actually find a way to pierce the darkness that remained inside of him in the same way he sent the afternoon sun to find its way through the crevices of this old barn?

—ᴍ—

Fiona drove down the highway on the north side of Clew Bay, looking for one of the brown road signs with the castle emblem, or waiting for her GPS to direct her. She supposed she could have read the directions, but her mind was on Rory. She'd avoided him all day, keeping to herself in the cottage, needing a little distance to get her head and heart together. This summer was about finishing her dissertation, not falling in love with a handsome Irishman. *Life is complicated enough without getting in any deeper with a man with baggage,* she told herself.

Everyone has some baggage, she argued back. *I have baggage.*

Like what?

Like having a constant internal dialogue! Being a bit OCD. Having to get straight A's all through college and grad school.

She let herself off the hook as she turned down a road that swept through a farm, with the ruins of the towering, black-stoned Bunowen guarding the top. After all, Kiernan Kelly was waiting for her halfway down a lane marked "private," and she had to get her head in the game.

Kiernan, dressed in a slim navy sweater, khakis, and boots, was talking to someone Fiona assumed was a caretaker. He was an older man in overalls, with one muddy boot up on the edge of an ATV. Clearly, he'd driven down the lane to greet Kiernan.

She parked behind Kiernan's BMW and got out. "Hello!"

He smiled, lifted a hand, and as she approached he said, "Fiona Burke, this is Timothy Barwicke, Lord of Bunowen."

The older man waved away the faux title as the joke it was and reached out a hand. "Happy to meet ya, Fiona. Ya can just call me Tim."

"Thanks, Tim," she said. "We really appreciate that you're allowing us to tour the ruins," she said, glancing back at the imposing mansion.

"Yes, well, there's little left of what I hear ye're lookin' for, but ye're welcome to see what ya can see."

"Thank you."

Kiernan shook Tim's hand and they moved to a gate that was marked PRIVATE PROPERTY: KEEP OUT, but had been unlocked.

"Just leave it shut behind ya!" called Tim. "I'll come back tonight to lock 'er up!" He roared off in his ATV, gravel scattering behind the small tires.

"Why did they decide to close this to the public?" Fiona asked Kiernan.

"Liability, for the most part," he said as they walked uphill through the clumpy, soggy grass. "As you can see, the place is little more than a gaunt ruin. If you have kids coming out here, daring to climb the walls, or others raiding for stones, you could see collapse." He gestured to a place in the outer wall that had been filled with a mishmash of stones to close up a gap. She followed behind him on a narrow path, taking in his assured, elegant stride. He had a hint of the Irish brogue, but it was subtle. She was pretty sure he played it up when he was on camera.

He was inarguably a handsome man, what the locals referred to as "Black Irish," with a serious dose of Latin blood. His ancestors perhaps the Spanish who once came to fish along these shores. His hair was longer, but styled in a wave that required product, despite his efforts to make it look natural. And his dark eyes—lined with dark, long lashes—were intent as he repeatedly glanced back at her, making certain she was faring all right.

They neared a massive, central round tower, with a doorway marked DANGER: KEEP OUT as one final warning. Fiona didn't find it disturbing. Had they been walking second- or third-story floorboards rotting away it would have been one thing, but walking among the roofless walls hardly seemed perilous at all.

"This way," he said, straddling an arched stone window frame and offering his hand.

She took it, noticing his strong, long, manicured fingers, and climbed into the structure to look about. Some of the walls remained remarkably true; others were crumbling.

"As you can see, these remains are the nineteenth century structure financed by John O'Neill in 1830," he said, ducking beneath a disintegrating doorway. "As recently as a hundred years ago, the structure was largely intact. But these coastal winds and weather can take buildings apart faster than most would believe."

Fiona looked around, trying to imagine it intact a hundred years ago, with floors and furnishings and lights and finished, refined doors. It *was* stunning how quickly a building could essentially dissolve. Unsettling, really. Thousands and thousands of Euros—essentially the modern-day equivalent of a million or more in this house, and now there was literally nothing left but three-quarters of the stones that had formed her foundations and walls.

"O'Neill was a member of parliament, right?" she asked.

He glanced at her, a trace of surprise in his eyes at her knowledge. "He was. But he never stood for re-election. Some said it was a gambling issue, others that he overstretched his resources in building this place," he said, slapping a wall. "But as the Great Famine closed in, he was forced to sell it."

Fiona followed him into the next room where the floor was thigh-high with ferns and weeds. "Who bought it?"

"A man named Valentine O'Connor Blake, who used it as a summer residence."

"It must've been quite the summer home," Fiona mused. She paused to look out the window, down the sweeping green hill and to the ocean, then up to the remains of the second story on her left.

"Quite," Kiernan agreed. He picked off a small, purple daisy from a nearby weed and offered it to her with a shy smile.

She took it, not knowing what else to do, but he was off again. He led her farther inward and while the wind abated with the walls providing shelter, the cold stones lent a chill to the air. A shiver ran down her spine.

Through a long hallway, they entered what must have been the central gathering place, with five windows on either side. "This is the only place you can see what might have been stones that Grace O'Malley or Donal O'Flaherty might've walked." He bent and grabbed hold of some grass, wrenching it from the mossy soil beneath, then pressed back a massive, wide-leafed plant so Fiona could peer among the foliage.

She crouched beside him and touched the broad, rectangular stone. Here and there across the floor, she could see hints of others between the greenery that was swiftly claiming reign within these ancient halls. "So the tower house would've been here? Right here?" she asked, spreading out her hands.

"Most likely."

She went to the central window and admired what had once been their view of the Atlantic, with a silver sheen from the wind upon it, and thought about how their territory had run from here all the way to Oughterard. "Those O'Flahertys certainly earned their title of the kings of Connaught," she said.

He joined her at the wide window, leaning on the far side and looking out. He had plucked a weed and was idly ripping off one bit of it at a time. "The Joyces gave them a run for their money. But the O'Flahertys really dominated the land, from here all the way to Galway's door. Surely you've heard what the medieval sign on the western gate of Galway read, right?"

"'From the Ferocious O'Flahertys, O Lord, deliver us,'" she quoted.

"Good girl," he said approvingly, folding his arms. "You have done your homework."

Girl. Homework. She shoved aside the patronizing comments from this man who was what—eight or ten years her senior?—and smiled sweetly. She would get what she needed from him and be done with him as soon as she could.

He might think he could charm her. Use her. Maybe even seduce her.

He was mistaken.

They continued to walk through the rest of the castle, then down past a World War I gun turret, to the ruins of an ancient stone circle—either to pen up sheep or provide a small fortress—and then on to a tiny chapel by the sea. As Fiona bent to run her fingers over the remains of a stone tablet on the center of the chapel floor, wishing she'd brought pencil and paper to do a rubbing and perhaps discover a clue to what it had once said, she looked up at him.

He was staring out the window, the wind ruffling his big, dark curls. He didn't draw her like Rory did—with his rugged, natural strength—but Kiernan was handsome in the way that made someone want to draw or photograph or film him. *There's a reason he's a TV personality.*

He caught her looking when his attention returned to her and smiled, as if he'd half expected it. She blushed and busied herself with rising and brushing the dirt off her hands.

"So tell me, Fiona," he said, as they left the chapel, "what sparked your interest in our pirate queen as the subject of your dissertation?"

She glanced back at him in surprise. "I mean, how could you not? Once you've heard of her? A sixteenth century woman who basically owned the west coast of Ireland and much of the sea beyond? Who reigned as a pirate queen for decades, managing hundreds of men and ships, as well as thousands upon thousands of acres of land? A woman who faced the queen of England—in person—but did not end up on a pirate's gallows, hanging from a noose? Now *that's* a woman I want to know more about."

He laughed, and the sound of it was pleasing, but curtailed somehow. Cultured. As if he was aristocratic, only allowing himself a certain level of levity in public. "Indeed," he said.

"When did the queen first draw *your* attention?" she asked.

"As a schoolboy in Dublin. She was but a blip in our history books, of course. I had to come here, to County Mayo and Galway to learn more."

"Did you go to college? Study her?"

"Only for a couple of years," he admitted. "Most of my knowledge has been outside the academic realm. Does that make you discount it?"

She was surprised at the note of defense in his question. No doubt he'd suffered his share of critics over the years. "Not at all. In fact, I've had my fill of the academy. I think

I've read every source available in regard to Grace and her life and times. What I seek is more of what I suspect you have found. The folklore, the stories passed down from generation to generation, corrupted though they may be."

"And that is the crux of it, yes? What is corruption and what is truth?"

"Exactly," she said, warming to what seemed to be their joint understanding. They began their walk back to their cars, side by side. "May I ask you some more pointed questions?"

"Please," he said, gesturing before them.

"Why are you so convinced that Grace O'Malley amassed a treasure?"

"It's simple," he said. "She had much of the lands and waterways that royals in other countries commanded, but with half the outlay needed in funds. With all that she was accomplishing in terms of honest trade and piracy, there had to have been a substantial sum amassed over time."

"But she had many men she had to pay. All of these castles and lands required protection, especially with the English constantly encroaching via Galway."

"True. But by my calculations, there would still have been plenty left over."

"Calculations?" she said, looking at him. "Do you have files or something I could look over? Reference, even, for my dissertation, as a source?"

He considered her. "Possibly."

She wondered what that meant. *What hurdles do I have to jump to be allowed in?* "I promise you that I am not going to begin my own treasure hunt," she said, lifting a teasing smile. "The only treasure I'm after is a university position."

But he did not return her smile. "Perhaps," he said.

He really thinks this treasure is worth protecting. She

guessed, after a few years on the hunt for it, she might be similarly invested and protective.

She'd have to proceed carefully, if she was to get anything pertinent out of him.

"Why is it, with so many castles between the O'Flahertys and O'Malleys, that you're convinced her treasure is near Rockfleet?"

"Because it makes the most sense," he said, his long legs taking even strides, his hands clasped behind his back. "Grace could protect Clew Bay from Clare, but if pressed, fall back if she had to. And inland, she had strongholds all along Lough Corrib, as well as to the north and south. In many ways Rockfleet was the central hub to her territory. I believe it's why she died there. To the last, she was ready to defend what was left."

"Local legends say it's there," she said, encouraging him.

"Absolutely. Along with the legend that anyone who discovers it shall encounter a headless horseman." He cocked a brow and gave her a wry look.

Fiona smiled. She'd read that too. "It wasn't enough to dissuade you, huh?"

"Maybe I've already seen such a ghost."

"Have you?" she said, turning to him with some surprise.

"That is its own story," he said, the tease of a smile on his full lips. They'd reached the gate and their vehicles. "Shall we continue this conversation at the pub?"

"Mr. Kelly," she said, waiting while he latched the gate. "You do know how to hook your audience through the commercials, don't you?"

"I would hope so, after three seasons," he said, referring to his television series. "So? Fancy a pint at the Axe & Oak?"

"Yes, okay," she said.

"Come with me," he said, lifting a hand toward his car. "I'll drop you back afterward."

"Oh, that's all right," she hedged. "If I drive myself I'll be halfway home." She flashed him a sweet smile and moved to her car, thinking through all they had discussed. She suspected he really hadn't yet told her anything she couldn't have culled from watching those three seasons of his show. Maybe with a Guinness in him he'd be more free with his information.

And hopefully, more on that financial front he'd figured out than the headless horseman tale.

CHAPTER 14

At the Axe & Oak, Kiernan and Fiona took a small table near a wood burning stove. She took a moment to peer around. Pubs were traditionally the meeting place for locals. Up by the bar, a group of men traded stories. Here and there were obvious tourists, as intrigued by the environs as she was, but dressed in brighter colors. Fiona had long figured out that the best way to blend in in Europe was to wear blacks, browns and neutrals.

The waiter arrived. "What can I get ya?"

"I'll have a Guinness. Pint, please. Fiona?"

"I'll have the same, but make mine a half," she said. "And I'll have your fish and chips."

"Sounds perfect," Kiernan said. "I will too."

"Good enough," said the waiter. "I'll have it all out to ya shortly." He moved over to take a credit card from one of the touristy couples who was lifting it up in the air, eager to get his attention. That was the thing with Irish pubs...they never wanted you to feel pushed out, so few brought your check before you asked for it. If you wanted to leave, you usually had to go to the bar and ask for the check.

Two more men and a woman came in, greeting others by the bar with the warmth of long-held friendships. There was shoulder clapping, banter and laughter.

Kiernan followed her gaze over his shoulder, even as he leaned forward on his elbows. "Would ya rather be over there?"

"What? Oh, no. I was just thinking that we don't really have anything like pubs in America. I mean we have bars, sure. But they're more for a cocktail after work, or where college kids gather to get drunk or find someone to hook up with. Not just this sort of warm, friendly atmosphere."

He took another long look over his shoulder, then turned back to her. "Those guys are here every night."

"You can tell. But they have a pint and head home, right?"

He pursed his lips. "Usually one. Two, if their wives will let them."

"How come more of their wives don't come with them?"

He shrugged. "It's always been more of a man's domain, but you see more women all the time." The waiter arrived then, delivering their dark, rich brews with a creamy foam on top. Kiernan lifted his glass. "To women in pubs."

"To women in pubs," she agreed. "What makes this your favorite?"

"Favorite in County Mayo," he clarified, twisting his glass. "I could take you to some others in other counties this summer, if you'd like."

She lifted her brow and tilted her head slightly, as if considering it. Was that a hint at a date? She didn't want to offend him, but there was only one thing she wanted out of him, and that was information. "Hey, do you think your friend Tim would mind if I go back tomorrow and do a rubbing of that stone in the chapel?"

He sat back in his chair and took a sip. "I could call him. I don't think he'd mind if it was just you."

"Only me," she promised. "That kind of thing as a visual reference in my dissertation would be very helpful."

"If it would help, there are a couple of other things in Rockfleet that might serve you well too."

She blinked. "*Inside* Rockfleet?"

He nodded. "I have the key. In fact, I believe I have the only extra key at the moment."

She could feel the satisfaction he had in that, even if he pretended to be nonchalant. "The local authorities gave you permission to enter?"

He shrugged. "It's good publicity for the county and Ireland, the longer my show airs. So I did a little negotiating, and yes, I ended up with a key. We've shot some brilliant segments inside for this upcoming season of the show."

"Why'd they close it? Did someone get hurt?" she asked.

"Ach, nah, it was just some eegit kid. He decided to climb a ladder that was off limits and fell. As he fell, the ladder hit the far wall and some stones fell down. The historical society didn't have the funds to man the location, to keep watch on visitors, so they elected to close it down. While it's sad for the public, it's a boon for me. I can give my own unique access via the show. And to friends, of course." He lifted his glass and she did the same for a silent toast.

Friends. That's all he was thinking about her, right? But she'd noticed his dark eyes roam over her as they toasted. She'd clearly have to keep this one in line. For a moment, she thought about Rory and his warning about Kiernan. But the man didn't feel like one who would take advantage of her. *Correction, he might try.* He was clearly a player and used to girls falling all over him. But he wasn't the first of the male species like that she'd met. And if he could get her inside Rockfleet, and there were additional rubbings to be made? That was worth whatever games she had to play.

She'd take him up on that offer to tour the interior of Rockfleet, but she'd take her time to ask. Instead she lowered her voice and leaned forward. "Now I think you were going to tell me a ghost story, right?"

"Right," he said, looking left and right as if to make sure no one was listening in. "This is between us only, though. Because it will be in the next season of my show and I don't want it leaked."

"Got it," she said. "My lips are sealed. But after it airs, can I quote you for my dissertation?"

He hesitated. "Speaking of that, I have something for you to look over." He fished inside his jacket pocket and pulled out a folded piece of paper, then offered it to her.

"What's this?" she said, squinting to see in the dim light of the pub.

"It's a confidentiality agreement," he said. "You understand. If I'm to be free in sharing information with you, I need to be certain that you will not use that information before I have the chance to do so."

"Oh, right," she said, scanning the legal mumbo-jumbo. At least it was brief. But her eyes settled on the paragraph that basically pledged she wouldn't publish or verbally share anything learned from Kiernan, without Kiernan's written permission first.

Sheesh. Paranoid much?

But on the other hand, she understood. And if he was working this hard to protect his information, surely it'd be something she could use. "Where do I sign?" she asked nonchalantly.

"There at the bottom," he said, handing her a pen.

She signed where he'd indicated and then passed it back to him. He tucked it into his pocket, then twisted his glass. "Now then, where were we?"

"Umm, the ghost story," she whispered.

"Are you one to believe in ghosts?"

"No," she answered honestly, sitting back in her seat. "Too much the academic, I guess."

"That was me too," he said, lifting a perfect brow that she swore had been plucked. "Until last fall, after we'd wrapped for the season. That was when I found something in Rockfleet that made me more certain than ever that Grace's treasure is about." He leaned forward, arms folded beneath him. "When that kid knocked the ladder against the wall and those stones fell, I discovered something no one else had seen before."

"What?"

"The ladder did such damage because it fell against a false wall," he whispered. "And as I tore more stones away, I discovered a chiseled arrow atop a bow. Pointing to that field we're searching again now."

"A chiseled arrow atop a bow," she repeated. "But it was covered up?"

"By light mortar and stones," he said, nodding. "That is why I am so certain we're heading in the right direction. This is my season I find it. I'm sure of it."

Fiona sat back in her chair and nodded. Her pulse had picked up. Could the man truly be on the right track? "Well, I'd love to get a rubbing of that too," she said.

She knew why he was so excited. The priest on Clare had said there was likely a clue to the treasure somewhere at Rockfleet. She was sure that Kiernan Kelly was not the first treasure hunter to scour every inch of the old tower, searching for such a clue. But he was the first to discover this. Could the arrow truly be pointing toward it?

"What is it?" he said, his eyes narrowing. "Do you know something of this? Have you run across something about this clue in your readings?"

"No," she said honestly. "Nothing in my readings. My mind is whirling. It's so exciting, Kiernan. No wonder you're so dedicated."

Fiona didn't know why she didn't share the priest's story from Clare, right then and there. She was no treasure hunter. That was more the realm of her old college roommate's cousin, Christina Alvarez. She was the one to find ancient Spanish galleons and gold doubloons... All Fiona was after were some fresh takes to include in her dissertation, right? And yet, something made her hold on to the priest's story. Perhaps for the same reason the priest himself didn't share it with Kiernan when he was with him. There was something about the man that made a person want to make him work for what he got, not hand it to him.

No, she'd see this arrow for herself, take some readings on direction, and see if it was somehow possible to interpret it as not pointing to the field, but rather to somewhere along Lough Corrib, where Father Michael believed the treasure might lay hidden. "I hope you find it this summer," she said. "But then, wouldn't that be the end of your show?"

"I can only hope."

He leaned back as the waiter arrived with plates loaded with fries and a huge fillet of fish, battered and fried to a golden brown. Then he grabbed bottles of malt vinegar, ketchup, and hot sauce from another table, set them on theirs, and was gone.

"After we find the treasure," Kiernan said, sprinkling vinegar over his fish, "we'll have a season full of interviews with experts, evaluating what we've found, and then the finale will be the auction."

Fiona dipped a fry in ketchup and smiled. "Then what will you do? Retire to some South Sea island?"

"With an occasional guest lecture to keep the coffers filled," he said, winking at her.

"Sounds like a nice life," she said.

"I hope it will be. We'll see."

"But what about this ghost?" She'd said it lightly, popping a delicious piece of perfectly fried cod in her mouth. But when she met his gaze, she saw that he was deadly serious.

He wiped his mouth with his napkin and leaned forward. "It was what made me absolutely sure we were on the right track. My cameraman even got footage of it." Again, he eyed those nearest to them, to make sure no one was listening in. He was so serious that Fiona found she was holding her breath.

"I know it sounds crazy," he said. "But I saw him. The headless horseman. We found the bow and arrow emblem and began filming immediately—as long as we could without drawing undue attention by any local farmers. And then I replaced the rocks, as best as I could, in the false wall. As we were leaving the building, the coldest wind I'd ever felt blew off of the bay. The kind that slices into ya and leaves ya shivering, ya know? The kind that takes your very breath away?" His brogue was growing more apparent, the deeper he fell into his story.

"We all felt it," he said. "It wasn't just me. The cameraman, the sound tech…we all literally took a half-step back together. And when we stepped out again, gathering on the front stoop of the castle tower to lock it up, we heard the horse whinny."

Fiona frowned.

"No, I know. I get it. It sounds mad. But all three of us would tell ya the same thing. There he was, atop a dark horse. For just a few seconds, hovering there, an apparition. And if we weren't chilled before, we were dead chilled then." He shook his head and lifted a hand. "I never want to see such a thing again."

Fiona tried to think of a logical explanation. Not that there was any true scholarly way to investigate a ghost story. "Why?" she asked. "Why would he appear to you?"

"Don't ya see? It's long been the legend, and we'd found the clue to the treasure," he whispered. "All I could think was that it was Grace's man, sent to warn us away. Or decide if we were worthy." He took a long sip of his beer. "We decided since he disappeared, rather than try to run us off, he figured we were the latter."

Or not a true threat, Fiona thought.

Not that she believed in ghost stories. To her way of thinking, ghosts—if they existed—were more likely demons, riding on the image of loved ones to gain access to the vulnerable...or a commonly held image such as this headless horseman. Something that the weary and vulnerable said they thought they saw, and the mere suggestion of it got the rest to think the same.

But the hint of this fresh, collective story about Grace and her ghostly guardian might prove pertinent to her dissertation. "If I give you and the show full credit in my dissertation, might I interview your cameraman and sound guy?"

He considered her. "When will you present and defend your dissertation?"

"This fall, after your show begins to air, right?" She could feel his hesitation. But clearly, the man was itching to share it with her. Perhaps because he hadn't met another as intrigued with Grace O'Malley as she was. Or because he wanted to use his knowledge to draw her in a bit closer, she acknowledged. A man such as this was not above using such things to weave a web around a woman…

"It was mad. I mean, I know it makes me seem dead mad. But I swear it's true. And it all began with me discovering that carving in the wall."

She nodded, hoping there wasn't a trace of disbelief in her eyes. But she knew that if people collectively heard a certain story all their lives, it was imprinted on their sub-conscious. Had one of them heard what he thought to be a whinny and suggested it to the others? Had another pointed to a shadow that for a moment did resemble a horse? That was how these sorts of stories grew, boosted by one person's account and then another's…

"You can't tell anyone of it," he said, taking a piece of fish in his fingers and pausing to stare at her. "I mean, I shared this with you in confidence. So that you might have some-thing fresh for your dissertation."

"Of course," she said. "I will keep it to myself. But I may write about it in my dissertation? I have your permission to do that?"

"As long as it isn't in print before September." He took another wary look about. "I get harassed by reporters. The rags, you know," he said, referring to the tabloids. "They're ready to write anything about me. And this sort of story…it needs to be carefully curated. We want to craft how it's pre-sented to the public."

"That's understandable," she said. "Thank you for trust-ing me with it."

He eyed her, and for a moment was deadly still. "I hav-en't made a mistake," he asked slowly, "have I, Fiona?"

"I don't think so," she said, shaking her head. Why was his gaze so penetrating? Piercing?

"Good, good," he said, his demeanor easing. "You must

come tomorrow, then. I'll show you the clue straight away," he said in an eager whisper.

"Oh, I can't tomorrow," she said, honestly regretful. "I have another interview."

"With?" he asked scornfully.

"Abigail Callaway. I'm to have tea with her at Westport House."

"Ahh, right," he said. "Just don't mention my name. She thinks I'm a quack."

"Okay," she said carefully. "Our friendship will remain our secret."

"Brilliant," he said raising his half-drained Guinness glass to clink against hers once again.

CHAPTER 15

Rory paced the floor that evening, waiting for Fiona to get home. Was she all right? Had she run into car trouble? Or was that Kelly simply keeping her out this late?

Kiernan Kelly. Images of him on magazine covers, tabloids, and the promos on the telly set Rory's teeth on edge.

But what right did he have to object to her being with him? What right did he have to feel this agitation, worrying about her so? As far as she knew, she and Rory were just friends. Hadn't he made that utterly clear to her?

And yet Grandda's words niggled at him, repeating over and over in his mind. Tugging loose his heart, a heart he'd worked for years to wrap and cover and wrap and cover some more. Anything to avoid discovering he was not as strong as his frame might portray, but rather as weak and fallible as the next man.

Especially when it came to beautiful wee redheads with bright blue eyes and an insatiably curious mind...

He was honest enough with himself to know that it was only because of her, and these growing feelings in his heart—a heart that maybe, somehow, wanted to be free of the carefully crafted shelter he'd built—that he'd made the call. Gone to Westport that very afternoon for his first session. Cara Deegan hadn't tarried. As soon as she'd gotten the run-down on his history, they'd conducted their first EMDR treatment, what Cara claimed was "the best possible method of putting PTSD in its proper box."

Rory was all for putting his PTSD in a box, and letting his heart out of another. He just wasn't really sure how that was going to happen, or how long it might take. Or if Fiona would consider him as anything more than a friend in the midst of dealing with it. Who would want a man who was so clearly physically damaged, as well as mentally and emotionally impaired?

Impaired for the time being, Cara had said. *But that doesn't mean you have to stay that way, Rory. Trauma doesn't disappear. But you can manage how you respond to the triggers that remind you of it. You can heal and manage it, in time. It doesn't have to rule your life.*

Rory sat down on his bed and let those words settle around him like a warm blanket. *It doesn't have to rule your life.* "Lord, God," he whispered, "don't let it rule my life any longer. Don't let it keep me from living the life ye've given me, with all it can be." He leaned forward and wearily rubbed his face. The first session today had been hard. He felt the repercussions of it like a physical beating, he was so tired.

He flopped to his back on the bed and stared at the cracked ceiling, then checked his phone again. No message from Fiona. Or anyone, for that matter. "Ye've cut yourself off from the world, man," he muttered. "What did ye expect?" Other than his parents, brother, grandfather, and Uncle George, he admitted to himself. For years he'd dodged the invitations of other teachers to join them at the pub or for a football match, or anything. He'd made excuses. Shut himself off. Placed himself in a pocket he thought was safe.

But now he wanted out. To be free of the memories that plagued and controlled him. To pursue Fiona, if she'd ever have him. But for himself too.

Meeting her, letting her in a little, seemed to create a crack in his carefully crafted armor. And after today he was wondering if he needed that armor at all. Sure, he'd pulled it close again, as soon as he'd walked out of Cara's office. But tonight? Tonight, he imagined letting it go. Little by little. Bit by bit. And the thought of it was not altogether as terrifying as he'd thought it might be.

A flash of lights across his wall brought him upright, hoping it was Fiona coming home.

But it'd only been a neighbor, passing by the farm on the way home.

I have to get out of the house, he thought, running his fingers through his hair.

—ᗰ—

Fiona drove back to Ballybrack, utterly worn out. It felt like she'd been gone all day, even though she hadn't left until mid-afternoon. *The repercussions of being with Kiernan Kelly for hours*, she surmised. The man wasn't all bad, she decided, just a lot. A big personality with a lot going on in his mind. Paranoia for one, certain that someone was going to steal something that was his. After signing that confidentiality agreement, she wasn't certain she'd be able to use a thing she learned from him or his crew in the coming days. But she would respond to his invitation to see what he'd found in Rockfleet, and conduct some interviews of her own.

She glanced up to the darkened windows of the farmhouse, a bit disappointed that the men inside were all asleep already. She felt a pang of missing Rory, after not talking to him since yesterday, and regretted not getting home sooner. Maybe their paths would've crossed then. Kiernan had gone on to order a second pint, then a third, all the time regaling her with tales of his career path, first as a private investigator and later as a television reporter. Apparently, he'd done some modeling gigs here and there too. He'd let that subtly slip, then swiftly covered it with a disclaimer that he'd found out that line of work wasn't for him. "Too superficial," he'd said, with a wave of the hand.

And yet somehow Fiona doubted that. He'd simply found something more lucrative to pursue. He might've truly wanted something more of depth in his work, but the man was almost manic in his desire to finally find the queen's treasure. It reminded Fiona of stories she'd read of the '49ers and their "gold fever." It truly was a sort of sickness, in his dark eyes. Hadn't she herself felt her pulse quicken when she heard the priest speak of it? Clearly, it was what drove people to watch his show, week after week, even though the only thing his crew managed to find were metal shoe buckles from the sixteenth century or the fragmented remains of a boat entombed in the mud beside the tower. Just the hint of history and truth behind his story was enough to titillate and keep his audience coming back for more.

He'd bent and kissed her on either cheek as they said goodbye—as so many did in Europe, especially after a shared pint or two—and said he'd expect her in two days' time back out at Rockfleet. He'd smelled nice, of clean linen and hair product that reminded her of being in a high-end spa.

But it was Rory she was thinking about, with his more earthy smells of soap and hay and puppies. She turned off her engine and leaned her head against the steering wheel. *You have no business thinking of Rory*, she told herself. *Missing him. Wondering why he didn't text you today. He's your friend. Not your boyfriend.*

Murphy ran around her car, tail wagging, eager to greet her.

Puppies, she thought. *You need a dose of puppies. That will shake all these jumbled feelings loose and let you sleep.* She *had* to sleep well tonight. Tomorrow was her meeting with Abigail Callaway at Westport. The last thing she wanted to do was arrive frazzled, especially after rescheduling their last appointment. Would she present Fiona with a confidentiality agreement too? After all, she made her living as the biographer of Grace O'Malley. Maybe she'd only refer Fiona to her books and web site.

Wearily, she climbed out of the car and shut the door. She'd retrieve her bag and purse after a visit to the barn. "Let's go see the babies," she said to Murphy, giving him a good rub. "Let's go see them."

As if understanding, he gave her a bark of excitement.

"Shhh, shhh!" She moved out with long strides to the barn, getting him farther away, hoping she hadn't awakened the household. They began their days early. She was just hoping that Patrick left a barn light on all night for Molly, when Rory opened the barn door, obviously having heard the dog bark. She could tell it was him by his silhouette, and as she drew closer, saw he held a tiny, wriggling puppy in one of his big hands.

"Hello," she said in surprise, and then leaned in to put her forehead against the puppy's. "And hello, little one," she added, rubbing its impossibly soft fur. The litter was still so young, their eyes weren't open. "Everything well with Molly and the litter?"

"Well enough," he said, lifting the one in his hand. "They're all getting as round as piglets."

"They *sound* like piglets too," she said, passing by him. "I thought I'd come for a visit to clear my mind."

"Hmmm," he said, following behind her after shutting the door. "I had a mind to do the same."

Fiona took that in, wondering what was filling his head. She looked up into the dark expanse of the barn roof and then down to the warmly lit stall that held Molly and her pups. There was something quieting and reverent about a barn at night. Especially with Rory here. Without him it'd be a bit creepy.

She smiled as she entered the stall and reached out to let Molly sniff her hand and give her a weary lick of welcome before setting her head back down to rest. For once, the puppies were not nursing, but rather piled on one another in haphazard fashion alongside their mama's belly, all snoring away.

Fiona picked up the nearest and cradled her close a moment. Then she settled down into a clean pile of hay, resting her back and head against the wall, feeling the puppy wriggle against her chest.

Across from her, he did the same with the one he held. "Was it a good day, then?"

"A good day, yes," she said. "And I have to say, Kiernan shared some pretty remarkable information."

"Oh?" he said, lifting a brow. "Something you can use for your work?"

"Possibly. He also made me sign a confidentiality agreement. He wants approval on any information I draw directly from him and how I quote him."

"Hmmm," he returned.

"Exactly," she said, smiling. "You know, you do that a lot." "What?"

"Hmmm," she said, in the deepest way she could, trying to imitate him.

"Hmmm," he said with a gentle smile.

"It's your all-purpose response, I think. Something to say as you decide whether you really want to say anything at all."

"Hmmm," he said again.

They smiled together.

"The farm wasn't the same without ya today," he said quietly, turning the puppy in his big palm and giving its chest a scratch.

"Oh?" she said.

"Murphy missed ya. Hung around your cottage all evening, as if he was worried ya weren't coming back."

"A sheepdog worried about one of his flock?" she said, watching him. Was he really saying that he had missed her?

"Could be," he allowed. He turned to the pen and gently set the puppy in with its brothers and sisters. "I should turn in. Grandda needs me early."

"Me too," she said. "I have that meeting tomorrow in Westport."

He reached for the puppy in her hands and set her among the others, then patiently waited at the gate as Fiona came out. He closed up the stall and walked out with her. Outside, the night was full of the most brilliant blanket of stars Fiona thought she'd ever seen. Earlier, it had been overcast, but night had brought crystal-clear skies.

"Oh my goodness, Rory," she said, taking his arm. "Just look at it." She stared up in awe.

"It is beautiful," he said. Then he took her hand and set it in his.

She glanced at him in surprise, but couldn't make out his face in the starlight. Still, she let him go on holding her hand, because it felt so good. So warm and comforting and right.

"Ye're trembling," he said, lifting her hand. "Are ye all right?"

"I'm shivering. It's a bit chilly out here," she admitted.

"But this is lovely." She didn't add *with you holding my hand. I think I've longed for it all day.*

"Come 'ere, lass," he invited gently, opening his arms. He wore a long barn jacket, and when she tentatively wrapped her arms around his torso, she felt the welcome collective warmth of being inside both his jacket and against his body, cradled in his arms. "Better?" he asked.

"Yes," she said, nodding, trying to get over her surprise at his invitation. She could feel the strong, quick beat of his heart beneath her cheek.

"Fiona, I have something to confess to ya," he said.

"Oh?" She looked up. Half-hoping he wasn't about to break up this newfound intimacy. Half-hoping he would. What was this? What were they doing?

He bit his lip for a second. "I'm not just feeling friendship toward ya."

"Oh. No?"

He paused a moment and tipped up her chin. As if he could see into her eyes in the dark? Or because he wanted to kiss her? "No," he said solemnly. "Are ya feeling only friendship toward me?"

It was her turn to pause. Because at that moment, she knew this wasn't just a platonic thing. And that scared her. But she had to be as honest as he. "No. Not just friendship," she whispered.

His fingers beneath her chin became his palm, cupping her cheek. "Ahh, lass," he groaned, cradling her against him. "Ahh, lass," he whispered again with a sigh, pulling her even closer.

"I know," she said, a bit bewildered they were having this conversation, but knowing exactly what he lamented. So little time a summer was, really. And afterward...

She banished the thought of leaving Ireland from her mind. Leaving him.

He didn't try to kiss her, much as she wished he would, pushing all her fears and worries out of her mind. After a moment longer of holding her close, he took her hand in his again, his cane with the other, and they made their way to her cottage.

Fiona paused at the car door. "I still have my stuff in here," she said, reluctantly letting go of his hand. She grabbed her purse and backpack and he accompanied her to the door, where she unlocked it, opened it, and tossed the bags inside. She flipped on the corner light. "Want to come in?" she asked, looking up at him. "Light a fire?"

He paused. "I don't think so. As much as I want to, I think it best to leave ya here now."

She swallowed her disappointment, suddenly every trace of her previous weariness gone. "See you tomorrow, then?"

"I hope so," he said, lifting a hand to trace her cheek and chin with the softest touch a man had ever given her. It sent shivers down her neck, shoulder, and out her arms. "Because truth be told, Fiona lass, I missed ya today even more than Murphy did."

She ducked her head. "Even more than that, huh?"

"Hmmm."

"Hmmm," she repeated.

They smiled together.

"Goodnight, Rory."

"*Lass oiche maith,*" he said in Irish, which she guessed might mean the same. And with that, he disappeared into the shadows beyond her front door.

CHAPTER 16

"Heard ya come in late last night," Patrick said, stabbing a bite of black pudding and placing it in his mouth. They'd managed to cook their breakfast on the new barbeque outside, using a fancy side burner. Until the kitchen was back together, they ate on the couch.

"Hmmm," Rory said. He concentrated on eating and not smiling. His lips seemed to have taken on a life of their own after he'd left Fiona last night, perpetually turning upward of their own volition. He believed he might have even smiled in his sleep. When he awakened, his cheeks ached.

She doesn't just think of me as a friend.

"Were ya checking on the dogs?" Grandda pressed.

"I was," he said.

"What dogs?" George asked from his chair, mouth hanging slightly open.

"Eat yer puddin'," Grandda said, pointing at the plate in his lap, apparently in no mood to placate his brother this morning. Ever since he'd gotten back from the hospital, the man had been more befuddled than ever. This morning, he'd arrived at breakfast in his pajamas and robe again, missing one slipper. Mrs. O would have a fit.

Absently, George took a bite as he was told. At least his hands didn't seem to be bothering him, even though they were still protected in a mesh gauze.

"I happened to get up for a cup o' water," Grandda said,

eyeing Rory again. "And saw Fiona walking to the barn. Did ye happen to meet up with the wee lass?"

Rory took a sip of his tea and considered him. Clearly, the old man knew the two of them had been in there together. Had he seen any more than that? "We did," he said at last, then cut apart his fried egg.

"C'mon, lad, ye're as open as a cockle at low tide. How'd her time with Kelly go?"

Rory grunted. "Made her sign some sort of confidentiality agreement, so she couldn't say much. But apparently it was worthwhile."

"Confidentiality agreement! How is a scholar collecting information able to abide by such a notion?"

"Kelly apparently wants approval over anything she quotes from him and the like. Since she's agreed to that, I suspect he gave her something worthy to chew on. She came home with a sparkle in her eye."

"For information about Granuaile, or because of who she found in the barn, petting the very puppies she went over to cuddle?"

He met his gaze. "It was all about Granuaile, I'm certain."

"Bah," Patrick said disapprovingly. "Come now. Appease an old man's curiosity."

"Hmmm," Rory returned. But at that, his lips curved upward again. She was right. He did use it every time he wasn't ready to say more.

They ate for a while in silence, and his grandfather apparently accepted the fact that Rory wasn't going to tell him more about Fiona. But then he asked, "How did it go with Miss Cara over in Westport?"

Rory felt the tease of his grin morph to a grim line. And yet despite how hard it had been, he still felt hope, real hope, for the first time in a long while on that front. "It went well," he said, lifting his cup. "I'm going back today. After the appointment, I'll pick up the cabinets ya ordered. Gerald called me and said they're in."

"Good on ya, lad. Good on ya," Grandda said approvingly. And he knew he was talking more about his appointment than the cabinets.

"Who is in Westport?" George asked.

"A friend who is helping our Rory," Grandda said. "Now eat your eggs before Mrs. O'Sullivan arrives and finds ya half-dressed."

Rory finished his breakfast quickly and rose. He grabbed the plastic bin they were using for dishes, and set it atop the coffee table, then set his dishes inside. "I'll wash up the breakfast dishes in a bit," he told Patrick.

"Off to check on the dogs, are ya?" Patrick teased, taking another sip of tea.

"Dogs? What dogs?" George asked.

Rory stepped out the door and took a deep, full breath of a perfect Irish morning. Birds were twittering, bursting out of the huge cottonwood that dominated the yard, and then disappearing back in, as if they were children trying to escape from home but called back in.

Murphy ran up to greet him, with his tongue hanging out of his mouth, as if he'd been rounding up sheep just for sport. And their two horses—Clyde and Claude—cantered along the field fence, shiny manes waving, obviously in high spirits themselves. It was as if the whole world was echoing the joy that had infiltrated his heart.

He set off toward the cottage, thinking he might invite Fiona for another puppy visit, and saw that Mrs. O'Sullivan was coming up the drive in her husband's rebuilt Mercedes.

The man was forever rebuilding engines and refurbishing old cars, and their cook was often driving the newest off the line...until it broke down again. Rory didn't know how many times his grandfather had hooked up an O'Sullivan vehicle behind his tractor and slowly hauled it home. She was just passing the apple trees when the engine hesitated, the car slowed, sputtered, and then emitted several loud explosions from the muffler.

He threw himself out flat across the gravel, as if he was being fired upon, covering his ears and head. Logically, Rory knew what had emitted the sound. He had just processed it in his brain. But his body reacted differently. Dimly he wondered if his hands could stop a bullet, or if it would simply pierce through the ligaments and into his brain, ending it all.

At the same time he knew this was madness. That it was only Mrs. O's old car, not anyone firing at him at all. But he seemed unable to do anything but this. To take cover, take cover, *take cover...*

She was there, then. Fiona.

He could hear her voice, but she sounded far away.

"Rory," she said gently, putting a hand on his shoulder and resting it there. "Concentrate on me, Rory. On my voice, okay? You're here. At Ballybrack. You are safe."

Ballybrack. Safe. Ballybrack. Safe.

Fiona.

He closed his eyes and rolled to his back. Put his hands over his face, trying to get ahold of himself as well as figure out what to do now. *Ya fool. Ye eegit. What have ye done now?*

He moved to his hands and knees, aware that Grandda had come out on the front porch, hesitating, witnessing his shame. Mrs. O stood uncertainly by her car door, looking their way.

"He's fine!" Fiona called. "Fine! Just tripped, I think!"

She was covering for him. His face burned with shame.

Fiona had his cane. Wearily, he took it, made it to his feet, brushed himself off, and then said, "A minute? Can you give me a few minutes? I just need to get ahold of myself."

"Sure. Of course," she said. "Want me to meet you in the barn?" she whispered, well aware that they had an audience.

"Fine," he bit out. Then more softly, "Yes."

She turned then and scurried to her door. Half-what? Embarrassed for him? Pitying him?

Rory closed his eyes, feeling the ache of what had transpired—both just now and years ago—like a fresh shrapnel wound to his very heart.

"Lad? Are ye well?" Grandda called.

"Fine! Fine," he called in irritation, walking stiffly toward the barn.

—⁂—

Fiona paced in her tiny cottage, wringing her hands. She knew Rory hated this part of himself, his history. He'd likely be chastising himself all the way to the barn, much as when he'd thought they were under fire on the island. Did he think he'd ruined things with her again?

And yet, if she was honest, wasn't there a bit of hesitation in her heart now?

To witness it once was concerning. To witness it twice was alarming. How often did it happen? How did he manage it at school? When he was driving?

It all seemed so incongruous to her. Everything about Rory was warm, reassuring, grounded, steady. This…this wasn't. And if she felt this unsettled by it, how much more did he?

The yard remained silent and still. She made herself

count to one hundred, and then grabbed her jacket and walked out to the barn, uncertain of what she should say or do. She found him in Molly's stall, seated in the hay as he'd been the night before. This time he didn't hold a puppy, but rather his head in his hands, legs akimbo.

She acted before she thought too much about it. She sat down between his legs and wrapped her arms around his barrel of a chest, resting her head on one shoulder. For a moment she wondered if she'd made a mistake, but then his arms came around her and held her close.

"I'm sorry, lass, that ye had to see that again," he said, every word a grief.

"It's all right, Rory. Really," she said. She let several moments go by, willing her comfort to seep into him. They listened to the pigeons moving about the rafters above. The puppies grunting and squirming for position as Molly laid down again.

"Do you want to tell me about it now?" she asked softly. "What just happened, in your head?"

He was silent a moment more. Then, "It's PTSD," he said. He swallowed hard. "There was a time when my buddy and I were fired upon. We took shelter in a family's home. We were on one side of the door, they were on the other. Bullets pelted the back wall, and I really thought we were going to die. But then the Americans arrived and saved us."

She considered that for several long moments. "So when you hear something like gunfire…"

"I'm back there, yes. But also…" His voice cracked and he brought his hand to his mouth.

She remained silent, waiting.

He blew out a deep breath and rubbed his forehead, his eyes wide and distant. "When I hear gunfire—or something like it—I go back to that day, yes, but also to another day. The day my mate Bryan died and my leg was obliterated by the mine."

She nodded, holding her breath.

"It's like I can *know* what it is—I knew that was Mrs. O's engine backfirin'. But for my body, it moves on instinct. I'm right back there, in that Afghan street." He shook his head. "I can almost feel the grit o' the dust in my teeth, Fiona. It's that real. I start sweatin' and my heart Euros dead out of my chest."

"Is it a panic attack, then?"

"I suppose so," he said, pushing back his hair. "Of a sort."

"How often does it happen?"

He looked down at her and gave her a rueful smile. "More often here than in Shannon it seems. It's been a year or so since it's happened in town." He bit his lip and finally let one arm drape around her, his fingers slowly stroking the small of her back. "I'm sorry if I scared ya."

"I'm fine," she said. "It's you I'm worried about."

"Hmmm," he said, and she felt the rumble of it in his chest.

They stayed there, resting for a couple more minutes, and gradually, Rory's heartbeat slowed. "Have you ever talked to anyone about it?" she ventured.

"Yeah," he said. "Years ago, when I returned, I saw a counselor for a while. But it didn't seem to help much. But yesterday I went to see another in Westport. A woman who specializes in treating PTSD. I'm returning today."

"That's good," she said, sitting up in order to see him better. "I know that takes a lot. I'm proud of you for jumping in."

He searched her face, and at that moment, he looked so full of sorrow that she might have done anything to ease his pain. He lifted a hand and as he'd done last night, gently traced her face from temple to chin.

She took his hand in hers and turned her lips into his palm, tenderly kissing it once, then lifting it to cradle her cheek so she could look into his eyes.

If anything, he looked more tortured than before. "Lass, I don't know if I can do this. If I am the man for ya."

"No?" she said, leaning closer.

"No," he whispered, slowly shaking his head.

But he didn't mean it. He was fighting it. She could sense it.

"No?" she repeated, now so close to his face that she could feel his hot, sweet breath, the tiny hairs of his mustache and beard tickling her chin.

His blue eyes searched hers. Then he gave in, leaning forward to close the gap and capture her lips with his own. At first quiet, gentle. Then as she responded, pulling her closer, deeper, as if falling into a pool he'd long desired to reach.

After a moment, he pulled away. "I'm complicated, Fiona," he growled. "Are ya sure ya want that in your life?"

"I suspect," she said, cradling his beard-covered chin, "that the trauma you've suffered is the only thing that makes you complicated. And that is something that can be negotiated. Especially if you're in therapy."

"But there is no guarantee," he said. "Therapy isn't magic."

"No," she said, considering that. She'd been to a counselor here and there to work through the comparison issues she felt with her brother. Seen friends dive deep to tackle bigger issues. She looked back into his eyes. "But I think if you're praying for healing, and if you do the work, therapy can do wonders."

"Ya think?" he said, casting her a tortured look.

"I do." She settled back against his chest and he stroked her hair, then rubbed her back.

"What about this being just a summer?" he said. "Is it truly worth startin' something we're not sure how we'd finish?"

She took a deep breath. "I don't know, Rory." She rose and gestured for him to rise and walk her back. It was getting late, and she couldn't miss her appointment for tea in Westport, no matter how much she wanted to finish this conversation. But there was no real end to this conversation, really. Neither of them knew where this would lead, or what they might do when they faced parting. "All I know," she said, taking his hand as they walked out, "is that this feels right."

He paused at the barn door and faced her, rubbing her hand. "This? Hanging out in a barn with a PTSD-riddled cripple?"

She shook her head and looked up at him. "No. Spending time with a lovely, intriguing Irishman, who'd better trim that beard if he wants to keep kissing this American."

A slow smile spread across his face and he stroked his beard, eyeing her all the while. "Aye? How short?"

"*Much* shorter," she said, stepping out ahead of him.

He pulled her back, up against his chest. "And if I do, I might steal another kiss?"

"Probably," she said, grinning up at him.

"Then consider it done," he said.

CHAPTER 17

Fiona sat across a perfectly set tea table from Abigail Call-away, madly taking notes. The woman had at first been a bit standoffish, but as they wandered through her finely curated exhibit—worlds better than the one on Clare Island—with the remaining stones of what had once been an O'Malley castle dungeon still visible in the basement, she had gradually warmed to Fiona. Dressed as one who belonged in the sumptuous, historical house, sipping from fine china, Abigail embodied class. But she also clearly felt at ease in her role as the preeminent scholar about the ancient pirate queen. She, too, had been to Oxford and Dublin, seeking out every rare document she could to flesh out what precious little they knew for certain about Grace.

"Tell me, Abigail," Fiona said, as the woman poured them both another cup of tea and took a cookie from the depleted tray of sandwiches and delicacies, "have you ever had the occasion to speak to Kiernan Kelly?"

He'd told her not to mention him. Fiona wanted to know why.

Abigail's perfectly plucked brows twitched almost imperceptibly. "Here and there," she said, with just a tinge of a lilt to her refined accent. "Given our lines of work, it's proven rather difficult to avoid him." She poured some milk into her tea and stirred it with a tiny, sterling spoon.

Fiona bit back a smile. Clearly, there was no love lost between them. "Do you think he might be right? That Grace amassed a treasure over time?"

Abigail lifted her spoon and pointed at her. "On that account, I do believe he could be right," she said, then set the spoon on the saucer beside her cup. "But do I believe he will find a buried chest full of Spanish gold?" She shook her head. "Grace ran an empire, and that empire required a great deal to finance, particularly in the end, as the British were closing in."

"I haven't been able to find record of those last two years before her death," Fiona said, "detailing how many men were loyal to her. And she seems distracted to me, traipsing off to attack MacNeil in 1597 in Scotland, just because he'd offended her."

Abigail nodded soberly. "She perhaps was suffering from some paranoia by that point. I've heard some speculate that after all her battles, she'd certainly suffered her share of concussions. One oral tradition holds that in her last years, she had the 'shakes.' That could have been Parkinson's, or Alzheimer's, and both might leave her prone to paranoia."

"Especially a woman who'd had to fight for everything she got, every step of the way," Fiona said, the idea taking hold. She sat back in her chair, teacup in hand. "And yet if she was paranoid, might she not have squirreled away some of her wealth?"

Abigail pursed her lips and lifted a thin brow. "It is possible."

"And if she had, do you believe she would have buried it at Rockfleet?"

"Possibly," she said. "But I believe she was more cunning than that. She did not rise to her position by doing the expected, did she?"

"No," Fiona whispered. "But where else might she have

hidden it?"

Abigail considered her a moment, then leaned forward. "Another oral tradition I recorded from an old man north of Sligo said that she left clues at several of her castles."

"A clue?" Fiona said, praying her face did not betray what Kiernan had told her, nor Father Michael. "Of what sort?"

"A picture of a bow and arrow, is how the story goes," Abigail said. She shook her head. "But I never found anything definitive that corroborated that story—no written record, no fresco, no etching—so I never pursued it nor wrote about it. The only thing related that I've come across is a stone with a bow and arrow etched into it, that might have originally come from Hen's Castle. It was found in the base layer of a manse's ruins on the western shore of Lough Corrib."

"Oh?" Fiona asked, managing to hid her excitement. "What was the name of that manse?"

Abigail thought about it and then shook her head. "That's been lost to the ravages of time. But it's due west of Hen's." Her eyes narrowed. "Have you run across anything like it?"

"I have not," Fiona answered honestly. "But I may know someone who has. When I'm at liberty to tell you more, I will."

The woman's gray eyes sparked with interest, but she gracefully let her off the hook.

Something niggled at the edges of Fiona's memory. Thinking of the exhibit below, as well as the one on Clare, she pulled out her phone and scrolled, looking for the pictures she'd taken on the island. Her heart began to pound. She enlarged the photo and showed it to Abigail. "Do you see this silver broach shown on Grace's mantle? Is that a figment of the artist's imagination, or something she might've really worn?"

Abigail took the phone from her and looked at the

broach, crafted in the form of a bow and arrow. "It could've been her broach. I'd read something about her favoring a bow and arrow as a mark of her territory. Perhaps the artist knew of it too."

"I see." Fiona paused, thinking about all this woman probably had in files and files at home. "Abigail, would it be possible for me to see your records for myself—especially those that might indicate some mental issues for Grace in those last years? Or specifics about her struggle to maintain her power? Or anything that might substantiate this emblem as uniquely hers?"

"Of course. Come and pay me a call in Dublin, and you're welcome to my library."

"That would be amazing," Fiona breathed. All that source material? It was a dream come true. "Perhaps I could book a room for a week. It sounds like you have a lot I'd love to read and record and catalog as references for my dissertation. As long as it wouldn't be an imposition."

"What is mine, is yours," she said. "Grace O'Malley is Ireland's treasure, not any one man or woman's, despite how someone like Kiernan Kelly thinks." Any trace of a smile disappeared from her face. "You watch yourself with that one, my friend. Agreed?"

"Agreed," Fiona said slowly, taking in the mixture of motherly care and what? A tinge of fear or wariness?

Abigail leaned forward, any trace of formality disappearing. "He's on the hunt for a treasure he believes might be worth millions," she said. "Men have killed for far less."

Fiona blinked. *Killed?*

Kiernan was obsessed. He'd long been on this hunt. But would he truly go to such drastic measures? After all, his whole life was public. She'd seen how he'd been casually recognized by so many at the Axe & Oak. While people didn't ask for his autograph, or ask him how things progressed out at Rockfleet, they'd been keenly aware of him. In the midst of that, how far could a man get off the track?

"Do you think I could go and interview that man you talked to north of Sligo? Hear his story for myself?"

Abigail shook her head, her gray eyes growing stormy. "I'm afraid not. He...died."

"Oh?" Fiona said, disappointment tamping down that hope. But something in Abigail's demeanor made her pause. "How did he die?" she asked quietly.

Abigail narrowed her gaze and looked to the window, as if troubled. "He fell from a cliff one night. Along a path he'd walked since he was a wee lad."

Fiona felt the hairs on the back of her neck rise. "Was he alone?"

"Presumably," Abigail said tightly.

"But you don't think he was."

"It was never proven," she said, so quietly that Fiona had to strain to make out her words. "But some said a dark haired man in a fancy car had come to call the afternoon before."

Fiona guessed what she was saying.

"Did Kelly know that you had interviewed that man?" she dared to press.

"He did not. Until today, I've never related that story to another soul. In fact, I've kept most of my sources to myself, aware that Kelly has done his own research. And in regard to this treasure..."

Abigail shook her head, seemed to gather herself, and opened her eyes a bit wider. "Well, enough of that. 'Tis all conjecture, of course. The constable found no evidence of foul play and perhaps Kiernan conducted his interview and left the man in peace. Just mind yourself around him, will you?" she said again. She wiped her mouth with a dainty linen napkin. "Come across to Dublin, have a look at my library and files. There is much more to tell about what we know of Grace's state of mind than there is about any supposed treasure. Your time will be far better spent with me than with the likes of Kiernan Kelly."

—⚂—

Abigail Callaway's words of warning echoed in Fiona's mind, but she still found herself driving out past Rockfleet, past the crew in the fields with their handheld metal detectors, patiently sweeping each square foot of land. She didn't stop and hoped Kiernan hadn't seen her car buzzing by—her little Up was pretty identifiable with her crushed bumper.

In an hour she reached the point along the water that neared the ruins on Hen's Island. She slowed, frequently pulling over to let others pass her by, until she finally saw what had to be the remains of the manse on the hill that Abigail had mentioned. She got out and climbed over the fence and up the hill. Most of Ireland was free for walkers to traverse, as long as they shut any gates behind them so the sheep didn't get out. And clearly no one had lived on this land in a very long time.

Her cell phone buzzed in her pocket, nearly scaring her to death, she was so wound up. She looked at the caller ID. *Rory.*

"Hello!" she said, resuming her climb.

"Hello. Are ya still here in Westport? I just finished my appointment and I wondered if ya might want to join me for a cuppa."

"Oh, that would've been fun," she returned. "But I'm so full from the Westport House tea that I don't think I'll eat or drink again until tomorrow. Besides, I'm out at Lough Corrib."

"Lough Corrib?" he said in surprise.

"Yes. Abigail told me about something that I thought I'd check out."

"Oh. Good," he said, sounding as if he was trying to be enthused for her, and yet was disappointed he couldn't see her. It made her smile.

She stopped walking and looked out to the lake, a dark gray today with a solid layer of clouds above. "Tell me about your appointment. Did it go well?"

"As well as a soul can expect," he said, sounding weary. "She says it has to get worse before it gets better."

"Well that's a slogan you wouldn't want to put on one of those inspirational posters at work, right?" She smiled as she heard his deep *hmmm* over the phone. "But she's probably right. You have to dig deep. Get to the bottom of things. Bring it to the light."

"Aye, that's the process, I guess."

"Think you'll stick with it?"

She held her breath, waiting for him to answer.

"I'm going to try, lass. As hard as it is…Well, for the first time in a long while, I think I have a sense of hope about it. This girl—woman," he corrected, "seems to believe this treatment works. And that makes me hope it will work for me too."

"That's good, Rory. I mean…it's great. I'll be praying that it will. Every day."

"Thanks. That means a lot." He paused. "May I see ya when ya get home?"

"Yes. I'll call you when I'm on my way, okay?"

"Brilliant. Take care."

She said goodbye and held the phone to her chest a moment. She so hoped the therapy would work for Rory. That he would find relief. Freedom. "Please Lord," she whispered. She wanted it for him, first. Regardless of whether there would be a long-term them or not. He deserved healing. Wholeness.

She continued her trek up the hill. Here and there were strewn stones, having either fallen from the crumbling wall or been pulled aside. Abigail had mentioned the emblem was etched into one of the foundation stones. Methodically, Fiona began at the corner of the remains of the house and scanned one section and then the next. At the far corner, she found it.

She bent and ran her fingers across the curve of the bow, the taut string, and the straight arrow laid across it. She rose and looked out across the breast-high wall ruins to the lake. It seemed to be pointing across and north. Northwest? But then she remembered the stone, while from Hen's Castle, had been raided and moved. Who knew where it had originally been laid there, and in which direction it pointed.

Fiona fished a piece of paper and pencil from her pocket, positioned the paper against the stone, and quickly shaded across the carved emblem, until it showed clearly in white relief against her gray expanse. She lifted it, holding it with two hands against the breeze that set it to fluttering. Was it a match to what Kiernan had found behind the false wall at Rockfleet? And were there others?

She made her way out of the manse, staring down three fluffy sheep with black faces that had stopped chewing, so intent were they on watching her. Like she was going to turn and come after them. She ran her hand across the swaying grasses, watching as a stream of cars roared down the highway toward Oughterard.

Oughterard. That's where she'd head next. Could she be so lucky as to find another bow and arrow on Aughnanure, the ancient stronghold of the O'Flahertys?

CHAPTER 18

It was growing dark by the time she left the black-rock walls of Aughnanure Castle, shooed out by a security guard who'd told her once before that they were closing, before coming back around to fetch her. Much of the castle had been rebuilt in the centuries following the capture of it from the O'Flahertys, so it was of little use to Fiona, particularly because she did not see any evidence of a bow and arrow emblem, nor even any potential false walls as there had been at Rockfleet. And the stern woman at the ticket booth wasn't moved by Fiona's pleas to have a look about the foundation stones, where no "guest" was allowed, regardless of her entreaties as a "visiting scholar" and flashing her university ID. She'd sternly told Fiona that she'd have to take it up with her boss, and that he wasn't available until next week.

Fiona walked across the bridge to the path along the river that led to the parking lot, but then realized that two small farms bordered the castle's land. She could see a man entering a small barn across the way, a hay bale on his shoulder. Hurriedly, she entered the parking lot and then strode down the road to enter the private drive.

The man was closing up the barn doors with a crossbeam when she approached. "Hello!" she called. "Sorry to bother you, but I was wondering if I might ask you a few questions."

He waited, skepticism lining his face as if he had to deal with tiresome tourists all the time. "This is private property, miss."

"Yes, forgive me. I'm Fiona Burke," she said, reaching out a hand, "and I'm doing some research on Grace O'Malley for my PhD in history back in the States."

The small man tepidly shook her hand.

"May I ask how long you've lived in this part of County Galway?" Fiona pressed on.

"All m'life," he said slowly, squinting at her suspiciously.

"Fantastic. How many generations back?"

He folded his arms and peered up at the trees. "Let's see. Back to my great-great grandda, I'd wager."

"Excellent. I am seeking source material from locals like yourself in regard to Grace O'Malley."

"Yes, well, ya know Donal O'Flaherty and herself were driven out." He waved toward Aughnanure.

"I do. But I assume you've been over to the castle," she said, gesturing herself to the tower through the trees, "many times."

"Aye. We used to play there as children, back before it was protected and all."

Fiona nodded, her pulse fluttering. She pulled the rubbing of the Hen's Castle stone emblem from her back pocket. "Can you tell me, have you ever seen anything like this, etched into any of the stones of the castle?"

He took it from her, his knuckles rounded with what she assumed was arthritis. "Ahh, this." He looked at her. "What is it? I've always had a wonder."

Fiona's pulse picked up. But it was clear he was offering her a deal. She would tell him something, and in turn, he might tell her what she wanted to know. "I...I think it had something to do with Grace O'Malley. That she might've made this mark in every castle she inhabited."

The man pursed his lips and nodded, still staring down

at her paper.

"So have you seen something like this in the dungeon of Aughnanure?"

"No," he said. "But as a boy, I saw it right there, under the bridge."

She glanced over in surprise to the arched stone bridge that led to the castle. "That bridge?"

"Aye."

"Has that bridge been there since the time the O'Flahertys reigned?"

"Ah, sure. The arch of the bridge collapsed at some point. And it might not have been a bridge at all, but rather a drawbridge, once. But the pillars on either side have been there for centuries."

She tried to hide her grin. "On this side of the water? Or the far side, by the castle?"

"This side, where it's better hidden against the embankment." He looked back to her paper. "Ya say ya believe this is the queen's mark?"

"It could be," she said. "I'm starting to wonder if I might prove it in time."

"Well, 'tisn't that somethin'."

"I so appreciate your time," she said, reaching out her hand. "If I have other questions, might I come and visit again? Or if you prefer, call or text you?"

"Ach, I don't do any of that fancy cell phone stuff. Stop by any time ya wish," he said. "And let me know how ye're farin' on that," he said, gesturing to her paper. "I'll be curious."

She nodded and left him then. At her car, she hesitated. Hers was the last in the lot. The farmer had moved into his cozy cottage. Might this be the only time she could wade into the waters and see under the bridge, without calling undue attention? The sun had set, but she'd learned that in this part of Ireland, twilight would hold for a good hour or two. *No time like the present,* she decided, pulling off her belt and shoes and tossing them in the back seat along with her rubbing of the bow and arrow.

Fiona looked down at her nice pants and silk blouse, wishing she had a change of clothes in the car. She hated to sacrifice them…but the closer she got to the castle, the more determined she became.

When she had first crossed the bridge today, she'd paid it little mind. After all, the pretty castle and its exposed, walled yard dominated one's attention. But now her head was filled with what this bridge once might have been. Clearly it could have been a drawbridge, the river used as both an access point to Lough Corrib but also a convenient "moat" to repel intruders. She made her way through the thick grass and prickly brambles to the upstream side of the bridge pillar, observing that the waters plunged deep and moved fast, despite their tranquil look. She bent to roll up her pants. Gingerly, she crept lower, trying to see under the arch of the wide, stone bridge, but eventually knew she was either going to have to return with a swimsuit or truly sacrifice the one nice outfit she'd packed for Ireland.

Because the only way to see under the bridge was to swim beneath it.

She paused, looked about, and hearing nothing but the squeaky call of a Northern Lapwing and the rushing sounds of the water around rocks, knew she just had to go for it. Biting her lip, she stepped deeper and then deeper still, holding her phone high in case she slipped. It was waterproof, but she didn't want to test it. And if there was something to see, she wanted to both take a picture and try and get coordinates so she could map out where the arrow pointed. With that in mind, she opened the map app. Supposedly, one could take a picture anywhere in the world and it would tell you exactly where you were, and the direction you faced. She'd try that first. Because judging from the swiftly moving water, if she didn't find something to grab hold of beneath, she'd likely drift right by.

The bank beneath the cold water was progressively slippery, the deeper rocks covered in a slimy moss. With each step, she clung to the rough bridge stones to her left, her phone grasped in her right. Thigh deep, she could finally peer underneath the arch. She clicked on the flashlight on her phone and shined it across the arch and down to the pillar.

There. Just as the farmer had mentioned, it was etched. But this one was now covered in a bright green moss, perhaps disguising it from any other archeologist or nosy child who managed to make their way beneath the ancient bridge. She switched to her map app and took several pictures, but they didn't show up well. The app flashed, as if ready to connect to the satellites dedicated to it and tell her exactly where she was, but Fiona wanted a straight-on shot, so that she could get the angle of the arrow right.

She considered how she'd get out on the far side of the bridge as the current took her. From the looks of it, these pillars plunged a good ten feet down below the surface. Or more. The waters were dark and cold. *Do you really want to do this?* she asked herself.

But once again, she knew this might be her only opportunity, given that it was the height of the tourist season. She'd grab hold of the brambles on the far side, or a tree limb, and pull herself out. She was a decent swimmer; she thought she might be able to keep herself mostly afloat with kicking alone as she drifted by. Gradually, she went deeper, trying to enter the water as steadily and with as much control as possible. The chill made her gasp.

What are you doing, Burke? she chastised herself. *Is it really worth this? If anyone finds you now, what will they think?*

Well, you're literally in deep… Holding her breath, she let herself sink to her neck in the water, turning to face the pillar as she did so. *The things you do for a killer dissertation…*

The water moved faster than she anticipated, so Fiona just held up her phone and took one picture after another, hoping she'd captured it. She was out and drifting down the river beyond the bridge before she had time to think further about it. Groaning, she tossed her phone up the embankment by a yew tree so that she'd have both hands free to get herself out. She missed a low-hanging branch and then avoided a bramble covered in thorns. The last thing she needed was to emerge bloody, as well as soaking wet.

Finally another low-hanging branch offered her the helping hand she needed. Grabbing hold, her body swirled to a stop, the water rushing past her shoulders now, and her legs pulling her downstream with a surprisingly concentrated effort.

"Hey! Hey!" called a voice from down the path. "Are ye all right?"

"I'm okay!" she called, inwardly groaning. The young man ran to a stop just above her on the bank, moving down through the thicket to reach out a hand. Behind him, a pretty young woman stopped, and Fiona ducked her head. It was the woman from Kiernan Kelly's crew; the man who now gripped her hand was probably one of them too. Would they recognize her?

With some effort, she gained a foothold and stepped

through the brush. "Thank you," she said, panting. The man continued to hold on to her as she moved slowly up the embankment, trying to come up with the right story to explain this away.

"Selfie gone bad?" said the blond woman, looking sympathetic, then upstream, following where she must have fallen in.

Selfie. Right.

"Yes," Fiona said ruefully. "It was going to be so awesome too. Now I'll have to file insurance for a drowned phone. I threw it up on the bank somewhere."

"Ya never know," said the man. "If ya find it, put it in rice tonight. It might come back."

"Good idea."

"Ye're shivering," said the woman. "I wish I had a towel." Her eyes settled on Fiona's face, then narrowed in puzzlement. "Have we met before?"

"I don't know," she said, pretending ignorance and rubbing her arms. "I have one of those faces. Everyone seems to think they know me!" She turned to walk back up toward the bridge, intent on retrieving her phone, as well as hiding her face from Kiernan's minions. She finally found the yew, and with relief, discovered her phone.

The couple had followed her.

"Good on ya," said the young man. "At least ye didn't lose it in the stream."

"Let's hope that rice trick works," she said, flashing him a small smile. "Thanks again. All I can think about now is getting into my car and running the heater full-blast." She waved over her shoulder, but she could feel the woman's gaze on her back, every step of the way to her car.

—w—

Rory busied himself that afternoon by concentrating on the kitchen, hanging new sheetrock, then taping and mudding it in preparation for the new cabinets. But he knew he'd been checking Grandda's old, plastic kitchen clock every hour, then every fifteen minutes in the last hour. He sighed in relief as Fiona's little car came up the drive at last, well after dark. Why hadn't she called? he thought for the hundredth time, swallowing a mixture of frustration, fear and hurt.

Was she thinking twice about seeing him tonight?

He had just decided to let her reach out to him when he saw her get out of the car, her hair and body plainly having taken a dunk. He blinked in confusion as she opened her back door, fished out flats that she slipped on to her bare feet, then a belt and piece of paper. She moved to the cottage, Murphy wagging his tail and circling her in joyous greeting.

Curiosity now had the better of him. He wiped off his hands, called, "Headin' over to say hey to Fiona!" to his grandfather and Uncle George, who were watching the telly at an ungodly volume level. He left through the swinging front screen door, letting it slam behind him.

The sound of it brought Fiona's head up as she unlocked the cottage door, and she flashed him a grin. He strode over to her as fast as the cane would allow and peered down at her. "What the devil happened to ya, lass?"

"I took a dip!" she said gleefully. "Come in, come in," she said. "Do me a favor and put the kettle on, would you? I'd kill for a cup of tea."

"I bet," he said, lifting her chin and catching her chattering teeth. He looked down her clinging, still-damp clothes, then back to her face with some embarrassment. The silk had settled over her soft curves, revealing more of her than he'd ever seen before. It set his pulse to racing. "Get changed," he said gruffly. "I'll get the kettle on."

He poured water into the old, chipped pot, trying not to think of Fiona undressing in the next room. Peeling off those trousers, unbuttoning that soft silk shirt... He swallowed hard and opened one of three small cupboards she had, looking for the tea to get his mind on higher things. "Jasmine or Irish Breakfast?" he called.

"Irish," she returned, her voice muffled, perhaps as she pulled a sweater on. "It sounds so good. I need something to warm my bones!"

She appeared in her doorway then, dressed in a fleece and jeans, her feet tucked into fuzzy slippers. She pulled a brush through her damp, tangled hair.

"So, are ya going to tell me how ya fell in?"

"It wasn't my plan," she said, tossing the brush back into her bedroom and coming closer. "I had a perfectly civilized tea with Abigail Callaway at Westport House. And then as you know, I headed to Lough Corrib."

He poured the steaming water into two cups and set a tea bag in each, then handed her one.

She held the cup in both of her palms and closed her eyes as she took a sip, as if willing the scalding heat into her bones.

"Come," he said, gesturing to the sofa. He set down his cup and cane and reached for the afghan, wrapping it around her shoulders. "Sit," he commanded softly.

Gratefully, she did as he'd asked. He sat down and wrapped an arm around her. "So the lough looked so inviting ya jumped in?" he prodded.

She cast him a teasing smile. "I'll get to that part of the

story, I promise. But when I was interviewing Abigail, she told me about a bow and arrow emblem, that might be tied to Grace. Remember how Father Michael said there might be a clue of some sort at Aughnanure?"

He nodded.

"I wondered if that etching could've been what he spoke of. She mentioned an old manse near Hen's Island with a stone with the same on it, saying it could have come from Grace and Donal's castle."

"Aye, many of the old ruins have been ransacked over time for building stones," he agreed. "Did ye find it?"

"I did." Excitedly, she leapt up and went to retrieve the paper from the table and brought it over.

He lifted it in his hands and studied it. "And so…"

"So then I headed to Aughnanure, hoping to find another. Because Rory," she said, gripping his hand, "Kiernan told me he found one at Rockfleet too."

"I don't follow ye, lass. So it might be the mark of our pirate queen. So what?"

"What if," she whispered, "the arrows point toward the treasure?"

He sat back in surprise. "Ye think they might?"

"Why not?" she asked, hopping up and pacing. "First, Kiernan seems utterly convinced that Grace had the capacity and wherewithal to amass a fortune. I think he'll share his research with me if I play him right."

Rory frowned at that. Kiernan Kelly didn't seem like the kind of man who would take "playing" well at all. Or he might take it as some sort of invitation from her.

"And Abigail believes it would've been a stretch, but possible. Toward the end of her life, Grace was in quite the precarious position as leader. She might've been facing internal struggles for power, as well as trying to fend off the English. Abigail believes that it could have been logical for Grace to squirrel away a fortune to fall back on, should the worst come."

"So Kiernan is on the right track," Rory said, a bit surprised. After all, it'd become a bit of a national pastime this last year to make a joke of it. Every tabloid told the same story—if he didn't find the treasure this year, his backers would not fund another season of his show.

"It appears so. But Rory," she said, perching on the edge of the sofa. "What if he's searching in the wrong place? What if..." She rose again, as agitated as a wee wren searching for lost seed among the grass. "Here, let me show you." She went to grab her phone and then the emblem rubbing. She handed the paper to him and then tapped on her phone, scrolled, enlarged a shot and handed it to him.

He looked from the paper to the phone. "The arrows are at different angles."

"Yes," she said, pleased. "Now there's no way to know where the arrow from Hen's originally pointed, given that it's been moved. But see how it's at about a 285-degree angle, pointing to the upper left quadrant?"

"Aye, as long as we don't have it upside-down," he said.

"But look at the bows. They're the same in both, as if cupping the arrow. This one in the picture," she said, leaning over his shoulder to look at the phone with him, "is pointing almost in the same direction, given the angle of the bridge. But more at a 300-degree angle northwest, if this coordinates-app is working."

He blinked up at her in surprise. "Bridge?"

"Yes, that's where I found it. Under the bridge of Aughnanure. I had no choice but to go in, clothes and all. I had the site to myself and a bit of twilight left to me. I seized the day and all that."

He laughed under his breath and shook his head. He reached out and took her hand, unable to wait any longer. Gently, he pulled her closer and into his lap, cupping her face. "Ach, I missed ya, woman. You're a bundle of energy, fairly alight with all this."

"You have *no* idea." She smiled and gave him a slow, soft kiss, then pulled back, her head clearly still in her treasure hunt. "I need a map! Do you have one?"

"Aye," he said, knowing he wouldn't gain her full attention until he'd wrestled through all of this with her in full.

He rose and then she snapped her fingers. "Wait! I have one!" she scurried to her room and returned with a road map, hurriedly unfolding it on the floor in front of the couch. She grabbed a pen from the table and circled Aughnanure, Hen's Island, and Rockfleet. Then she set out her phone and pulled up a compass app, using the edge of the phone to draw a solid line from Aughnanure northwest at 300 degrees, then a dotted line from Hen's Island at 285 degrees.

She looked up at him, blue eyes wide, and then back to the map.

Rory eased his way down to sit on the coffee table in order to get a better look.

The lines intersected at the foot of a mountain just south of them.

He huffed a laugh and leaned over to point at the brown marking on the map that denoted a mountain. "Do ye know what this peak is called, lass?"

She shook her head.

"Devilsmother."

And then she laughed too. "Do you think…Is it possible…"

"Is it possible that the pirate queen hauled her treasure to a mountain that came to be called 'Devilsmother,' and buried it? Perhaps. But we need to find more of these emblems and compare the trajectory of their arrows," he said, reaching behind him to pick up her rubbing. "Ye're sure there wasn'a one at Westport House? Down in the basement, where the remains of the castle are?"

"No, I don't believe so. Precious few of the original stones remain. It's mostly the dungeon."

"Bunowen?"

"Same."

"Then where else? Are there other O'Malley castle remains?"

"There's Ballynahinch, down south. And the one out on Achill." She rose and paced, wringing her hands.

Ach, how he liked to watch the lass work something over in her mind. She was as smart as she was beautiful, and he itched to reach out and grab hold of her again. But he knew she wouldn't welcome it, and he was determined to let this thing between them unfold slowly. To not force it. To allow God to weave together their hearts—and a way forward for them—or to help them determine that they were but friends for a season.

Oh God, he prayed silently, *don't let it be just-friends.*

She turned to him, biting her lip. "I need to go back to Rockfleet tomorrow. Kiernan told me he'd found that emblem. I think he'll show it to me."

He nodded. "I'll go with—"

"No, Rory. I need to go alone." She moved toward him and rested a hand on his shoulder, even as he began to shake his head. "I have to. He invited me. And I signed a confidentiality agreement. He wouldn't let you in anyway."

"That's all right. He can know I'm outside, waiting for you in the car."

It was her turn to shake her head. "No. I need to do this. I don't want you to spook him. I can handle it. I'll just go and see it for myself, try and snap a coordinates pic, and be out."

He swallowed hard. He knew he hadn't earned a place in her life yet that he could be more insistent, but something about it really made him uneasy.

Really, *really* uneasy.

Still, the last thing she needed—or likely wanted—was an overreaching boyfriend. He took her hand in both of his. "Ye'll go to Rockfleet and be back straight away?"

"Straight away."

"Ya won't get a notion to drive off to some other site without tellin' me?" He bent to kiss her knuckles and pull her closer.

"No," she said. "Hey! You trimmed your beard."

"Aye, I did," he said, feeling the crackle of anticipation.

She sat down in his lap then, stroking his temple, his cheek with her light, small fingers. "Then what are we doing, talking of Rockfleet?" she whispered huskily, leaning in for a kiss.

CHAPTER 19

Fiona tossed her bag in the back of her VW the next morning. Rory emerged from the house, wiping paint from his hands on a rag. Clearly, he was painting the kitchen the soft green Patrick had chosen, in preparation for hanging the cabinets.

"When I get back, I want to see it," she said as he came closer.

He glanced over his shoulder. "It's looking good," he said. "Though it has George in a fit. He thinks we've forgotten it should be the old gold. It's like he can't make out his home in the midst of the missing cabinets and the taller ceiling, especially now with that color."

"He'll get used to it," she said. "That green is supposed to be a soothing color."

"I hope so." He paused. "You're heading to Rockfleet now?"

She heard the edge in his tone, but chose to ignore it. They'd gone through this already. "I got a call from the landowner of Bunowen Castle. I'm going to run by there to do a rubbing of a book sculpture in the chapel down by the water. It's probably the Ten Commandments or the like, but I thought I'd check. It's so worn from the weather and open windows, it's impossible to see more. Then on to Rockfleet."

He reached out and tucked a stray strand of hair behind her ear. "Do me a favor?"

"Sure," she said slowly.

"Text me when ya head to Rockfleet, and when ya leave? Just so I have an approximate time you arrived? And when I should get worried?"

She patted him on the chest, realizing anew how big and brawny he was. His protective care touched her heart, even if it irked her mind. "I can do that. But honestly, Rory, Kiernan is not going to make any move on me that I won't allow. He has people all around. And with a new season on the line, the last thing the man needs is a scandal."

"Hmmm," Rory said.

She stepped up on her tiptoes and gave him a quick kiss. "See you later." Then she moved around him, opened her door, revved the engine, and headed off, feeling his gaze follow her until she was around the bend.

It made her smile as she drove. It had been a few years since she had felt this…giddiness. This thrill, every time she saw him. And the way he looked at her…it sent a shiver of delight running down her spine. He was so intent, keen. It felt like he was as aware of her and her wellbeing as he might be of himself.

Not that he'd figured himself all out. He was just starting on the PTSD front. She wondered if he kept with it, how much progress he'd make this summer. But then she reminded herself that there were no *promises* of progression at all. Could she live with something like that long-term? How else did it affect him? Did he have nightmares? Might he only let her in so close before he set her aside, not wanting to make himself any more vulnerable?

It wouldn't be all magically fixed, come fall. She knew that. And it was surprisingly okay. For once she wasn't looking at a relationship, judging where it was going to go and how fast. With Rory, she only wanted to enjoy what time she had with him. She'd let God take care of the rest. For now, she'd concentrate on her research and her dissertation.

Was this a wild goose chase? Would her time be better spent heading to Dublin and looking through Abigail's library? She told herself she'd do that next week. For now, she had to follow through, before Kiernan changed his mind. She drove out to Bunowen, parked where she had beside Kiernan when they'd come out, let herself in through the gate, and walked across the field.

Fiona entered the tiny chapel, glad for a slight break from the constant, cool wind off the foggy sea. She ran her fingers through her damp hair, feeling it curling, and wished she had a band to pull it back. For a moment she remembered Rory tucking a strand behind her ear and smiled. For such a big man, he had the capacity to be amazingly gentle.

She set to work, rubbing segments of the big slab, a page-width at a time. But when she was finished, all she found were remnants of lettering, impossible to make out. No arrow and bow as she had hoped—that much was clear. She wandered down to the older stone fort, taking in the gray, thin stacked flagstones that were so common in ancient structures around here. Even more so out on the islands. She shielded her eyes and looked out to the hundreds of shallow hills that filled Clew Bay. "Where'd you put it, Gracie?" she muttered under her breath as she walked back to her car. For all she knew, her treasure could be on one of those tiny, nameless islands.

Now that would keep Kiernan busy for a while, she thought, picturing him with a shovel digging on one sandy dune and then another. She checked her watch. This had been a bust, but what was ahead set her heart racing a bit. Could she find a way to sneak in a picture on her app at Rockfleet? Or would he be watching her the whole time? And would that woman and man from his team—the couple that had fished her out of the river yesterday—be on site?

If they hadn't recognized her before, they would today. She was sure of it.

Whatever. She'd continue with her story of a selfie gone wrong and laugh it off.

In half an hour, she saw Rockfleet in the distance. She drove past it, noting the location of the team—one man short now—and up to the top of the hill where Kiernan's trailer and the big satellite disc perched. After sending Rory a brief text that only read "HERE," she knocked on the door and he emerged, as if he'd been waiting on her. He flashed her a bright smile and gave her a hug, kissing her on both cheeks. "How are you this fine morning?" he asked, pulling on a flat Irish cap and leaning an arm against the trailer.

"I'm well," she said.

He waved down at Rockfleet. "I suppose you're eager to see her, eh?"

"I could barely sleep," she admitted.

He gestured to the path and they walked to the road and then down it toward the castle. He tucked his hands into his tweed jacket with leather elbow patches, calling to mind a university professor. For the first time, Fiona wondered if he had donned such an outfit just for her. The other two times they'd met he'd worn more casual clothing. "I hear you were out at Aughnanure," he said.

She glanced at him in surprise. *So much for wondering if I'd be recognized.* "Yeah, I ran into a couple of your people there. They helped fish me out. Totally embarrassing."

"Yes, well, with the amount of water in Ireland, it was

bound to happen. I've ended up in the muck down there a few times myself," he said, pointing to the marshy waters around the castle.

"Still not as bad as falling in up to your neck," she said, hoping to just own this story now. Better not to appear as if she was hiding anything.

"They said you were trying to take a selfie?"

"Guilty as charged," she said. "Proof that I need a buddy on any site visit."

"I could do that for you," he said easily. "Where to next?"

"Oh, I don't know," she hedged, not really wanting to make another date. "I know I want to see the other castles associated with Grace, but I need to get some writing done too. And I'm supposed to head to Dublin to visit Abigail Callaway at home. She invited me to peruse her research materials."

"Nothing like seeing the real thing in comparison to reading about it," he said. "That woman thinks she knows everything about Grace O'Malley," he said over his shoulder, taking the walkway to the castle door. "Let's just say, your time is better spent with me."

She hoped her face belied nothing but innocent interest and admiration. Because inside, she was recoiling. She might have turned and walked away, if he wasn't about to give her access to the interior of a house Grace had once inhabited. The key squeaked and rattled in the lock and then he pulled open the creaking, heavy door. She walked in, gazing about in wonder. Taking in the massive, sloped fireplace. The slotted windows, perfect for defense. Wider windows to give one light as well as a viewpoint to Clew Bay and the hills in all directions.

She jumped and looked back in surprise as the door slammed shut.

"We don't want any tourists barging in," Kiernan said, pocketing the key after he locked it.

A shiver of trepidation ran down her spine. *Locked in the castle with him*. Would anyone hear her if she cried out?

"Uhhh, I'm afraid I'm going to have to ask you to open that again. I get claustrophobic." She lifted her hands, hoping her lie wasn't written all over her face. "Sorry. It's a real issue. If anyone comes in, I'll come down and shoo them out myself."

He hesitated, but then turned, unlocked it, and left it open a few inches. "All right?"

"Better," she said, wishing she could prop it open all the way. But that would feel weird.

He passed by her, moving to the curved, stone staircase. "I assume you want to see the rest of it before we go down?"

"Absolutely." She followed him up the narrow, crumbling, spiral stairs, only wide enough for one person at a time, a defense strategy from ancient times, giving the man upstairs an advantage.

The second floor was made of wood timbers and planks, which had obviously been replaced recently. There was another fireplace. "Would this have been the guards' quarters?"

"Likely," he said. "The family slept on the next two floors."

After she took a slow video of the floor, she followed him to the next, and finally the stone flagged fourth floor. Kiernan fished another key from his pocket and unlocked the contemporary padlock on an arched doorway, letting the wooden shutters open wide. Fiona rested her arms on the edge of the eastern wall, looking down to the river and marsh below, then out to the bay. It would have been a fine viewpoint for Grace, indeed. And from this door, they could've loaded cargo into the castle that was too difficult to carry up the narrow stairwell.

Kiernan joined her to lean on the far edge. "You know what she said to Richard from the ramparts above, after their year of trial marriage, don't you?"

"'Richard Bourke, I dismiss you,'" she said. Fiona held up a finger. "But only once her men had secured the tower and her ships were anchored below."

"Clever woman, eh? A bit like my ex-wife."

Ex-wife. "I suppose. My dissertation is largely about how Grace sought freedom from men's rule most of her life. She grew up with an abusive half-brother. No doubt, she suffered more abuse as she sailed with her father."

"That's true," he said. "Her fellow sailors weren't apt to look kindly on sailing with a female."

"And then she was married off at sixteen to Donal."

Kiernan turned and folded his arms. "Do you not think she loved him?"

"Maybe. In time, I believe she respected him, at least. But my thought is that the only man she ever truly loved was the lover she fished from the sea."

"Hugh de Lacy," he said.

Fiona nodded. "She was forced to be with Donal. She married Richard for political gain. But Hugh? Maybe he was the lone man who stole her heart."

"If she had one," he grunted. "The woman was said to have killed hundreds of men in battle."

"I think it was hundreds upon hundreds," she corrected. "When you count up how many battles she undertook. I mean, maybe it wasn't all by her sword. But if you counted cannon fire too…"

A slow smile spread across his handsome face. "Come,"

he said, moving to a far door. Again, he fished out his ring of keys and unlocked another padlock. "This way," he said, pointing through the open doorway to a tiny stairwell that led upward. "It's quite safe."

Deciding she'd likely never get this offer again, Fiona followed him up to the roof. At the top, there was a hatch door. He shoved it and it fell open with a clatter. When she climbed up beside him, she slowly took in the three-hundred-and-sixty-degree view. From here she could see Clare Island, as well as the waterways around the hundreds of islands, and then up into the hills. "Oh my," she said. "To think Grace walked these very ramparts…It's amazing."

"Indeed," he said, stepping closer. "It would have given her quite the strategic view."

"The roof wasn't thatched?"

"There's some evidence that it had an iron roof, though it rotted away long ago. But see here?" he said, pointing down. "Those are original stones. We believe this was a wall walk for guards."

Fiona pulled out her phone and took some pictures. "This is awesome," she said, shaking her head. Never had she dreamed she could get to the *roof* of Rockfleet—let alone her basement. A surge of gratitude welled. "Thanks, Kiernan. This is so amazing."

"It is," he said, his eyes lingering on her with a shared smile.

No matter how you felt about someone, Fiona mused, *a shared passion went a long way to bridge the gaps.* He followed her as she walked the perimeter of the roof, the parapet stone guardrail only coming as high as her thighs.

"Grace divorced Richard, but she obviously remained friends with him," she said over her shoulder. "I think later she might have felt a bit badly about taking this castle."

"Why do you say that?"

"Because of their ongoing relationship. She helped set him up to become the successor to the clan MacWilliam in 1571," she said. "If she was helping him to become the most powerful chieftain in Mayo, they couldn't have been bitter exes at that point."

"True. Too bad her efforts failed."

"They were pretty much doomed with the English closing in. Irish politics had gotten infinitely more complicated."

Clearly, she wasn't sharing anything he didn't know already. But it felt good, right, to be thinking through her theories, right here where Grace had lived her life.

"So was all that evidence of a softened heart, or two enemies forced back to solidarity in the face of a greater encroaching enemy?"

"Now *that* is a good question," she said, giving him an admiring nod then looking to sea. It would be good for her to tackle in her dissertation. She'd have to think about it some more.

"Mind if I take your picture?" he said.

She glanced at him in surprise.

"You look more the quintessential Irish girl than an American at the moment," he said, gesturing to her and the sea beyond her.

"Sure," she said, a little embarrassed.

"Thanks," he said, snapping the photo then pocketing his phone in the front of his tweed jacket. "Ready to head down?"

They made their way down the plank to what would have been Grace's room, then down the curving stone staircase to the main floor. He gestured to a hole in the floor, with a new, metal ladder sticking out of it. He grabbed hold of the top of it. "Too tall now to do further damage. I'll go down and hold it for you though."

He climbed down it with the ease of one who had done so a hundred times before. Then he looked up, waiting.

She glanced at the door again, and then gave herself a little shake. She was being paranoid. He'd wanted to lock it for exactly the reason he'd told her. No doubt tourists tried the door every day. She took to the ladder and reached the bottom, then looked around the dark room, blinking as she waited for her eyes to adjust. "Dungeon?"

"Dungeon, pig pen, storage room, who knows." He pulled out a flashlight and shone it around the room, the same width as the main floor above, of course. But it was infinitely more cold with the damp of the water seeping through the walls. Moss and mold clung to the stones all about them.

"But here is what you've come to see," he said, gesturing to the northern wall.

And there it was. An emblem that perfectly matched the one she had found on the Hen's Island stone, as well as beneath the bridge. "Wow," she breathed, stepping forward. She discreetly fished in her pocket for her phone, hoping it could capture a picture in the dim light. She couldn't ask permission; she knew he'd deny her. And there was no way to find the app without him seeing it. She'd just nab a pic and then figure out the angle of the tower wall when Kiernan wasn't around.

"It's huge," she said. *Probably five times as big as the others.*

"You sound surprised."

"Do I?" she returned, rounding her eyes in what she hoped looked like an innocent expression. "I mean, it must've taken quite a while to carve." She backed up to better see it, as well as get behind him. "Can you show me what you think is important?"

He seemed pleased by the invitation to show off his knowledge. "If you see here," he said, pointing to the bow, "I believe this represents Grace. And the arrow? Well, I hope 'tis pointing to her treasure."

She pressed the button of her camera just as he pointed to the arrow, then swiftly dropped it into her pocket as he turned to face her.

"But isn't that pointing farther north than where your crew is searching?"

"True," he said, looking up again. "But the northwestern fields are the closest land. We've already covered the river and embankment and road to the west, and made our way upward to where they are now. Twice."

"Do you really think she'd make it as obvious as that? Why point out your treasure? Would you not want it to be a secret?"

He frowned and folded his arms and then looked to her. "Well, no. At first I didn't. Until we found this, we were looking all about the castle."

"But it doesn't make sense, does it?" Fiona said. "She'd know exactly where her treasure was laid, as would some of her trusted men. So for whom did she leave these—this," she swiftly corrected herself, wincing inwardly, "emblem?"

His eyes narrowed at her for a long moment, then he studied the carving again. "Well, it was hidden behind the false wall. And I believe she did not really hide away a fortune for herself, but rather for her descendants, those she hoped would rise up and fight in her stead against the British." He ran his hand across the remains of the false wall. "With this, she could wait until her deathbed to choose who was worthy to tell. And because it's still here, I believe she never found anyone worthy."

"And this is why you're searching so diligently now in the northwest field."

"Yes," he said. Were his eyes lingering on her overlong? As if trying to discern the secrets within her?

Fiona could feel a damp sheen of sweat forming on her forehead, despite the chill. She brought a hand to her nose and rubbed it. "I'd love to stay down here, but the smell is not good for my allergies. And…as I said, tight spaces aren't my fave."

She was moving to the ladder when he caught her wrist.

"Fiona," he said, eyes narrowing. "Do you know of other emblems like this one?"

"What? No," she said shaking her head, even as she felt her color rise. "Let go of me." She looked down at his hand, holding her wrist, but still, he didn't release her.

"You would tell me if you had?"

"Of course. *Now let go of me.*"

He did so, then, and rubbed his temple. "Sorry. I get a bit worked up over things like this."

Fiona forced a smile. "I was thinking of a picture I saw of her over on Clare." Fiona pulled out her phone and scrolled to the pictures from the exhibit there—carefully avoiding the folder with the photos from the bridge—then enlarged the same portrait she'd shown Abigail. "Check it out," she said, offering it to him as if she didn't have anything to hide. She looked around and mentally held back a shiver of fear, thinking of the old man on a cliff in the middle of the night, falling to his death. Down here, no one would likely hear her scream. And he had the only extra key on a closed site.

"I know that portrait," he said. "But I've never noticed the broach before."

"Cool, huh?" she said, taking back the phone. "I think you're definitely on the right track."

She moved to the ladder and had taken one step when his arms came around either side of her and she froze. But after an awkward second, she realized he was only holding the ladder for her. Right? Or was he messing with her? Getting too close on purpose? *What* purpose? With frustratingly trembling hands she took hold of the rungs and began climbing, gaining speed—and oxygen—the farther she got from him. She forced a smile when he emerged after her, but his demeanor had cooled toward her. Clearly, he knew something was up.

Fiona opened the door and tried to relax, not rush, pretend everything was cool. She forced herself to slow down as she crossed the walkway to the road, while he locked up the tower. On the other side, she had to wait for him, pull herself together, continue to pretend everything was exactly as it should be. "Thank you for showing it to me, Kiernan," she said, clinging to truth amidst her lies. Wasn't that the best way to maintain a cover-up? "I'm so grateful that I got to see it." She turned and walked backward up the road, staring at the tower. "It's even more amazing, now that I've been inside."

"It was my pleasure," he said, joining her on the road.

"Say, aren't you down a man on the team?" she asked, noting again that there were four when there had been five.

"I had to let Dylan go," he said.

"Oh? Why?" she asked, hoping to get him talking. Anything to keep quiet herself. But Dylan had been the one who had talked to *her and Rory.*

"He talked to too many people," he said pointedly. "And he'd signed the same confidentiality agreement you did."

She could feel the heat of his gaze. "You remember that agreement, right, Fiona?" he said, taking her elbow. "I mean, I don't want to get too anal about it. But this," he paused to gesture about, "has taken too long and too much for me to be anything less than protective about it. Do you understand?" He paused to turn and face her.

And in that moment, Fiona found her footing with him again. He was scared, really. Fearful that he'd poured his life—and his image—into this project, and it would all come to naught. Didn't she really fear some of the same with her dissertation? If someone was threatening to destroy all she'd written over the last few years...she might be a tad pushy herself in defending it.

"I understand, Kiernan. And your secrets are safe with me. I won't publish anything that you haven't read first, nor had the chance to televise to your audience. Honestly, I'm sure you're miles ahead of me on this. All I'm looking for are clues to how Grace interacted with the men in her life. And if you're right...if she gathered this treasure in order to fund a future rebellion, that would be an interesting part of my theme to explore. I mean, she had declared one son dead to her, buried her lover, denied her powerful husband his rights...who was left to her? Who was dear to her? And if you're right, why were they not found worthy in the end?"

"If a woman hates all men—which Grace understandably might have—would any of them have been deemed worthy?" he asked.

"Another good question," she said, "and perhaps why her treasure still awaits you."

"Fiona," he said, pausing by her car, leaning against her door, arms crossed. Blocking her, almost. "Would you be willing to guest on a few segments of my show? My producers tell me I need something fresh this season." He reached up and tucked a strand of her hair behind her ear, in an eerily similar move to Rory that morning. She fought not to stiffen. "And *you*," he said, "are fresh and bright." Holding her hand, he took a step away, looked to the horizon, where the sun was sinking and lifted his other hand. "I can see it now. You and I, walking and talking theories about the queen. The American audience would eat it up."

She smiled and pulled her hand gently away, tucking it in her front pocket. "Gosh, you flatter me! But I'm afraid," she said, opening the door and sliding in, "that I'm just a history nerd working on her PhD. Not some sort of television personality."

He held on to her door as she took hold of the handle. "I think you're selling yourself short. C'mon. Just one?" he pleaded. "Try it and see what you think? You've promised to show me what you wrote that pertains to my own findings. In the same way, I could show you the footage before it even goes into editing. If you don't care for it, we wouldn't use it."

"I'll think about it," she said, mostly so he'd release her door.

His smile faded. "See that you do."

And then at last, the door slammed shut.

CHAPTER 20

When she got back to Ballybrack, she parked her car and felt her phone vibrate, indicating a text. She opened up her messages and blinked, staring at the picture Kiernan had taken of her from the roof of Rockfleet. "See?" his text read. "You have a face meant for film. Join me on set! It'd be fun."

She frowned at it a moment. It wasn't that it was a bad picture—she actually loved it—but was she going to regret the fact that Kiernan now had her phone number? She guessed that he could be persistent if he got an idea in his mind. "Thinking about it," she texted back. "Thanks again for the tour of the tower." With a sigh, she switched her phone off and headed over to the house to say hello to Rory and see what he'd accomplished in the kitchen today.

"Hello," she called, as she knocked and let herself in. "Rory?"

"In here," he called.

She moved into the kitchen and found him on a ladder, painting the ceiling. "Oh gosh, Rory. That looks amazing!"

He smiled down at her. "Thanks to you and your HGTV design advice."

She turned in a slow circle. "This room feels huge now, without that drop ceiling!"

"It does, doesn't it?" he asked. With obvious pain, he made his way down the ladder.

"Want me to help?" she asked. "I'm awesome at painting."

"Sure," he said. "If ya want to tackle the edges, it'd be great."

"Not a detail guy, huh?"

"No. I'm more into the broad swath painting."

"Clearly," she said, noting how he'd not finished either the green walls nor the white tin ceiling all the way to the edges.

He moved over to her and bent to give her a quick kiss, smiling down at her. She smiled back up at him. How'd he do that? Convey that he'd missed her and was glad to see her all with one long, smoldering look? It made her wish he didn't have paint all over him, because she was seriously in the mood to give him a proper kiss.

"How'd it go with Kelly?" he asked.

She rounded her eyes in excitement. "Rory, he's found the same emblem in Rockfleet."

"Exactly the same?"

"Bigger. Four or five times bigger than those from Hen's and Aughnanure. But the same, yes. It was hidden behind a false wall."

"Hmmm. Could there be a false wall at Westport House too?"

She shook her head. "No. I looked it over pretty careful-ly. It's all raw stone there."

"Did you get a picture of the one at Rockfleet?"

"Yes!"

"Without Kiernan seeing ya?"

"I think so." She pulled out her phone to show him. She'd captured a blurry image, but it was clear enough. But then she saw there was another message from Kiernan. She clicked on it and saw that it was another picture of her with her hand on the wall inside Rockfleet, a picture she hadn't known he'd taken. How many had he?

"Hey, that's a nice picture," Rory said, looking over her shoulder.

"Yeah," she said, but nothing more. She didn't want to freak him out. *Apparently I wasn't the only one taking covert pics inside Rockfleet*, she thought.

She was about to go to her camera roll to show him what she'd captured when another text rolled in. "There's good money in it," Kiernan had written. "What grad student wouldn't welcome that?"

"He's texting ya now?" Rory said, catching his name, before she scrolled away.

"Apparently. He has it in his head that I should do some guest spots with him for this season of the show."

"Hmmm."

She left it at that, moving to her photo files. Finding it, she lifted it for him to see. "Think it's good enough for us to figure out angle and coordinates? I didn't have time to pull up my app."

He took it from her and stared. "Do ya think ya were dead-on? This isn't from an angle?"

"It's as close as the bridge shot," she said, taking his arm to draw closer and stare at it with him. "I was probably off a bit, but maybe close enough to get the angle of the arrow? To me it looks like it's pointing northwest."

"Maybe we can land on the coordinates using Google Maps."

She nodded. "I want to go to Achill Island tomorrow. See if there's anything at Carrick Kildvanet."

"Ye'd think there would be pictures on the Internet if there was."

"True. I just want to poke around myself. Aughnanure is

the perfect example of it not being where you'd expect. Want to come with me?"

He cast her a sorrowful glance. "Wish I could. I'm taking Grandda and George to Galway tomorrow for a follow-up on his hands, and to pick up the countertops. Could ya wait until Tuesday?"

She shook her head, disappointed. "No. I think I'm heading to Dublin that day. I got a message last night from Abigail that it'd be the best timing."

His gray-blue eyes searched hers, as they both did the math. What was this? she wondered. The idea of being apart from him tomorrow, then the following week, actually hurt a little. She shook her head. She'd have to get a grip on that. If she couldn't handle a week apart, how would it be when she had to leave for the States?

"That's cool the countertop is in already," she said, forcing her tone to be bright.

"We're cooking on the barbeque tonight," he said. "Want to join us?"

"Yes, but the proper American language is that you're 'gonna fire up the grill.'"

"Ahh, yes," he said. "We're gonna fire up the barbeque and slap some ribs on," he said, in a mangled American-Southern accent.

She laughed and cocked her head. "It's a start. What can I bring?"

"Can ya do some sort of side dish?"

"I can do that. But I gotta go to the store. Need anything else while I'm out?"

"I think we have the rest. I have ribs and barbeque sauce. Salad makings."

"Got it. I'll go do that now and then come back in some

grubbies to help you paint for an hour or so before dinner."

"Fantastic," he said. He looked down at his paint covered hands. "I wish I could give you a hug," he said.

"That's all right," she said. "There's always tonight." With a flirty smile, she backed out of the kitchen and made her way back to her car, in a hurry now so she could get to town and back to spend as much time as possible with Rory. Somehow, even painting seemed romantic if it was by his side.

Her phone buzzed again and she pulled it out. It was another message from Kiernan, with another picture of her, looking up. "A face made for film," it read.

She took a long, deep breath, trying to steady her nerves. "Is this gonna be a problem?" she muttered. The hair on the back of her neck stood out. Because something told her this wasn't only the third covert picture he'd snapped of her.

—⁂—

In town, Fiona had grabbed a detailed road map of Ireland, and stopped briefly at a coffee shop to determine the exact coordinates of Hen's Castle's four walls, as well as that of Rockfleet's tower. That night, after their dinner of some pretty massacred, burned ribs, she'd distracted Rory from his failure at his first try as a barbeque master by spreading out the map and drawing lines in the trajectory of where the Hen's stone would have pointed, regardless of which wall it had been on. Together, they discounted the two lines that pointed east and south, out of O'Malley territory. Then they drew the line northwest of Rockfleet.

Rory pointed at Devilsmother. "So the lines, if they're right, might actually skirt either side of our mountain."

Fiona agreed. "So much for us going treasure hunting

just up the road," she said.

"We could still take a picnic up there, when ya get back from Dublin," he said.

"I'd like that," she said. "As long as you bring those cheeses you brought last time, I'm in."

"That's all it takes, does it? A bit of cheese is the way to your heart?"

"Well, a bit of cheese served up by a handsome Irishman."

They'd kissed for a long moment before turning their attention back to the map. He'd tapped it, showing where all three lines might intersect, up off County Mayo's northwestern point, among a group of islands. "Now that's a more believable hiding spot for Grace's treasure," he said, circling them. "But the question is, which one?"

She'd not slept much after that, tossing and turning until her sheets and blanket were a rumpled mess, thinking again and again of the map and the group of islands off of the Mullet Peninsula. Now she was on the road to Achill Island—accessible via a bridge—hoping against hope that there'd be another bow and arrow emblem somewhere on or near the ancient O'Malley castle. Grace hadn't built the tower—her ancestors had a hundred years prior. But she'd frequented it during her years of dominating Clew Bay. Regardless of whether or not she found anything, it was good for her dissertation research.

You gotta get your head back into the paper, Fiona, she told herself. *Just this one last stop, then you need to set the treasure aside and concentrate on Grace.*

For the tenth time, she wished Rory was with her. She kept thinking back to their trip to Clare, and how fun it'd been to have him by her side. She stopped in the tiny village of Knockmore for a sandwich—a yummy brie, bacon jam, and arugula combo—and was daydreaming of her next picnic with him, when she pulled up to the castle site.

Frowning, she stared at the orange cones that appeared to be blocking it off, as well as a policeman in a bright yellow-green vest, bending over to speak to the driver in front of her. That car made a U-turn and passed by her, the driver looking none too pleased. She pulled up and rolled down her window.

"Sorry, miss, the site's closed today," he said.

"Oh? What's happening?" She looked down the hill and could now see a big satellite dish on top of an RV—an RV with Kiernan Kelly's logo on it.

The guard saw she'd seen it. "He's coming in by helicopter any minute," he said apologetically. "He should wrap by this afternoon. Maybe ye can come back tomorrow?"

She shook her head, frustrated. "I know him. Mind if I park over here and say hello?"

The guard looked skeptical, but he gave her a brief nod. "Just stay behind the line down there," he said, pointing to where other locals or fans of the show had gathered.

Fiona pulled into a small gravel lot and got out, shielding her eyes to look for the helicopter she could hear approaching. *Oh brother*, she thought, as the chopper circled above them. She knew what he was after. She'd seen him do the same on the show—making it look like the only way to get to these ancient towers was to arrive by helicopter.

She groaned inwardly as the chopper hovered a hundred feet above them. A cameraman leaned out the open door, and Kiernan appeared, one booted foot on the runner of the helicopter, his hand on the upper part of the doorway. Filming, of course. An intro? Then he came out to stand on the runner and a woman beside Fiona gasped. Another did the same as he hopped off, swiftly rappelling down to the grass beside the castle.

Well, that's totally Bear-Grylls of you, she thought. She supposed he needed to up the drama factor, in case they didn't find the treasure this season.

Another cameraman moved out from behind the castle, capturing his landing. She was too far away to hear what he was saying, but Kiernan moved his hands about, clearly talking as he unhooked his cable and gave the chopper a double thumbs-up. Then he moved toward the castle, while probably giving an introduction to the O'Malley family connection. She thought about hopping in the car and heading back to Ballybrack, but then wondered if he might wrap up this segment sooner than later. *Besides, I'm gone all next week.* She checked her watch. *I'll give it an hour*, she thought.

It looked like the crew was setting up another shot on the other side of the castle. While they did that, Kiernan spotted the small crowd and climbed the hill to speak to them. The two women beside Fiona squealed in excitement. Others fished in their purses and pockets for something to get his autograph. But as he began to sign postcards and other paraphernalia—even a man's "In Search of the Pirate's Queen Treasure" T-shirt—he saw her there, in back.

"Fiona!" he cried, his face splitting in such a wide grin of delight that the crowd practically split like the Red Sea, parting before her. "Come, come," he said, waving her forward.

Reluctantly, she moved to the line. He took her hand and led her to the corner, where a stern-looking female guard stood. "This one's with me," he said, pulling her around the corner post and finally dropping her hand. "What are you doing here?"

"Well, I didn't realize you were filming here today. I'd

come out to take a look at the old O'Malley stronghold."

"Sorry about that," he said, looking contrite. He glanced back at the crowd, feeling what Fiona did too—all eyes on them. Many were taking pictures of the two of them, and for the first time, Fiona saw a man with a professional looking camera. A journalist?

Kiernan wrapped his arm around her shoulders and guided her down toward the castle. "I'll tell you what. Do a test segment with me right now and you can have full access," he said, waving up at the tower. "Solo."

She squirmed away. "I don't know, Kiernan. I'm more of the behind-the-scenes kind of pirate queen fan."

He let out a scoffing laugh and touched her chin. "How many times do I need to tell you?" he said, taking a step closer and whispering in her ear. "You do not have a behind-the-scenes face."

She smiled and took a step away, flattered, in spite of herself. He was looking even more handsome than usual, with his brown-black hair dancing around his face in the wind. But he was staring intently at her. He reached out and took her arm, then tucked her own windblown hair behind her ear. "Give my makeup and hair gal a minute and they'll have you ready. Then just ten minutes on camera. Please. Just to resolve my curiosity."

"I don't know," she repeated, again stepping away. "It's just really not my thing."

"Please," he said, clasping his hands and leaning toward her. "I'd consider it the biggest favor. After we wrap, I could even take you up in the chopper for a tour. This part of the coast is magical by air."

She frowned over her shoulder, watching as the helicopter landed up on the hill. "Well, I guess…" she began slowly.

"Brilliant!" he said. "You've made my entire day!" He grabbed her hand and led her over to the trailer, introducing her to the makeup artist and hair stylist inside. "Ladies, this is Fiona Burke. She's going on with me in fifteen. Can you give her a quick once-over?"

"Yes, Mr. Kelly," said the women in unison.

In short order, they applied more collective makeup and hair product than Fiona had worn all month. "Sorry about this," said the makeup artist, painting on a deep rose lip gloss. "I know it seems like a lot, but it really makes ya look yer best on camera."

Fiona's heart fluttered double-time. She really didn't know what Kiernan wanted from her. What was she supposed to say? Why had she even agreed to this?

Another woman popped open the trailer door. "Is she ready?"

"Yes," said the makeup artist, finishing up with a huge, soft brush full of powder.

Fiona sneezed.

"Don't do that," she complained. "Ye'll muss your mascara!"

"Doctor Burke?" asked the woman at the door. "I'm Anne Donnovan, Kiernan's producer," she said, offering her hand.

"I'm Fiona Burke. I'm a grad student, but not quite a doctor of anything yet." She came outside and walked down the hill with Anne.

"That's all right. Kiernan tells me ye'll earn that title this fall, right?"

"If all goes well," she said hesitantly.

"Gotcha," Anne said, scribbling notes on a piece of paper on a clipboard. "But by the time we air, ye'll have it, and it'll look better on screen to have a name with that 'doctor' title beneath."

"I guess that might—"

Anne interrupted her, asking the spelling of her last name, then thrusting the clipboard into her hands with a place to sign, allowing them to use her image.

"Listen, I have no idea what I'm doing," she said to the producer, as she signed.

"No worries," she returned, taking the clipboard and tucking it under her armpit. "Ye're in professional hands. Now, just wait for Kiernan right in there." She pressed her forward, through the dark doorway of the castle, and as she waited for her eyes to adjust, Fiona was immediately captivated by the soaring, vaulted ceiling. She turned in a slow circle, taking it in, before she realized she wasn't alone. Kiernan stood in the corner, slightly behind his cameraman.

Filming her. He nudged the cameraman. "Did you catch that?"

The man nodded, lifting an appreciative brow and lowering the camera to peer in the small review screen.

"Brilliant!" Kiernan said, looking at it with him. "I told you she'd be a gem on film, right?"

"Wait, you were filming me already?"

"Yes," he said excitedly, moving over to her to take her hand, then bent and kissed it. "You, my dear, are so beautiful. And that look as you came in the door, that utter sense of wonder...that's exactly what I want my viewers to feel when they watch my show. I swear, you're going to help me make this season the best yet. Even before we find the treasure." He pulled her close and kissed her on either cheek. "You're doing me the hugest favor. I won't forget it."

She pulled away, trying to remember that he'd given her

access to Rockfleet, and now this castle too. "Okay. But I really don't know what I can say that would be worthy of film."

"You might be surprised," he said, folding his arms. He reached out and moved her chin one way and then the other. "Be sure to capture her from this side," he told the cameraman.

"Got it."

Fiona shifted nervously. "I'm not really sure, Kiernan…"

"Do me a favor," he said, as a sound guy with a long, fuzzy-covered mic moved inside. "Just start telling me stories. Look around the castle, much like you were just doing, as you talk about it. Pretend it's just you and me. Like we were at Rockfleet. Forget the camera and the sound boom is even here. Just concentrate on Grace and your passion for her history. I'll lead you."

So Fiona began, starting a bit rough, but as she warmed to her stories, she got more and more excited. He bantered with her, leading her with good questions, and in minutes, it began to feel rather easy. When she finished her third tale, he lifted a fist in the air. "That's a wrap," he said. He strode over to her and hugged her. "Thank you so much," he said, pulling back to look at her with utter admiration. "That was perfect. Perfect. Now let me get some footage in myself, so they don't give my show to you. We'll head out in an hour on that tour. I have someplace you must see. You'll be wild for it."

"Okay," she said, finding it hard to turn down such an intriguing offer. "Do you mind if I look around while you do so?"

"Please," he said, gesturing with his palms up. "My castle is your castle."

CHAPTER 21

Kiernan ended up taking several hours to film his remaining segments, and their helicopter tour—what Fiona had thought would be a brief trip along the coast—became a two-hour affair, culminating with landing on Nephin, the tallest mountain in Mayo. Fiona had to admit it was pretty cool, getting out and looking around in amazement. From there they could see another massive land-locked lake below them to one side and Clew Bay to the other. As she took some selfies, with the iridescent Lough Conn below, Kiernan photo-bombed her shot. She'd laughed, in spite of herself. He was kind of sweet when he was being goofy, rather than taking on the whole I'm-a-cool-television-personality-persona. After spending the afternoon with him, she decided that all the rumors of him being somewhat dangerous for women were likely unfounded. Clearly, he was charming. And he'd probably just left some broken, bitter hearts behind him. As for the old man who'd fallen to his death? Kiernan was determined to find Grace's treasure, but Fiona couldn't see him resorting to murder for it.

Time seemed to evaporate and it was with some dismay that she realized the sun was setting when they returned to Achill. He walked her to her car. "Come by Rockfleet in a few days. We'll do another segment there."

"I can't," she said, glancing at her phone when it buzzed. A message from Rory. His second. She looked up at Kiernan.

"I'm heading to Dublin."

"Oh, right," he said, his enthusiasm dampened. He snapped his fingers. "I have a segment I want to film at Howth. Would you like to join me there?"

She hesitated. She really didn't want to get in any deeper with this guy. But the chance to see Howth House, the place where they reportedly still set an extra place setting each night, all due to the promise made to Grace O'Malley…?

"C'mon," he coaxed, putting a hand on her shoulder. "It's going to be a grand affair. A fancy ball, seven course meal, the whole nine yards."

"I don't know," she hedged. Couldn't Abigail Callaway get her in to Howth, with no strings attached? "I don't have a ball gown." Her one fancy outfit had been ruined with her dip in the river. Not that it was even ball-worthy…

"Let me take care of that," he said, putting a hand on her car roof as she slid into her seat. "Anne can find the right dress for you."

"No, that's all right, Kiernan."

"Hey, I have a costume budget," he said, tossing her a cavalier grin. "Think about it. You earned a thousand Euros today. That'd be another thousand."

Her mouth dropped open. A thousand Euros? For an afternoon's work?

He laughed, seeing her face. "See? Sometimes television work can pay off. I'll call you."

"Okay," she said, still thunderstruck. If she earned even two thousand Euros, it'd pay for her cottage all summer. And student loans were piling up. This seemed like easy money. "Thank you. Thank you so much."

He shut her door then and crossed his arms, looking pretty self-satisfied. As she drove off, her phone rang, and she fished it out of a pocket and set it in the holder, speaker on. "Rory," she answered. "Sorry. Bet you were worried about me, huh?"

"Just making sure ye're not in a ditch somewhere," he said.

"Not yet," she said, smiling. It was good to hear his voice. "I'm heading home now."

"Where are ya?"

"Just leaving Achill now."

"Just now? Didn't ya get there this morning?"

"I did," she said, thinking how she could best say this, knowing Rory wasn't Kiernan's biggest fan. "But when I got here, I found out that Kiernan Kelly had the site closed down. He was filming a segment for his show."

"I see," Rory said slowly. "So then…ye spent the whole day with him?"

She paused, hearing the unspoken questions behind that one he'd voiced. "Well, yes. But it wasn't like that." But even as she said it, she admitted to herself that it had *kind of* been like that. Kiernan had been super flirty all afternoon. "We're just friends," she said quickly.

"Friends. With a tool like Kiernan Kelly," he said flatly.

"Hey. I think he's gotten a bad rap. He's not all bad."

"Hmmm," Rory returned.

"Look, can we talk about it when I get back?"

"I'm not sure I'll be here. Two of the puppies are sick and Doc Ames is on holiday. I'm heading back to Galway to a twenty-four hour clinic. Grandda is staying here with George."

"Oh, no!" she said. For a variety of reasons. First, out of fear for the sweet little things. Second, in disappointment that she might not see Rory tonight. She was leaving for

Dublin the day after tomorrow. "So, tomorrow, then?"

"I'll whip up some scones," he said, his voice finally softening. "I'm a better baker than I am a barbequer."

"Sounds perfect. I'll cook some eggs and we'll have breakfast together. Then maybe we can hike Devilsmother tomorrow afternoon?"

"That'd be grand," he said. "As long as these puppies are on the mend. If not, between them and Uncle George, I'll probably need to keep close to the farm."

"I understand," she said. "If so, I'll stay with you."

"That'd be good, lass," he said. "I have to say, I'm not lookin' forward to this comin' week without ya."

"Me neither," she said tenderly. "It's kind of surprised me. How fond I've become of you, so fast."

"Fond, eh? Well they say absence makes the heart grow fonder, right?"

"That's what they say," she returned. "But I'm not really looking forward to testing that theory out."

"Ach, me neither. Me neither."

"Text me tonight when you find out about the puppies, okay?"

He agreed and they hung up. Fiona couldn't sleep until she heard from him at one a.m. The puppies had contracted a virus and were admitted to the pet hospital.

"That's awful," she texted.

"Once they're situated, I'll be home," he texted back. "Still on for breakfast tomorrow?"

"Nine a.m.," she returned. "Don't forget my scones."

—⁓—

But when he arrived at her door, he didn't have scones in

hand. He looked grim.

Her first thought was the puppies. "Oh, no," she said, letting him in. "What's happened?"

"Maybe ye can tell me," he said, pulling a newspaper out from under his armpit. He went to her coffee table and opened it to the entertainment section.

Fiona's mouth dropped open. The headline read, "Kiernan Kelly's Mysterious New Love Interest" and beneath it, five different pictures. Kiernan kissing her hand. Kiernan giving her a hug. Kiernan whispering in her ear. Kiernan leading her to the helicopter by the hand. And more.

"I-I can explain," she said.

"Can ye?" he said tightly, folding his arms.

"This-this isn't what it looks like," she began. "I was working for him. He's going to pay me two thousand Euros!"

"That doesn't look like work to me," he said, thrusting a finger toward the paper.

"Hey!" she said, her embarrassment turning to anger at his assumption. "You weren't there! You don't know how this all came down. And you know what these papers are like," she said, flipping it closed to see the cover. She knew Uncle George found the tabloids entertaining and received it every day.

"Yes, I know," he agreed. "But their stories usually begin with a kernel of truth. And Fiona, those pictures…"

Her face burned. It was true. Had their roles been reversed, what would she think if he'd had some woman in his arms? Was filmed, kissing her hand? Holding her hand? "Look, things kind of got ahead of me…"

He shook his head, looking completely disgusted. "I told ya to watch yourself around that one, didn't I?"

"You did," she said, again growing angry. "But it really isn't your place, is it?"

"Hmmm," he said, staring down at her. "Ye're right," he said, taking a step toward the door. "It's not that ye're officially my girlfriend. I have no right. Ye're free to see whom you please."

"Rory," she said, running a hand through her hair, her mind in a whirl. "You've gotten this wrong." She moved closer and touched his arm. "Please. Can we not just talk this through?"

"I don't think there's any more to say," he said. "Ye went to the castle, and that jackeen somehow worked ya with his smooth ways, didn't he?"

"Well, I wouldn't say—"

"Then what *would* ya say happened, Fiona?"

"He paid me, Rory. Convinced me to do a segment on camera with him, just telling stories about Grace. What you see in those pictures? That was just him, getting excited."

"Hmmm. So what happened after ya finished filming? Why were ya getting into his helicopter?"

"He took me on a tour," she said, not liking him pressing in this way. Making her feel defensive, when it was so unfounded. "It was all totally innocent. We went to the top of Nephin. Along the coast. Then he took me back to my car."

"And that's it?"

Fiona hesitated. He was asking if she was going to see him again. And she hadn't quite figured out what to do about Kiernan's invitation to Howth. "That was all that happened yesterday," she said. "I swear."

His blue-gray eyes searched hers, his mouth still in a grim line. "I have to go back to Galway. Another puppy has come down with a fever."

"That's terrible," she said, again for multiple reasons. He was leaving again. They wouldn't have time to work this out before she left. "Do you want me to go with you?"

He shook his head. "I don't think so. I need some time, Fiona. Time to let this settle."

Anger made her heart pound. "Take all the time you need," she said, opening the door. "Maybe it's good I'm going away this week. Because I don't need to be in a relationship if I'm not trusted."

He paused in the doorway as if thinking about saying something more, but then moved into the yard without saying anything at all.

Fiona slammed the door behind him, and then sank to the floor and burst into tears.

—∿—

The virus appeared to stop with the third puppy, thankfully, but Rory had a hard time finding a reason to smile that next morning. When he came out to see her little VW Up gone from the parking spot in front of her cottage, he hesitated, leaned an arm against the barn doorway, and dropped his head with a sigh. He rubbed the bridge of his nose, feeling the headache he'd suffered all night ramp up.

Patrick stopped beside him, followed where he'd been looking and then glanced at Rory. "So she's off to Dublin?"

"Yes," Rory said miserably.

"I noticed ya two were off-kilter yesterday," he said. "I'd kind of thought ye'd spend yer last day together."

"I wanted to. But then I heard something on the radio, and opened up Uncle George's paper."

"The Dublin rag? What'd ya see there?"

"A full spread of Fiona, with Kiernan Kelly."

"With Kiernan Kelly or *with* Kiernan Kelly?"

"They made it look like she was *with* him. Which is what I heard on the radio too. It's got them all in a frenzy, wanting to know who the mystery girl is."

"Bah. Ya know how they like to gossip about that one. Ya didn't blame her for it, did ya?"

Miserably, he met his grandfather's gaze, and Patrick took a long, deep breath through his nose and patted his shoulder as he let it out. "Ach, lad. I know ye haven't had a girl on yer arm in some time, but surely ya remember that much. A woman wants to be trusted, even as a man does."

"Ya didn't see the pictures, Grandda."

"I don't need to see the pictures t' know that girl has her heart set on ya, lad, not some peacock on the telly."

"Ya didn't see *them* together," he pressed, remembering the anger that had driven him yesterday.

"Did ya?" Patrick asked. "Truly? Or did ya simply fall for what it looked like, just as yer great-uncle with dementia might?"

Rory didn't miss the cut. And Grandda was right. He'd been a fool, even looking up the article. He'd half-believed the story, even before he'd opened to that spread. Believed the story, and doubted her.

"I've been played the fool before," he said. "When Elizabeth—"

"Fiona Burke is not the same woman as yer ex-girlfriend, ye eegit," Grandda said. "Now go after her and apologize. Tell her ye were a fool, and ye'll never doubt her again." He faced him and pushed him. "And if that Kiernan Kelly is making a move on her, ye get there and remind her that ye are too. Fight for her, laddie, if ye know what's good for ya."

Rory shook his head. "I dunno, Grandda. Maybe we just need some days to let it settle."

Patrick snorted. "Now that is the worst idea I believe ye've ever had. Women don't let this sort of thing settle. For them, it *simmers*."

Rory watched him walk off, heading back to the house. Was he right? Should he really set off after Fiona? He didn't even know where she was staying. He rubbed the back of his neck, suddenly feeling every lost hour of sleep he'd suffered the last couple of nights, three-fold. Or was he truly just depressed that he'd let Fiona go on such a sour note?

CHAPTER 22

Fiona threw herself into the bounty that was Abigail Calla-way's library with a single-minded determination to focus on her dissertation again, rather than Rory O'Malley. She'd spent the first day half-sick and half-mad at their last exchange. And she'd ignored every single one of the twenty texts Kiernan had sent her, as well as his heartfelt phone call, apologizing for the fake news story and begging her to join him at the Howth ball. "Just as friends," he'd said. "Completely platonic."

Meanwhile, during the next four days, Rory hadn't both-ered to even send a text.

At the moment, she didn't want to have anything to do with either man. And besides, Howth was open for tours on a daily basis. She could just buy her ticket and see it. Although she knew it would hardly be like experiencing it as a guest to the ball... She picked up her phone and did an Internet search on Howth, searching for images. She soon found pictures of the sumptuous ball room, with its gilded pillars and upstairs gallery, as well as the enormous, coffered ceilings. *It's like something out of a fairy tale*, she thought, imagining herself there.

Not that she had anything to wear. No, at this point, it was too late. She wouldn't even know where to start shopping for a dress.

Your head belongs in your dissertation, not on a fantasy ball, Fiona.

She tossed aside her phone and went back to Abigail's bookshelves. Her library was enormous, and one entire wall was dedicated to books that all related to Grace O'Malley. Many of them were rare volumes, dating as far back as the seventeenth century. For those, she pulled on special cloth gloves and paged through them carefully, as she'd agreed with Abigail to do.

The woman had greeted her when she arrived, showed her to the library, and then largely left her alone. If she'd heard anything of the fake story about her and Kiernan Kelly, she said nothing about it. But then Abigail Callaway was hardly the sort of woman to follow the gossipy newspapers and reports. She was far too erudite for that.

Each afternoon, promptly at three, she arrived with a silver tea tray and shared an hour's conversation with Fiona, asking what she'd turned up. Together, they talked of various aspects of Grace's life, and as they finished, Abigail would pull another five or seven or twelve volumes from her shelves for Fiona to peruse. There were books on the clans of Mayo and Galway. Books on piracy in the sixteenth and seventeenth century. Books on the complicated relationship between the Irish and the English. Books on the immigration of many to Scotland in the fourth century. Books on women of power in Granuaile's era, beyond Elizabeth and the pirate queen. Books on family dynamics in a bygone age. Books on sixteenth century weaponry and warfare. Books on sea-faring and military strategy.

That afternoon, when Abigail came with their tea, Fiona sat down across from her in what had become her favorite wingback to sit in and read. The light coming in through the huge window at her side was perfect—not too glaring, but bright enough to illuminate even the older, darker pages of text. "What are you delving into today, Fiona?" asked the woman, pouring hot, steaming tea from her silver pot into a delicate china cup.

"Ahh, currently, I'm reading about the rules of succession, descent, and distribution of property and titles in the sixteenth century."

"Oh, my. That sounds dry and tedious."

"You know it isn't," she said, raising her cup in a silent toast to the only woman in Ireland who probably found equal interest in such a topic. "Not when you're thinking through how Grace managed to hold on to all she did in an era that was one-hundred percent patriarchal."

"Well," Abigail said, taking a sip of her tea, "at first she was only able to secure her position because her sons were too young to take Donal's place as chieftain when he died."

"True. I'd give my eyeteeth to go back in time and see how she managed to keep that position, even as they came of age."

"It didn't hurt that she turned on one of her own sons, when he agreed to aid the English."

"That must've been devastating for her," Fiona said.

"Agreed. And that goes to your dissertation's point, does it not?"

Fiona nodded. "Just one of many men who betrayed or disappointed her over time."

Like Rory, she thought. How was it that he couldn't even pick up his phone to call or text her? Was he so stubborn? So willing to let go of what they'd started together?

"Not all men disappointed or betrayed her, remember. She surrounded herself with many who remained true to her for decades. Fought to the death for her."

"True," Fiona said. "But that must've made the betrayals

all the more bitterly surprising, don't you think?"

"Aye. A body settles in to power after time. It feels natural. So when someone disregards that power, it's very unsettling."

Fiona sat back in her chair. "I ran across a story about how Grace was very nearly trapped inside the tower on Achill by the English, due to a manservant who betrayed her. An O'Donnell I think his name was?"

"Oh, yes." Abigail finished her tea, set down her cup and went to the library shelves. She pulled a red-leather volume and then a ragged, brown hardback from the shelves and set them on the research table in the middle of the room. "You can find more about that in these two books."

Fiona shook her head. "You're a wonder. I wish I had started my dissertation here. But then I would've been intruding upon you for a year or more."

"I'm glad to be of aid to a fellow scholar," Abigail said. She picked up her tray. "Back to it?"

Fiona sighed. "Yes. I'd better do so. Thank you so much for this opportunity, Abigail. And for the daily tea. You really don't need to do that."

"Not at all. It pleases me to have our daily discussions. Are you in need of anything else?"

"No, thank you. I'll just let myself out at five. May I return tomorrow?"

"Return any day you wish, as long as you wish. This is no imposition at all." She swept out of the room and Fiona looked happily about. As much as she loved being in County Mayo, absorbing the land and waters in which Grace had lived, she could truly spend weeks in Abigail's vast library. Already, she'd added a good two thousand words to her dissertation, and for the first time, held real hope of making progress on it before she returned home.

Better this than wild treasure hunts. She'd gotten carried away, distracted, by the idea that there really might be treasure out there. *The only treasure you need to concentrate on, girl, is that piece of paper with a big, fat PhD on it.*

She sat down at the research table and opened the first book on the history of Carrick Kildavneet and the O'Malleys who built her. At the center of the volume was a signature of glossy white paper, with a number of photographs. As she often did, she began there, and discovered nineteenth century pictures of the castle when the interior had been far more intact. Back then, the floors were still in place. Full of holes, and probably treacherous to walk because of rot, but still there. Fiona was turning the pages when she paused and hurriedly turned back.

Because there on the top floor, beneath the window overlooking what appeared to be the coast to the north, was a stone with a bow and arrow emblem on it.

Mouth dry, Fiona took a picture of it with her phone and then raced through the book, trying to find out what had happened to it. Clearly, the castle had been raided over time. By archeologists? Was the stone in some museum? Or in some private collection? Because Fiona clearly remembering looking up to that window the day she was there with Kiernan, and it hadn't been there.

Thoughts of Kiernan brought those pictures the rag photographer had taken back to mind. Him kissing her hand. Whispering in her ear. His promises of future payments. She let her head fall into her hands, thinking again of the ball the following night. Another thousand Euros would be a boon for her. Staying in Dublin was not cheap, and while Abigail had offered her guest room, she already felt like she was pushing her luck, coming over every day from eight to five. For the first time, she could make money on her education, even before she got her PhD.

Forget it, Fiona. You don't have anything to wear, remember?

But as she stared at that image, and swiftly did a Google map search to figure out the castle coordinates, and just where that emblem had once pointed, she was right back into daydreaming about finding Grace O'Malley's treasure. *Forget a thousand Euros. There could be thousands and thousands somewhere out there...*

Not finding any reference to an excavation of the castle or removal of key artifacts to a museum, Fiona shut the volume and turned to the next. Hours later, she carefully re-shelved all the books she'd taken out during her day of study, backed up her dissertation and notes files on a thumb drive, adding the historic picture from Carrick Kildavneet. Might she find similar pictures of Bunowen? She'd look for that tomorrow.

Her phone buzzed and she realized she had two unseen messages. One was from her mom, and the other from Kiernan. But nothing from Rory.

Why was she still hoping to see something from him? It had been days since their bitter parting. If he hadn't apologized by now, he probably didn't intend to.

Her mom's message was newsy, telling her about her cousin getting married and hinting—not so subtly—that maybe she needed to spend less time buried in the past and more time giving the present men in her life some attention.

She opened Kiernan's. *Please don't leave me going stag to this ball, lass. I'll be the perfect gentleman. We can talk Granuaile all night and sneak down to the harbor she used to use to avoid the British navy. Pick you up at six?*

She laughed under her breath. Clearly, he was not the sort of man to give up easily. But if she did this, he'd come after her all the harder to guest on more of his shows. He'd see it as her defensive walls crumbling and press his advantage. And while he could be quite charming, she didn't want to be profiled in the gossipy newspapers all summer long. The last thing she needed was the paparazzi following her everywhere she went. Rory would definitely not be into that.

Rory. So she was already thinking about forgiving him, even without an apology. Thinking of being with him again. She wished he was there, then, pulling her into his arms, apologizing to her in person. He wasn't the kind of man to text, or hang out on the socials. He didn't even have accounts. She'd looked.

Quickly, she typed a response to Kiernan. *I don't think they'd welcome an American in jeans at that party. And something tells me you have a few more girls you could invite. But thanks for thinking of me!* She pressed send and then gathered up her things and headed back to her inn, thinking of little else than a piping hot beef pie for dinner and an early bedtime.

—⁂—

Rory trudged into Cara Deegan's office, not wanting to be there at all. It'd been a long day already. George was constantly agitated, remembering now about "that girl in the cottage"—when he couldn't seem to remember her at all before. Rory'd stayed up half the night to spell Patrick, because again and again, George tried to go out in search of her. "She didn't get home, laddie," he'd said, pointing out the window to her dark cottage, face drawn in anxiety.

"Somethin's happened t' her."

"Fiona's in Dublin," he'd said over and over again. "She'll be back."

He'd settle, begin to doze, and then rise to begin again. Over and over and over again.

Cara looked up at him, her hazel eyes filled with concern as he sat down. "Are you sick?"

He shook his head and sank back into his chair. He thought that amusing. This was only his fifth session, and he already thought of the big, leather chair as "his." Did all her clients do that? "Not sick," he said. "Only weary. My great-uncle lives with my grandda and suffers from dementia. He got all worked up last night and wouldn't go to sleep."

"Oh?" she said, perching in her usual place as well—the corner of the sofa nearest him, a small coffee table between them. "What got him worked up so?"

"Fiona's off to Dublin to do some research. He was worried she was missing."

He reached for the glass of water that she'd set down beside his chair without asking, not wanting to meet her gaze. He'd avoided talking about Fiona—and their argument—last time he was in.

"How long is she gone?"

"Another few days, I think," he said. He cast her a rueful smile. "Uncle George needs to forget she ever moved in, or Grandda and I aren't likely to sleep until she returns." He rubbed the back of his neck. "On top of that, my grandfather and I got into it this morning. He's gonna need some help when I head back to Shannon. But he wants to do it all on his own." He shook his head. "The farm's already a bit much for him, even without George on his hands."

"That's challenging, working through those aging parent

issues, for any family. Older folks dislike talking about it, because it brings to mind their own mortality. What about your parents? Could they come and join ya for that discussion?"

He nodded. It was a good suggestion. "I can call them. See if they'll come for a visit. They intended to anyway. But Uncle George…it upsets my mum to be around him long. They used to be quite close."

She gave him a sympathetic look. "That's hard. But ya shouldn't have to shoulder such responsibilities alone, Rory. Your mum and dad need to step up. And you need to be brave enough to ask for help."

He frowned. *Brave enough to ask for help.* He'd always thought of courage as soldiering forward, even if you had to do so alone. But she was right. Admitting that you weren't enough, that you needed reinforcements or guidance was its own sort of courage. Wasn't that why he'd come to her in the first place?

"I'll do it," he said, patting his legs. "Now maybe we can get on to the EMDR?" He wanted to get it done and get back. Maybe he'd turn in early tonight, get a head start—

"Maybe," she said, taking a sip of her tea. "But for us to address that old trauma most effectively, we need to address any current trauma. Is there something else? Last time you came in, I felt like something was off. Was it all this stuff with your uncle?"

He frowned at her, pretending ignorance. Could the woman see through to his very soul? It made him uncomfortable, how intuitive she was. *You need to be brave enough to ask for help.* Didn't he need some help on the Fiona-front too? Wasn't that half the reason he hadn't been sleeping since she left, even before Uncle George got worked up?

And Cara sat there, waiting, clearly wise to his internal

struggle. It filled him with admiration…and irritation.

"Last time I came in, Fiona had left. And we didn't part on good terms." From there, he told her everything. What he'd heard, what he'd read, what he'd said, what she'd said.

"And now, Rory?" Cara asked, no trace of condemnation in her tone. "What are you thinking and feeling about all of that now?"

"I'm thinking I was too ready to believe the worst," he admitted.

She nodded thoughtfully. "Tell me. How did your last romantic relationship end?"

"I'd just gotten back from Afghanistan. And I found out my girlfriend, Elizabeth, had been seeing my best friend. For six months. They just couldn't find it in them to tell me until I was home."

"Ouch," she said, wincing. "That must've been very painful."

He nodded.

"How long ago was that?"

"Five years."

"And ye've not had a relationship with a woman since?"

He shook his head.

"By design?"

He thought about that. He'd decided he just hadn't run across the right woman in all this time. But he also knew he'd done nothing to encourage any relationship. Until Fiona. "I guess ya could say that."

"A bit of self-protection, ya think? So that ya don't get hurt like that again?"

He didn't answer and stared at his clasped hands. He knew she was right.

"Could you have perhaps leapt to conclusions about Fiona and Kiernan because that is what you half expect?"

"Hmmm."

"Does Fiona deserve your doubts, Rory?"

He shook his head.

"Have you reached out to her since she left?"

Again, he shook his head.

"Think ya maybe should?" she asked brightly.

CHAPTER 23

Fiona returned to her inn after another long day of study and opened the dark wooden door, wondering if she should have the fish and chips tonight at the pub, rather than the delicious steak and ale pie she'd ordered three nights running. She was trudging up the stairs when she heard her name.

Turning, she blinked in surprise. It was Kiernan, dressed in a tuxedo.

"Kiernan," she said, a mix of surprise and dread surging through her. "How-how did you find me?"

He grinned and came over to the staircase. "I'm a treasure hunter, remember?"

She stared at him in confusion, until he lifted his phone. "I stalked you on Instagram," he admitted, looking at once sheepish as well as a little proud of himself. "This inn has a pretty unique exterior."

She stared at him, even as she remembered posting the picture yesterday morning as she headed out. It had been such a brilliant, beautiful morning, and the front of the inn looked so charming with their bountiful red flowers. She'd taken an artsy shot of it and the doorman, dressed in black livery. "That's a little creepy," she said.

"Is it?" He flashed her his trademark smile. "Or is it dedication?"

She studied him, still trying to decide. "I can't go with you tonight. I told you I have nothing to wear."

"Anne took care of that," he said, turning to grab a plastic dress bag from a settee by the door. "She needs me to go to this Howth party. See and be seen, you know. And she knew I wouldn't go alone." He lifted it. "All I ask is that you try it on. If you hate it, I'll head off stag, I swear, and leave you alone. At least, until you return to Mayo and do that other segment with me at Rockfleet. If you like it, you earn some money for talking Grace O'Malley all night with others, and helping me sow goodwill in a beautiful, historical mansion that you have to see for yourself."

She closed her eyes and shook her head. "You are impossible. You know that, right?"

"Impossibly handsome, you mean," he said, casting her a practiced, smoldering look as he fingered the lapel of his tux. "Or impossibly smart? Is that what you meant?"

"If you got me something red, I'm not going."

"It's not red," he said, offering the dress bag to her.

She took a deep breath. From the corner of her eye she saw two teens taking pictures of them with their cell phones. "Come up to the second floor. There's a lounge area at the end of the hall. You can wait there until I see if it fits."

"Brilliant!" he said, taking her backpack from her shoulder to carry it up for her. Together they climbed the stairs. Obediently, he sat down on the settee at the end of the hall and Fiona went to her room, unlocked the door and closed it behind her. She leaned her head against the door for a moment. Did she really want to do this? If Kiernan got his way now, he'd likely be impossible in the weeks to come. And yet…a thousand Euros. Just to show up on his arm at the ball.

She went into the bathroom, hooked the hanger on a hook behind the door and unzipped it.

Her mouth fell open. Inside was a high-necked, sleeveless royal blue gown, with an hourglass cut and thousands of beads across the bodice. It was gorgeous. She checked the size. A four. The heels were only a half-size too big, fixable with a bit of stuffed Kleenex in the toes. How had Anne known?

She supposed producers had to figure out that kind of thing all the time.

But was Anne trying to orchestrate more tabloid media coverage in throwing them together again? Was she paying her because the show would benefit that much? *No publicity is bad publicity*, was the old adage.

She doubted the family who owned Howth Castle would allow any paparazzi near. There might be socialite photographers, but not anyone who'd publish their photos in the newspaper Uncle George received. That was as far beneath them as it would be for Abigail Callaway.

And Kiernan had mentioned stealing away to a pirate cove beneath the castle. How cool would that be? While the castle was open for daily tours, she doubted that meant she'd have access to the grounds. When might she be able to see a secret cove that Grace O'Malley had frequented? It was really another unprecedented research opportunity, when she thought of it that way.

But what would Rory think?

Of her going out with Kiernan, research excuse or no?

She turned to look for her backpack, to fish out her phone. To check one last time to see if Rory had bothered to call or text her.

Her backpack wasn't with her. She opened the bathroom door and glanced about the room before she remembered.

Kiernan had her backpack.

Which meant he'd had access to her phone for the last fifteen minutes.

He wouldn't have checked it, would he? Even if he'd tried, she had a passcode on it.

Yeah, a passcode spelling G-R-A-C-E. What would be the first thing Kiernan Kelly would guess? She groaned and put her hands to her face.

Her heart pounded. If he had opened it…If he had seen the covert picture she'd taken at Rockfleet, those from the manse, Aughnanure, the research picture from Achill Island…he'd know what she'd been up to. And suspect the worst.

But the longer she stayed in her room, fearful of facing him, the longer he had to search it. If he was searching it at all. She forced herself to put a hand on the brass knob and turn it. Smiled, willing herself to look nothing but an eager date for the night.

Kiernan lifted a dark brow and gave her a blatantly approving look as she approached, his dark eyes drifting from her hair—which she'd swept into a chignon and pinned—down to her black heels, peeking out from the long slit of her skirt. "You, Doctor Burke," he said, rising and taking her hand, "are stunning."

"Thank you. Ahh, there it is." She bent down to her backpack, sitting on the settee beside him, and unzipped the top, fishing out a lipstick, pretending to not even think about the phone, which was blessedly in one of the side mesh pockets, just as she'd left it. "I'll just toss this in my room," she said, turning to carry the pack back to her room. He followed behind, leaning against the door frame. Had the zipper been more open than the last time she'd zipped it? She pulled out the phone, but then paused.

It was in the left pocket of the bag. Not the right.

She always, always put it in the right.

As she turned, her eyes caught his in the mirror above a desk and she stilled. He was staring at her. But in kind of a cold, detached way. If she'd been feeling hesitant a moment before, now she was feeling full-blown caution.

Focusing in, he seemed to catch himself and flashed her a smile. "Ready?"

Slowly, she turned and grabbed her purse, regretting this. Wishing she'd kept saying no, even when he showed up here tonight. Something was…off. But how could she stop now? It'd be too awkward. She'd pretty much accepted she was going, the moment she stepped into the hallway in the gown.

She locked the door and in the hallway, he offered her his arm. As they strode down the thick central carpeted hall with its high, turn-of-the-century ceilings, lined with heavy mouldings, her mind raced. She bit her cheek, feeling the tension rise between them. Halfway down the stairs to the lobby, she paused. "Kiernan, is something wrong?"

"Wrong?"

"While I was changing…You didn't search my bag, did you?"

He paused on the stair beside her and frowned. "Why would you ask that?"

"Because my phone was in a different place than I left it."

He smiled. "Maybe you just forgot where you'd put it." He held on to her arm and pulled her a little closer. "Why?" he asked lowly. "Are you hiding something, Fiona?"

She faced him and searched his dark eyes.

He knew. He'd seen the pictures of the bow and arrow emblems. His eyes were rife with suspicion, blame, fury.

She tried to pull her arm away, but he held on tight.

"Come," he said, dragging her forward. "Let us go some-place private to discuss this." His eyes drifted down to the lobby, full of guests. A couple passed by them, giving them an admiring glance.

"I-I don't think so," she said, trying to pull her arm away again.

"I must insist," he said, pulling her down another step, leaning toward her. "We're going to go somewhere and you are going to tell me everything you know. *Everything.*"

Avoiding being isolated with someone threatening was a Self-Defense 101 basic. At least, without a fight. She wrenched her arm away from him and said loudly, "No, Kiernan!"

Several people looked their way.

Kiernan scowled and faced her. "Are you going after the treasure yourself?" he seethed. "Is that what you're up to? All under this guise of research for your dissertation?"

"What? No!" *Well, maybe,* she thought inside. Had that been her intention? Not really. But she'd just stumbled upon these emblems…and it'd been so intriguing. "Listen, I just found that one from Achill in a research book today," she said, wanting to soothe him. Because his eyes held frighten-ing intent. She had to calm him down if she was to get away from him. "I was going to tell you," she said. "You're the treasure hunter, not me." She flashed him a smile. "I thought I'd tell you tonight."

He studied her, clearly not believing her for a second. He turned, so his back was to the crowd below, blocking their view of her. He leaned in. "If you were going to tell me, you would have when you'd found the one beneath the bridge," he ground out. "Tell me the truth. Who are you working for? Gerald O'Malley? Did he send you to infiltrate my camp? Or was it Abigail Callaway? Has she teamed up with Gerald?"

She frowned, seeing the paranoia take hold in his eyes. She'd read a few articles by Gerald O'Malley, but had not met the man. Nor had Abigail mentioned him.

"Do you know what this will do to me, if it gets out? I'm the face of this treasure hunt," he said, pointing a thumb at his chest. "I have to find it this summer or it's over. You know that. All I can think is that you're trying to steal it out from under me."

Rage radiated off of him.

"This is over. I think you should go now," she said loudly.

"Oh, no. No, no, no," he growled, grabbing her arm again and sliding an arm around her back, forcing her down another step. "This is far from over."

He pulled up short when a man was standing in their way, two steps down. A big man.

Rory.

"I think she told ya to leave," Rory said, the veins at his temple rising in his fury, staring hard at Kiernan. His legs were spread out, his knuckles white on the head of his cane.

"This has nothing to do with you," Kiernan said, dragging her down a step. "Get out of our way."

"Do ye want to go, lass?" Rory asked, glancing at her, then down to the grip Kiernan had on her arm, her waist. His face grew more red.

"No. I don't want to go with him." She tried to catch her breath, tried to figure out how to diffuse this situation. "Kiernan, listen…"

"Let her go," Rory said. "Now."

"Get out of our way," Kiernan said, trying to pass him. Fiona practically fell as he dragged her.

Rory reached out a hand and spread out his palm on Kiernan's chest. "Ye're not going anywhere with her."

Kiernan pushed her to the side and moved to punch Rory, but Rory got in the first blow. Kiernan doubled over in pain and then with a sneer, dived into Rory. The two went down, rolling over and over down the staircase. Fiona screamed.

Rory had dropped his cane. At the bottom landing, he struggled to rise, but Kiernan was faster. He punched Rory across the cheek.

"Rory!" Fiona cried. She picked up the cane and tossed it to him.

Just as Kiernan moved to strike again, Rory stabbed the blunt end of his cane into the man's belly. Kiernan gasped, bent over and stumbled backward. Rory got to his feet, standing between him and Fiona. When Kiernan took another step in his direction, Rory punched him, sending him reeling off the stair landing and into a group of onlookers in the lobby. He was on his side and appeared to be out cold.

Rory looked back to her, and offered his arm. She sank against him, relief flooding through her, even as some people raised their phones, taking pictures, video. The desk manager was on the phone with the police. The doorman knelt and checked Kiernan's pulse. "He's alive," he said.

As if hearing him, Kiernan rolled to his back and blinked slowly, clearly trying to figure out where he was and what had happened. Gradually, his vision cleared and he made to get up, but Rory limped over to him and pressed the tip of the cane to his throat. "Stay where ya are. When the police get here, ya can get up. But not before."

Sirens blared, swiftly growing closer. In another minute, two cops burst inside. "What's happened here?"

"I'll tell you what happened," Kiernan said from the ground, squirming out from Rory's cane. "I've been assaulted. With a deadly weapon."

"Hmmm," Rory said, pulling away the cane and giving it an appreciative glance. "Never thought of it that way before."

"This man tried to force me to go with him," Fiona told the female officer. "When I refused, he tried to drag me down the stairs. This man stopped him. When he did, Kiernan started the fight."

The officer looked Fiona up and down, taking in her fine gown, Kiernan's tux, and Rory's jeans and sweater. "Ya weren't headin' out on the town with that one?" she pressed.

"I was. Until he began to threaten me," she said.

"I see. I'll need ya both to come to the station and give us a full statement." She looked at the gathering crowd, all taking pictures with their phones, then back to Kiernan. "Is that who I think it is?"

Fiona nodded grimly.

"Then that statement will be all the more important," she said.

CHAPTER 24

Fiona and Rory were finally alone. They sat in the police station, on a cold, plastic bench, waiting for clearance to head home for the night. Rory offered his hand and she took it, then slid closer. He put his arm around her and kissed her head. "Ah, lass, are ye all right?"

"I'm-I'm okay," she said. "I'm so glad you came." She looked up at him. "Why did you come to Dublin tonight?"

He shifted in his seat a little. "I got your new bumper. Figured I'd best let ya know or ya might stay in Dublin for the rest of the summer. Mrs. O told me where I could find ya."

She smiled. "So it's all due to my bumper arriving, huh? It was nice of you to make the drive to tell me in person."

He gave her a rueful smile. "Well, and there was the fact that I owed ya a sincere apology," he said, looking into her eyes. "I was an eegit, leaping to conclusions, last week. And then I was nothin' but a stubborn fool, for days. Can ya forgive me?"

"Probably," she said, squeezing his hand.

"So do ya want to tell me why ye're in this particular get-up tonight?"

She grimaced as she looked down at herself. "I owe you an apology too. Kiernan convinced me to go to a dinner and ball out at Howth. I'd told him no several times, said I had nothing to wear, and then he showed up with this." She gestured down to her dress. "I basically caved. Anne was offering me another thousand Euros just to be his date for the night. But I should've listened to my gut, Rory. I should never have said yes. While I was changing, I think he searched my phone. Found my pictures of the other emblems, plus more. He thought I was trying to get to the treasure myself. Steal it from him. I don't know what he intended, but he was furious on those stairs. If he'd gotten me outside, alone…"

He pulled her closer. "I'm glad he didn't."

"Yes, me too."

They sat for a moment in silence, the buzz and hum of the station filling their ears, but not their thoughts.

"Kiernan Kelly is a first-class cad, but I have to say, his producer has a good eye for dresses. Ya look like a princess."

She smiled and looked up at him. "So you're not angry? That I was going to this thing with him tonight?"

He shook his head. "I'm sure ya had your reasons. And as far as ya knew, I was still playing the sour, dejected fool back at home."

"He said there was a secret cove Grace O'Malley used by Howth. He suggested we sneak away to find it."

"Is that all it took?" he asked, raising a brow. "I have a friend who is a Howth ancestor. He could get ya in."

"Oh, that'd be grand." She breathed a sigh of relief, so glad they'd found their footing again, regardless of what a mess this evening had turned out to be.

"What *do* ya intend to do with the information on the emblems, Fiona?" he asked.

"I don't know," she said, shaking her head. "After all of this, all I want to do is finish up my research at Abigail's and then return to Ballybrack to write and name puppies and help you put the kitchen back together again. Oh and picnic at Devilsmother and in that pirate cave you told me about."

"Sounds good to me." He squeezed her hand and then lifted it, palm up. She spread her fingers across his, then intertwined them, delicious bolts of electricity shooting up her wrist and arm as a result.

A female desk sergeant came out to speak to them. "The captain says ya can go, but be aware there's quite a bit of media awaitin' ya."

Fiona groaned. She hadn't thought of it. But memories of all those cameras filming Kiernan Kelly go down were bound to reach TMZ in time. She could just imagine how it had all appeared.

"It's all right," Rory said, tightening his grip around her shoulders. "We'll get through it together."

She nodded. "I hope so," she whispered.

"One more thing," the sergeant said as they rose. She lifted a key drive in a plastic evidence bag. "Is this yours, Miss Burke?"

Fiona stared at it in surprise. Her backup drive! "Yes!"

"We found it in Mr. Kelly's pocket. When we took a look, we thought it might be yours. Since it's evidence of theft, and corroborates your story of how he was threatening you because you had discovered clues to the O'Malley treasure, I'm afraid we'll have to keep it for a bit. Will that be a hardship?"

"No," Fiona said. "I think I have everything on my laptop and phone. It's just a backup."

"Ye'll be staying in Dublin for a few days?"

"A few. I'll wrap up my research and head back to Mayo then."

"Good enough. We have your cell numbers, and we'll be in touch."

Rory rose, a bit ahead of Fiona. "Ready?"

She sighed. "Got your deadly weapon in hand?"

"Right here, lass," he said, picking up the cane.

—⟡—

If Fiona had thought the news coverage of her day on Achill with Kiernan had been something, it was nothing like what followed in the days to come. The inn manager asked them to leave the next day, tired of the throng of reporters in his lobby, all trying to interview his guests and snap pictures of Rory and Fiona.

Together, they made a pact not to read anything that came out. But their phones rang constantly with calls from family members and friends, all saying they'd seen it on the news. Abigail Callaway graciously offered them rooms at her house for a couple of days, and they settled in there, never leaving. In time, the paparazzi faded away.

One night, Abigail sat across from them at the research table. Rory had done additional calculations on the trajectory of the stone emblems on a more intricate map, and where they crisscrossed was among that group of tiny islands on the northwest corner of Mayo.

"You think it's really possible?" Fiona asked Abigail.

The woman sat back. "It's not impossible," she said. "But there are twenty islands in that region, maybe more. You've seen how Kelly's operation has invested countless man hours and money into the hunt by Rockfleet. It'd be a great deal more expensive out there."

"And what's to keep him from doing this very thing himself?" Rory asked, waving to the map. "He has pictures of Fiona's finds."

Abigail arched a delicate brow and steepled her fingers. "He does not have the permission of the Irish Land Authority."

"Is he seekin' it? Do ye know?"

"My sources tell me he has not. But his attack on you, as well as the charges of larceny, cost him his position as host of his show. Even if he wishes to go after it, he must be scrambling for financing. And then he needs to make it through the Land Authority gauntlet, and let's just say that shall not be easily accomplished. They were none too pleased with what he's done around Rockfleet, and it appears he bribed a few officials in order to keep the castle tower his own private set."

Fiona sat back. "I don't think I have it in me to be a treasure hunter. As you said to me, anything of Grace O'Malley belongs to all of Ireland. And if her treasure is out there, it should go to benefit the Irish Historical Museum."

Abigail nodded in approval. "So are you saying I may give this information to them?"

"Absolutely," Fiona said.

"Perhaps, if something is found," the woman said carefully, "I could encourage them to pay you a finder's fee."

"That'd be fantastic," Fiona said. "I'd use it to pay down my student loans." She glanced at Rory. "University professors of history don't exactly make the big bucks."

"At least ye'll make more than Irish secondary school teachers," he said.

"Let's hope," she said. "If I land a position."

"You could capitalize on this a bit more," Abigail said. "After you defend your dissertation, you could return and do a guest circuit among the universities, lecturing on Granuaile."

"True," Fiona said, her eyes slipping to meet Rory's. It was a nice thought, having a reason to return after the summer was over.

Because the more time she spent with him, the more she had a hard time thinking about leaving him.

For a few weeks, Fiona did little other than visit the now entirely healthy puppies—which she named Maeve, Milo, Meg, Maury, Maude, Mickey and Moira—take a long mid-morning walk with Rory, then settle in to write for the afternoon. Rory got her new bumper on to her VW Up, so that the rental company never had to know she landed in the ditch, and together, come evening, they practiced better barbeque skills.

She weathered meeting his parents, who seemed to take to her all right, and she was relieved when Rory told her his parents intended to move in with Patrick and George come fall. They all agreed to figure out what they ought to do next in order to best care for George—but it could wait until next Summer.

By the beginning of August, she felt her dissertation was complete, and yet she was in no hurry to return home. Any thoughts of it only made her rush back to ways she could get back to Shannon—or at least Galway—so she wouldn't be so far from Rory.

They were on a boat, heading out to the tiny islands where Grace's treasure might lay, and it was a brilliant day, in the high seventies, the sun warm on their faces. They carried no shovels nor sonar equipment; Fiona only wanted to see the small isles for herself. Rory steered the boat between and around a number of them, then slowed by the biggest one. When they could see the rocks below, he threw out an anchor. Then he reeled in a small dinghy, helped her in, and pulled the ripcord to rev up the small outboard engine. They skidded onto the rocky beach minutes later and she clambered out, held on to the boat while he made his way out, and together they hauled it farther up on the beach.

They climbed to the top of the grassy knoll and looked about. Rory enfolded her in his arms. "Our own private isle," he murmured. "I can see why the queen might have favored this place."

"Me too," she said, turning to wrap her arms around him as they looked together to the mainland. "There's not enough land to cultivate nor run sheep on. And I bet she could have stolen over from the coast, even in the dead of night, so that no one was ever the wiser."

He took her hand and together, they made their way around the circumference of the small isle, looking for any clue that anyone at all had visited. But all they found was washed up plastic trash from the waves, piles of seaweed, and here and there, some shells.

"Were ya hoping to find another emblem?" he asked, kissing her hand.

"It would've been cool, right? Or a big X. Isn't that how all pirates marked their treasure maps?"

"Something tells me Granuaile did things differently than the average pirate."

"But of course she did." She stopped at the highest point on the island, looking out to the wild expanse of the Atlantic, wondering what courage it might have taken to board a sixteenth-century galleon and sail off for Scotland or Spain.

He stood behind her and wrapped his arms around her shoulders. She held on to his wrist with one hand, thinking how happy she was here. With him. But before she knew it, she would be leaving for the States. "I don't want to leave you, Rory."

"Hmmm. And I don't want ya to leave."

She turned to face him, looking up into his eyes.

He traced the line of her face, from temple to jaw. "Fiona Burke, I'm in love with ya," he said solemnly.

"In love with me?" she whispered.

He nodded. "I am. Do ya...do ya have feelings for me?"

She smiled and pulled him closer, feeling a bit shy. "I think you're all right."

He didn't share her smile, too intent upon his subject.

"Rory. I came here to learn all I could about Grace O'Malley. I never expected to fall in love with her ancestor."

"So ye are?" he asked, his ruddy brows forming an arch of hope.

"I am," she said.

He grinned, kissed her, then wrapped her in his arms again. This was part of what she loved most about him—the feel of being utterly cherished. As if he couldn't hold her close enough. "But Rory, what are we going to do? I only have a few weeks left."

"I've thought of that," he said. "With Mum and Da moving in with Patrick and George this fall, things at Ballybrack will be taken care of for a while. So I sent off my resume to a few private schools in and around Boston."

She pulled back in surprise. "You would do that? Come with me?"

"If they—and you—would have me. Because, lass," he said, brushing a tendril of windswept hair from her face, "I haven't waited twenty-nine years to find ye, only to lose ya now."

"I don't think you could lose me, Rory," she said, "even with an ocean between us."

CHAPTER 25

Three weeks later, Rory had heard nothing from one of the private high schools, received a definitive no from the second, and a request for a phone interview from the third. But Fiona was getting nervous; she only had two weeks in Ireland left. Was it not going to work out?

She was ready to defend her dissertation. She had practiced her speech in front of the puppies and the cows and horses. Rory had asked her any question he could think of. Abigail randomly texted her others. Grad school friends texted her queries on methodology and ideology.

"I think I'm ready," she said, taking Rory's hand as they left the barn. "To face the board. But not to leave you."

"I'm not ready for that either," he said miserably, pulling her into his arms and kissing her forehead. She knew they were both silently praying that the phone interview, due to happen in a couple of days, would be the answer.

They looked to the rocks at the base of Ballybrack as a car entered. It was a fancy black BMW sedan and pulled up in front of Fiona's cottage. With a shared glance of curiosity, they set off to meet the visitor.

A woman emerged first, from the passenger side door, and it took Fiona a second to place her. Kiernan Kelly's producer, she remembered. Anne was in a slim khaki pant suit and heels. A man emerged from the driver side door, dressed in a button-down shirt, open at the collar, and jacket. Fiona briefly considered her own grubby jeans and worn sweater, what she'd taken to calling "barn clothes," but truthfully, what she ended up living in, most days.

"Hello!" the producer called, striding toward them. "I'm Anne Donnovan." She reached out a hand to shake Rory's hand, then Fiona's. "I met Fiona on Achill Island," she said to him. "This your farm?"

"My grandda's," he said.

Fiona crossed her arms. Why were they here? In the back of her mind, she kind of always expected some blow-back. A lawsuit from Kiernan Kelly or those who had backed him.

"You're a hard one to find," Anne said.

"By design," Rory put in casually. He stepped slightly forward, in a protective way.

"Good choice," Anne said, tossing a smile to her compatriot, who gave them a nod of approval. "Listen. Is there someplace we can sit down and talk?"

"Yes," Fiona said, gesturing to her cottage. "Please come in."

The four of them went in and settled on the tiny sofa and the two chairs that Rory and she brought from the café table a few feet away. They sat down, facing the newcomers.

Anne leaned forward. "Listen. We'd like you to accept our apologies for how Kiernan acted. He hasn't been himself the last couple of months, and we've come to find out that he has some…issues that need to be addressed. He's off to do that."

Fiona narrowed her gaze. Issues? A mental breakdown? Drug addiction? Despite her best efforts, she'd caught a few reports. One had Kiernan checking into a clinic in the Seychelles. "I'm only glad it wasn't worse than it was in the end," she said.

"Well, we appreciate your grace," Anne said.

"As well as your insights," the man put in. "You made more progress in getting closer to Grace O'Malley's treasure in one summer than Kelly did in the last two years."

"Yes, well, that remains to be seen, doesn't it?"

"Regardless of whether it's hidden among the Inishmore islands or not," Anne said, "you uncovered enough fodder to fuel another season of the show."

"The problem is that we're short a host," he said.

"Which is why we're here," Anne said. "You were simply brilliant on camera. Brilliant. Fresh. Enthusiastic. Kiernan wasn't wrong when he decided you'd shine on our show."

"We think our audience would be in the palm of your hand," said the man.

Fiona frowned. "Wait. Are you…"

"We are offering you the job as the new host for our show," Anne said.

Fiona glanced at Rory and he smiled in surprise, opening his hands. As if to say, *this is all up to you*. Her mind raced.

"I-I need to return to Boston in a couple of weeks. I'm due to defend my dissertation on Grace, in order to receive my PhD."

"We know," Anne said, and Fiona belatedly remembered discussing an appropriate title for her guest spot. Anne shared a glance with the man and smiled at Fiona. "It would be perfect. We'll tease the audience with a few clips we've already recorded. But then you return, a full-fledged historian, and lead us on the hunt that hundreds of thousands have been following."

Fiona stared at her. "I have no television experience."

"I know," she said. "That's what's so brilliant about you. There is nothing fake about your presence on film. Only raw passion for our pirate queen. Trust me, our audience is going to adore you. And after Kiernan's despicable behavior, they'll love that it's you taking his place on the show."

Fiona sat back, considering it all.

"Wouldn't you like to be there, when we find it? See this to the end?"

"I-I…maybe. Well, of course I would. But do I want this to be the next step of my career? I'd thought I'd find a university position…"

"Which you can do next year or the year following, right?"

The man unbuttoned his jacket and leaned forward. "Miss Burke," he said seriously. "We think you're the woman for the job. And frankly, our show is on the brink of failure unless we can see this through. How much would it take for you to sign on the dotted line? To commit to a year in Ireland? That's all we ask. A year."

She glanced at Rory and her first thought was *room and board. Just room and board and the ability to be near this man for another year.* But then she stilled, recognizing this was an amazing, God-granted opportunity to provide and keep them together.

"Might I call in some reinforcements? Abigail Callaway? And a professional operation called Treasure Seekers? I know a nautical archeologist. She's a friend of a friend. She and her husband, Mitch Crawford, have uncovered a couple of massive Spanish finds."

"Absolutely," Anne said, warming to the idea. "All of that would be excellent film fodder."

"And lend us newfound credibility," said the man, nodding.

As well as potentially earn you access via the Irish Land Authority, Fiona thought.

"But we'd have to come to terms with them, of course," added the man. "Contractually."

Financially, Fiona interpreted. "Understood." She glanced at Rory and grinned, inwardly thinking *going for broke!* She leaned forward herself. "Here's my offer. You pay off my entire student loan, my room and board here on Ballybrack Farm—or elsewhere, if we're on location—and I'll give you a year here in Ireland. Wherever you want to go, whatever you want me to do. If you allow me to bring in my own experts, mold this show in a new direction, I'll do it."

The man sat back. "How much are we talking in student loans?"

Fiona silently calculated, and then named the number.

The man's eyebrows shot up, and then he glanced at Anne.

The producer lifted her hands, clearly leaving it to him.

He returned his gaze to Fiona, studying her for a long moment. "We'll do it." He rose and offered his hand.

Fiona stood and took it, recognizing something monumental had just happened. But all she could think about was Rory. She looked to him and grinned.

She'd found a way for them to be together.

Or rather, God had.

EPILOGUE

A year later, they were married on a green hill behind Ballybrack's barn, with the mountains ringed in a few clouds above them, and in the distance, the Atlantic shimmering in the sun. Despite her producer's offer to pay for a large, luxe, media-friendly wedding, Rory and Fiona chose to have more sheep—and dogs—than people in attendance. But the people most important to them both were there.

As Father Michael gave his brief message and Rory's hand covered hers, Fiona's heart swelled with gratitude. She was so grateful...grateful for this opportunity to come to Ireland at all. Grateful to have arrived at just the right time. Grateful to have secured a cottage on this farm, with a chance to meet her beloved. And then for the provision to keep them together through the show this last year. There was even word of a potential assistant professor position opening up at the university come spring. But overall, it was Rory she was most grateful for, of course. She felt as if she'd been given the greatest treasure ever in him, even though the queen's still eluded her.

Thank you, she prayed silently, as she turned toward Rory and repeated her vows, smiling through her tears. Because Rory and his people were now hers, and Ireland, her home.

And at that moment, she knew she felt it every bit as fiercely as Grace O' Malley once had herself.

HISTORICAL NOTES

Grace O'Malley's most famous biographer is Anne Chambers. I have never met her, so my fictional character is not based on her, only the idea of what someone like a contemporary biographer of Grace might be like. If you'd like to read Chambers' biography, look for *Grace O'Malley*, or you can check out her web site at graceomalley.com.

The emblem of a bow and arrow is a figment of my imagination. There are bows and arrows on her grave stone on Clare Island, but as far as I know, there is no such historical record of Grace O'Malley wearing such a broach and there are no such markings on any of the sites noted (so don't go diving into the river by Aughnanure to check!) In addition, the islands of Inishmore are also fictional. The description of the abbey, exhibits, Rockfleet, Aughnanure, and other sites are described to the best of my knowledge, utilizing either personal visits or what I could scrounge from the Internet and pictures. In some cases, it's entirely a figment of my imagination. In addition, there is scant evidence that Grace spent much time at the O'Flahertys' Aughnanure. There is more reference to her living on, and defending, Hen's Island.

—⁓—

ACKNOWLEDGMENTS

Many thanks to my proofing crew—Melanie Stroud, Amanda Lamb, Sharon Miles, Shaina Hawkins, Shannon Talbot, Lisa Mattox, Julie Grant, Alyssa Grant, and Elizabeth Hoyer. In addition, Myrtle Honeyman kindly assisted me with Irish dialect and details.

WANT TO CONNECT WITH ME?

Visit my web site, www.LisaTBergren.com, and subscribe to my enewsletter. I promise not to overwhelm your in-box, and you can get a free e-book!

You can also connect with me via:
Facebook.com/LisaTawnBergren
Instagram and Twitter: @LisaTBergren

—⚊⚋—

Did you enjoy this book?

Reader reviews make a huge difference for authors, because it helps us sell books (and therefore, keep writing). Please consider adding your honest response on the retailer's site where you purchased this novel. You don't need to summarize the book—just a line or two about what you liked best works really well. (And if you want to get *extra* credit—virtual gold, shiny stars and heart-eyes from me—copy and paste that review on Bookbub.com and goodreads.com.) Thank you so much!

—⚊⚋—

Look for other titles in this series, available now!

Once Upon a Montana Summer

Once Upon a Caribbean Summer
(previously published as *Treasure*)

Once Upon an Alaska Summer
(previously published as *Pathways*)

Also by Lisa T. Bergren

Breathe
Sing
Claim

Glamorous Illusions
Glittering Promises
Grave Consequences

Waterfall
Cascade
Torrent
Bourne & Tributary
Deluge

Remnants: Season of Wonder
Season of Fire
Season of Glory

Keturah
Verity
Selah

Lisa T. Bergren is the author of over sixty books, with a total of more than three million books sold. She writes in many genres, from romance to women's fiction, from supernatural suspense and time travel YA to children's picture books. Lisa and her husband, Tim, have three big kids and one little, white, fluffy dog. She lives in Colorado but loves to travel and is always thinking about where she needs to research her next novel. In the coming year, she hopes to get to Hawaii, and sometime soon, dreams of a return to Italy. To find out more, visit LisaTBergren.com.